U0559926

浙江省社科联社科普及课题成果（23KPWT03YB）

 浙大城市学院教育基金会校友专项基金 资助出版

历代杭州西湖诗词一百首
（中英对照）

顾　问　　罗卫东

主　编　　张梦新　　柏　舟

副主编　　孙福轩

编　委（按姓氏笔画排序）

　　　　　吴　琳　　宋旭华　　金首红　　宣飞峰

　　　　　姚逸超　　徐　晔　　黄成蔚　　宿玉村

英译审校

　　　　　殷企平　　颜钟祜

歷代杭州西湖詩詞一百首

千鹤

张梦新 柏舟 **主编**

Zhejiang University Press
浙江大学出版社
·杭州·

序 言

One Hundred Poems
on the West Lake in Hangzhou
Through the Ages

Preface

"江南忆，最忆是杭州……"白居易道出了多少人对杭州的热爱！杭州，这座中国历史文化名城，有着数千年的历史，自首次出现"杭州"这一名字，已有1434年的历史。在中国人的心目中，杭州是人文之美、山水之美、生活之美兼具的首善之地，是美美与共的人间天堂。

　　杭州之美，首在西湖。杭州因西湖而美，因西湖而兴，"杭州之有西湖，如人之有眉目""未能抛得杭州去，一半勾留是此湖"……对于杭州，对于西湖，历代文人骚客可谓情有独钟，诗、词、歌、赋、书、画、印……以各种不同形式咏之颂之。其中，又以诗歌为甚。

　　历朝历代，歌颂杭州、赞美西湖的诗词到底有多少，无法确切计数。其中，妇孺皆知、耳熟能详的精品名篇应不下百首。白居易、苏东坡、欧阳修、杨万里、辛弃疾、柳永、林和靖等古代名人，都留下了无数金言佳句。经过千百年的传诵，这些诗词名篇都已脍炙人口，成为今人认识、欣赏、体味、理解杭州和西湖之美，抒发情感的经典表达。

　　山水人文之美，非诗歌不能描述；诗词之美，非真景实境不能验证。身处杭州西湖，实景的美和诗词的美，相得益彰；天地的奥妙与人心的幽微，互动而感。身与心、情与境、感与想、行与识共同创造出了无与伦比的体验，正所谓，物我两忘，天人合一，这是在世界上其他城市所无法获得的享受。不过，这样美妙而又深刻的感受，似乎只有在中国人的心灵里，在中文语境中才能产生，这又不能不令人感到十分遗憾。

　　尽管杭州这座城市的内在精神气质很难被异文化的游客所体悟感受，但历史上杭州的社会经济之繁盛、山水人文之形态美，是早就打动过很多异域人士的。据记载，最早来到杭州的西域人是印度

"Memories of the South of Yangtze River, the most unforgettable place is Hangzhou prefecture..." Bai Juyi expressed how deeply people love Hangzhou! Hangzhou, a famous Chinese historical and cultural city, has a history of thousands of years, and it has been 1434 years since the name "Hangzhou" first appeared. In the minds of Chinese people, Hangzhou is the most preferred place with the beauty of humanity, landscape and life, and is a paradise on Earth where beauty and harmony is shared.

Firstly the beauty of Hangzhou is mainly attributed to the West Lake. Hangzhou is beautiful because of the West Lake, and flourishes because of the West Lake. "The West Lake is to Hangzhou, what eyebrows are to a person", and "Why am I leaving Hangzhou so reluctantly? It is the West Lake that holds me up so firmly" ... The literati, especially poets of all ages have a special liking for Hangzhou and the West Lake, and they have celebrated it in various forms with verses, lyrics, ballads, rhapsodies, calligraphy, paintings and seals... Among them, poetry is the most popular.

It is impossible to count the number of poems that have been written in praise of Hangzhou and the West Lake throughout the ages. Among them, there must be no less than a hundred well-known and familiar poems. Bai Juyi, Su Dongpo, Ouyang Xiu, Yang Wanli, Xin Qiji, Liu Yong and Lin Hejing are just a few of many ancient famous names who have left behind countless exquisite and elegant poetic lines. Throughout the centuries, these famous verses and lyrics have taken hold of people's hearts and become a classic expression of how people today know, appreciate, savour, and understand their love for the beauty of Hangzhou and the West Lake.

The beauty of landscape and culture can't be described without poetry, and the beauty of poetry can't be verified without real scenery. When people are in the West Lake of Hangzhou, the beauty of real scenes and poetry complement each other; the mysteries of heaven and earth interact with the subtleties of the human heart and they sense each other. The combination of body and mind, emotions and environment, feelings and perceptions, and impulses and consciousness has created unparalleled experiences. As the saying goes, both subject and object are dissolved; nature and man are one. These are pleasures that cannot be obtained in other cities in the world. However, it is a great pity that such a wonderful and profound feeling seems to arise only in the Chinese mind, in the Chinese context.

In fact, although the city's intrinsic spirituality is difficult for visitors from other cultures to appreciate and feel, the prosperity of Hangzhou's society and economy and the beauty of its landscape and culture have long inspired many people from different cultures. According to records, Huili, an Indian Buddhist, was the first person from Xiyu (the Western Regions) coming to Hangzhou. In the early fourth century, he arrived at the ancient Qiantang, which was still a small county in the mountains, settled in the Lingyin area, and fell in love with this "hidden place of immortals", building

的佛教徒慧理，4世纪初，他来到当时还是山中小县的古钱塘地界，在灵隐一带落脚，并爱上了这片"仙灵所隐"之地，建造了灵隐寺这座名刹。他在这里一心修佛讲经传法，一直到圆寂。慧理和尚在杭州的山水中找到了安息之所，飞来峰前的慧理之塔便是见证。

在慧理和尚之后，至今约一千九百年的时间里，来自海外的形形色色的人，旅行者、留学生、商人、传教士……无不对杭州留下美好的印象，其中，有马可波罗、白图泰这样用文字记录下杭州，使其美名远播于海外的旅行家，也有卫匡国、司徒雷登这样把杭州作为最后归宿地的传教士。

人类的心灵是共通的，人类的审美也有一定的共性。山水之美、自然之美、建筑之美，即便完全不了解中国文化的外国人，也可以不经解释直接去感受；不过，对于人文底蕴、风土人情的理解，如不经过理想的语言中介，就不能达成。尤其是，对于中国古诗这样通过汉字载体呈现出节奏美、音韵美、气质美、内涵美的表达形式，如果没有优良的翻译，就绝不能达到令异文化人士心领神会的效果。

摆在读者面前的这本《历代杭州西湖诗词一百首》（中英对照），是凝聚了作者张梦新教授和柏舟教授心血的作品。两位教授既是我的学长，也是多年的老朋友。他们两人几乎一辈子生活在杭州，对这里的山山水水，熟悉得不能再熟悉，热爱得不能再热爱；他们对杭州的美了然于心，又凝结成浓得化不开的感情，最后转化为通过古诗英译向域外传播杭州之美的行动者。

梦新兄早年师从我国著名古代文学大家徐朔方教授攻读博士学位，先后在浙江大学人文学院和浙大城市学院传媒与人文学院从事古代文学的教学和研究工作，是中国古典文学专业的博士生导师；柏舟兄长期从事英语教学与翻译工作，他本人就是创作中文古体诗

the famous Lingyin Temple. Here he continued to practise Buddhism and preach the Dharma until his death. Monk Huili found his resting place in the landscape of Hangzhou, as witnessed by Ligong Tower in front of Feilai Peak.

In the 1,900 years or so since the death of Monk Huili, travellers, students, businessmen, missionaries and other kinds of people from overseas have been deeply impressed by Hangzhou. The city's reputation has been widely documented by travellers such as Marco Polo and Ibn Battuta, who wrote about Hangzhou and made it famous overseas. And there are also missionaries like Martino Martini and John Leighton Stuart who took Hangzhou as their last resting place.

The human psyche is mutual, and so are some aspects of human aesthetics. The beauty of landscapes, nature, and architecture can be directly felt by foreigners who have no understanding of Chinese culture. However, the understanding of the Chinese cultural background and local customs cannot be achieved without an ideal language intermediary. Especially for ancient Chinese poetry, which presents beauty in rhythm, rhyme, nature, and connotation through Chinese characters, it can never be understood by foreigners without excellent translation.

The book before the reader is *One Hundred Poems on the West Lake in Hangzhou Through the Ages* (Chinese-English). It is a work that embodies the hard work of the authors, Professor Zhang Mengxin and Professor Bai Zhou. They two are my senior schoolmates and long-time friends. Both of them have lived in Hangzhou almost all their lives and are familiar with and love the hills and waters here. They knew the beauty of Hangzhou by heart, and this condensed into strong feelings, which eventually transferred into the action spreading the beauty of Hangzhou abroad through English translations of ancient poems.

In his early years, Professor Zhang studied for his PhD under Professor Xu Shuofang, a renowned scholar of ancient literature in China. He has been engaged in teaching and researching ancient literature at the School of Humanities of Zhejiang University and the School of Media and Humanities of Hangzhou City University. He was a doctoral supervisor of Chinese classical literature. Professor Bai has been engaged in English teaching and translation for a long time. He himself is an expert in ancient Chinese poetry and has published multiple collections of his own poems. He has gained insights into the cross lingual transformation of poetic imagery. The two professors jointly led the completion of this book, which is really a perfect match.

They also invited their friend, Professor Yin Qiping, another native Hangzhouer, to proofreading through the book in manuscript. Professor Yin has studied English literature for a long time, and his moral character and knowledge are always valued by scholars. His gatekeeping has also increased the quality of this book.

的高手，曾经出版过多部自作诗集，对于诗词意境的跨语种转换自有一番心得。两位仁兄联袂领衔完成了本书，真可谓是珠联璧合。

他们还邀请了好友、另一位地道杭州人殷企平教授对书稿进行审定。企平兄长期研究英语文学，人品学问素为学林所重，他的把关又为本书的品质增加了保障。

翻译难，译诗更难，而将中文古诗译成别国文字，那是难上加难！同样一首诗，一千个译者就有一千种译法。任何翻译，某种意义上都是译者的二次创作。这样的再创作是否成功，归根结底还是要看读者是否认同，是否喜爱。我衷心希望本书不只是杭州西湖古诗英译的拓荒之作，更是被英语世界的读者们接受和传诵的名篇名译。

进入 21 世纪的杭州，是一座面对世界更加开放、国际化程度日渐提升的城市。西湖、良渚古城遗址、大运河先后被列入《世界遗产名录》，G20 杭州峰会（二十国集团领导人第十一次峰会）的成功举办，进一步提升了杭州的国际知名度和美誉度。再过几个月，举世瞩目的第十九届亚运会就要在杭州西湖之畔隆重开幕了，这不仅是一件体育盛事，也是一件文化交流的盛事。

把杭州亚运会办成具有"中国特色、浙江风采、杭州韵味、精彩纷呈"的文化盛宴，是全国人民的共同愿望。而讲好杭州的故事，让更多的外国友人更好地认识杭州、理解杭州，进而更好地认识中国、理解中国，则是每一个杭州市民当仁不让义不容辞的共同责任。在这个背景下，这本书的问世，自有一番特殊的意义。衷心希望该书的出版为杭州亚运会增添一份特殊的光彩。

是为序。

罗卫东

（全国政协委员 浙大城市学院校长）

2023 年 5 月 1 日

Translation is difficult, translating poetry is more difficult, and translating an ancient Chinese poem into another language is even more difficult! There are a thousand ways to translate the same poem for a thousand translators. Any translation is, in a sense, a second creation by the translator. Whether such a re-creation is successful or not ultimately depends on whether the reader agrees or likes it. I sincerely hope that this book will not only be a pioneering work in the English translation of the ancient poems of Hangzhou's West Lake, but also a famous translation that will be accepted and celebrated by the readers of the English-speaking world.

In the 21st century, Hangzhou is a city that has become more open to the world and increasingly international. The inscription of the West Lake, Archaeological Ruins of Liangzhu City and the Grand Canal on *The World Heritage List* and the successful hosting of the G20 Summit in Hangzhou have further enhanced the city's international popularity and reputation. In a few months, the 19th Asian Games will be held in Hangzhou on the shores of West Lake, which is not only a sports event but also a cultural exchange event.

It is the common aspiration of the people of China to host the Hangzhou Asian Games as a cultural feast with "Chinese characteristics, Zhejiang style, and Hangzhou charm". It is the shared responsibility of every Hangzhou citizen to tell the story of Hangzhou well, so that more foreign friends can better know and understand Hangzhou, and thus better know and understand China. Under this background, the publication of *One Hundred Poems on the West Lake in Hangzhou Through the Ages* (Chinese-English) has its own special significance. I sincerely hope that the publication of this book will add a special glory to the Hangzhou Asian Games.

For this, I write this preface.

Luo Weidong

(Member of the National Committee of the Chinese People's Political Consultative Conference,

President of Hangzhou City University)

May 1, 2023

前 言

One Hundred Poems
on the West Lake in Hangzhou
Through the Ages

Foreword

东南形胜，三吴都会，钱塘自古繁华

杭州，位于中国的东南沿海，京杭大运河的南端，它是浙江省的省会，全省政治、经济、文化的中心，名列国务院公布的首批国家历史文化名城名单。早在十万年前，杭州地区已有古人类栖息；而距今约八千年的跨湖桥遗址和距今五千余年良渚文化遗址的发现，则使杭州沐浴了中华文明曙光，让人由衷感叹杭州渊源深厚的历史与独特的魅力。

杭州自秦始皇二十五年（前222）建置钱唐县，至隋开皇九年（589）始用现名。唐末，钱镠在杭州建立了吴越国，杭州成为雄踞东南十三州的都府。宋高宗南渡后于绍兴八年（1138）正式定都杭州，杭州成为南宋帝都，历时一百四十余年，一跃成为全国的政治、经济、文化中心。至元朝，意大利著名的旅行家马可波罗游历杭州，盛赞杭州是"世界上最美丽华贵的天城"。

新中国成立后，特别是改革开放以来的杭州，更是容光焕发、大放异彩。被联合国人居中心授予"联合国人居奖"，先后获"国际花园城市""全球十大休闲范例城市"等殊荣，并连续十一年入选"魅力中国——外籍人才眼中最具吸引力的中国城市"，连续十五年被评为"最具幸福感城市"。2016年9月，杭州成功举办了举世瞩目的G20峰会。

自2015年9月获得第19届亚运会主办权以来，杭州市政府和杭州人民就积极地进行亚运会的筹备与建设，深入实施亚运城市行动，努力把杭州亚运会办成一届"中国特色、浙江风采、杭州韵味、精彩纷呈"的体育文化盛会。

Located in the southeast with beautiful mountains and rivers
And being the metropolis of Wuyue State,
Since ancient times, Qiantang has been a prosperous city.

Hangzhou, located on the southeastern coast of China and at the southern end of the Beijing-Hangzhou Grand Canal, is the capital of Zhejiang Province, the local political, economic and cultural center, and it is also one of the 24 first-batch National Famous Historical and Cultural Cities designated by the State Council. As early as 100,000 years ago, there were ancient humans living in the area of Hangzhou; and the discovery of the Cross-Lake Bridge site about 8,000 years ago and the Archaeological Ruins of Liangzhu City 5,000 years ago has bathed Hangzhou in the dawn of Chinese civilization, which makes people sincerely marvel at the profound history and unique charm of Hangzhou.

Hangzhou was established as Qiantang County in the Qin Dynasty (222 B. C.) and took its present name in the ninth year of Kaihuang Period in the Sui Dynasty (589 A. D.). At the end of Tang Dynasty, Qian Liu established the Wuyue State in Hangzhou, which became the capital of the thirteen southeastern states. Hangzhou was the capital of the Southern Song Dynasty after Emperor Gaozong transferred here in the eighth year of Shaoxing Period (1138), and it became the political, economic and cultural center of the country for more than 140 years. During the Yuan Dynasty, the famous Italian traveler Marco Polo visited Hangzhou and praised it as "the most beautiful and luxurious city of heaven".

After the founding of New China, especially since the reform and opening-up, Hangzhou has been glowing and shining. It has been awarded the "UN Habitat Award" by UN-Habitat Center, and has won laurels such as "International Garden City" and "Top 10 Global Leisure Model Cities". It has been selected as one of the "Charming China—Most Attractive Chinese Cities in the Eyes of Foreign Talents" for 11 consecutive years, and has been rated as "the happiest city" for 15 consecutive years. In September 2016, the 11th G20 Summit was held in Hangzhou, which attracted worldwide attention.

Since winning the right to host the 19th Asian Games in September 2015, Hangzhou municipal government and Hangzhou people have been actively preparing for and constructing the Asian Games, striving to make the Hangzhou Asian Games a sports and cultural event with "Chinese

浙大城市学院是浙江大学与杭州市人民政府合作创办的全日制本科院校，也是新中国历史上名城名校名企合作办学创举的结晶。作为大运河畔一所正在创建全国百强的大学，为杭州亚运会建设献计出力是全校师生共同的心愿。在罗卫东校长的支持下，我们部分老师决定编写本书，把它作为杭州市献给杭州亚运会的礼品书。

三月莺花千里梦，半林风月一囊诗

　　在诗词选录方面，本书首先注意采录历代的名家名作。比如唐代的李白、王昌龄、白居易、李贺，宋代的柳永、苏轼、陆游、辛弃疾，元代的关汉卿、赵孟𫖯，明代的高启、汤显祖、袁宏道，清代的黄宗羲、陈维崧、林则徐和近代的康有为、章太炎等作。这些名家名篇，如同璀璨的群星，熠熠生辉。

　　其次，注意选用杭州本土作家的作品。如罗隐、周邦彦、朱淑真、于谦、厉鹗、袁枚、洪升、龚自珍等都是杭州人。这些作家和他们的作品，能从多角度向读者展示杭州的山水人文，彰显杭州深厚的文化底蕴。

　　最后，注意选录那些与杭州关系密切，并为世人所熟知的作家作品。他们或曾在杭州为官，造福一方百姓，如白居易、苏轼，以及曾任杭州知州、疏浚西湖并修建杨公堤的杨孟瑛；或长期隐居杭州的，如林逋、俞樾、黄公望；或死后葬于杭州的，如于谦、张煌言、章太炎、秋瑾、李叔同等人。

江山也要伟人扶，神化丹青即画图

　　本书诗词在内容上大体分为四个方面。

　　一、吟咏杭州特别是吟咏西湖山水景物的诗词。杭州西湖是中国著名的风景名胜区、国家5A级旅游景区，被列入《世界遗产名录》。杭州自南宋时就形成了西湖十景。经过历代不断增添，到清乾隆时期已增至三十二景。20世纪80年代和21世纪初，杭州市又先后评选出了"新西湖十景"和"三评西湖十景"。在传统西湖景点的基

characteristics, Zhejiang style, and Hangzhou charm".

Hangzhou City University is a full-time undergraduate institution founded by Zhejiang University in cooperation with Hangzhou Municipal People's Government, and it is also a model under the cooperation of famous city, university and business in China. As a university striving for the access to the top 100 universities in China, it has long cherished a wish to contribute to the construction of the Hangzhou Asian Games. With the support of President Luo Weidong, we decided to compile the book *One Hundred Poems on the West Lake in Hangzhou Through the Ages* and on behalf of Hangzhou offer it as a gift to the Games.

In mid-spring, warblers sing in flowers sea, taking you into dreams;
A clear wind and bright moon urge you to be poetically gay.

In this book, our major concern is the selection of those masterpieces of famous writers through the ages, for example, Li Bai, Wang Changling, Bai Juyi and Li He in the Tang Dynasty; Liu Yong, Su Shi, Lu You and Xin Qiji in the Song Dynasty; Guan Hanqing and Zhao Mengfu in the Yuan Dynasty; Gao Qi, Tang Xianzu and Yuan Hongdao in the Ming Dynasty; Huang Zongxi, Chen Weisong and Lin Zexu in the Qing Dynasty; and Kang Youwei and Zhang Taiyan in the modern era. These famous writers and their masterpieces are like a group of stars shining brightly.

Secondly, attention is paid to the selection of works by some local Hangzhou writers, such as Luo Yin, Zhou Bangyan, Zhu Shuzhen, Yu Qian, Li E, Yuan Mei, Hong Sheng, Gong Zizhen. Their works can show readers the profound humanities and cultural heritage of Hangzhou from multiple perspectives.

Finally, attention is paid to the selection of writers who are closely related to Hangzhou and are well known to the general public.They have served as officials in Hangzhou, benefiting the people, such as Bai Juyi, Su Shi, and Yang Mengying; or long-term recluses in Hangzhou, such as Lin Bu, Yu Yue, and Huang Gongwang (the painter of *Dwelling in the Fuchun Mountains*); or those buried in Hangzhou, such as Yu Qian, Zhang Huangyan, Zhang Taiyan, Qiu Jin, and Li Shutong.

Mountains and rivers shall also be graced by great men;
When the colours of red and green are spiritualized, a picture is produced then.

The poems selected for this book are generally divided into four aspects:

1. Poems describing Hangzhou, especially the scenery of the West Lake. The West Lake of Hangzhou is a famous scenic spot in China and a national five-A tourist attraction, which is included on *The World Heritage List*. The "Ten Scenes of the West Lake" in Hangzhou has been known since the Southern Song Dynasty. Through successive generations, the number of scenes was increased to thirty-two during the Qianlong Period of Qing Dynasty. In the 1980s and the beginning of 21 century, Hangzhou citizens selected the "New Ten Scenes of the West Lake" and the "Third Nomination

础上又增添了新的景观。其中，大多数在我们选编的历代诗词中都有反映。

二、与杭州的风情民俗相关，表现杭州特色的诗词。如钱江观潮，元夜看灯，孤山探梅，柳堤踏春，清明品茶，六月赏荷，月夜泛舟，山影栖霞等。这些正是杭州西湖独有的文化特色。

三、歌颂、凭吊英雄豪杰，抒写志士豪杰爱国爱民情怀的诗词。如蒙冤而死的伍子胥、岳飞、于谦；为民族大义而英勇捐躯的张煌言。书中收录的辛弃疾、张元幹、王阳明、秋瑾等人的诗词，无不让人感受到其中的英豪之气。

四、一些咏物寓情、感时抒怀，反映当时社会现实的作品。如林升的《题临安邸》，文及翁的《贺新郎·西湖》，文徵明的《满江红》等，谴责正是统治者的苟安昏庸、荒淫无道，导致了宋朝的灭亡。

以上所举这些诗词，内容丰富，题材各异，异彩纷呈，蔚为大观。就形式看，既有古风、绝句、律诗，又有词、曲等诗体；就风格看，诗有雄健、沉郁之分，词有豪放、婉约之别。无论是写景、论事、还是抒情，都能从这些作品体察到作者的那一份修养和怀抱，体现中华文明中人与自然和谐共融的精神特点。这些诗词，好似颗颗璀璨的珍珠，串成光彩夺目的项链，既浓缩了杭州的历史与沧桑，展现了杭州的文化风貌，也折射出杭州的人文精神和历史文化传统。它们让人窥斑见豹，领略到中国诗词无穷的艺术魅力和情趣，更让读者感受到中华文化的博大精深。

欲把西湖比西子，浓妆淡抹总相宜

本书最大的特点，是采用了中英文对照形式。在版面设计上，采用左（中文）右（英文）页对应的形式，以方便读者中英文对照阅读。在体例上，有作者简介、诗词正文、注释和阅读提示四个部分。其中"阅读提示"重在简要介绍作品的思想内容和艺术特色，并作扼要的提示。为了方便外国读者阅读理解，我们省略了部分中文注释的翻译，并将能增进外国读者对诗词作品理解的一部分注释内容安排在英译阅读提示中。此外，我们还挑选了一些历代杭州西湖山水风景的名家

of Ten Scenes of the West Lake". New landscapes have been added to the traditional West Lake attractions. Most of them are reflected in the poems we have selected and compiled through the ages.

2. Poems related to the folk customs of Hangzhou, such as tide watching of Qiantang River, lantern viewing on the Lantern Festival, plum blossoms appreciating on the Isolated Hill, spring outing on the willow embankment, tea tasting in the Qingming season, lotus flowers enjoyment in midsummer, boating on the moonlit night, sunset glowing above the mountain shadow. They are culturally what the west lake owns.

3. Poems glorifying and memorializing heroes and expressing their patriotic ambitions, such as Wu Zixu, Yue Fei and Yu Qian who died a wrongful death; Zhang Huangyan, who died bravely for national interests. The poems of Xin Qiji, Zhang Yuangan, Wang Yangming, Qiu Jin and others included in the book make people feel the heroic spirit.

4. Some of the works that reflect the social reality of the time by chanting and expressing emotions and feelings, for example, Lin Sheng's poem "Written on the wall of Linan inn", Wen Jiweng's "Hexinlang", and Wen Zhengming's "Manjianghong". These poems condemned that it was the rulers' extravagance and incompetence that led to the demise of the Song Dynasty.

The poems cited above are rich in content, varied in subject matter, and beautiful in a variety of ways. In terms of form, there are various poetic styles such as old free style and metrical style, including ci (a kind of Chinese classical poetry conforming to a definite pattern, the length of its sentences changes with the tune of music, also being called long-short ju) and qu (a form of verse popular in the Yuan Dynasty, also known as yuanqu). In terms of its features, poetry can be divided into vigorous and gloomy styles, and ci can be divided into those of being bold and graceful. Whether it is about writing scenery, discussing matters, or expressing emotions, you can find authors' cultivation and breadth of mind from their works. These poems, like dazzling pearls, are strung together into a necklace, which not only concentrate the history and vicissitudes of Hangzhou, but also show the cultural style and reflect the humanistic spirit of Hangzhou. They provide a glimpse of the infinite artistic charm and interest of Chinese poetry, and make readers feel the profoundness of Chinese culture.

To compare the West Lake to Xishi, the ancient beauty,
Any makeup would be suitable, light or heavy.

The most important feature of this book is the use of Chinese-English bilingual form. In terms of layout, the left (Chinese) and right (English) pages correspond in parallel to each other, so as to facilitate readers' reading in both Chinese and English. In terms of structural arrangement, the book is divided into four parts: the author's introduction, the body of the poem, notes and reading tips. Among them, the reading tips focus on briefly introducing the ideological content and artistic characteristics of the works, and providing brief hints. In order to facilitate foreign readers' understanding, we have omitted the translation of some Chinese annotations and included some of the annotations that can improve foreign readers' understanding of the poems in the English

画作和书法作品作为插图，让读者在阅读诗词佳作、感受诗情画意的同时，也能通过画面，欣赏到杭州和西湖的美景。虽然书名冠以"历代"，但是本书所录诗词的下限止于近代 1900 年以前出生作家的作品，现当代作家的作品只能割爱了。

未能抛得杭州去，一半勾留是此湖

本书的顺利出版，我们要衷心感谢杭州市亚运会组委会的大力支持；感谢浙江省社会科学界联合会的大力支持；感谢浙大城市学院和浙江大学出版社的大力支持；也要感谢殷企平教授和颜钟祜教授一丝不苟地审核了全部英译文本。我们还要特别感谢中国工程院原常务副院长、浙江大学原校长潘云鹤院士欣然为本书题写书名；感谢浙大城市学院校长罗卫东先生为本书作序。所有这些都增添了本书的光彩。

当年大诗人白居易曾说："江南忆，最忆是杭州。"我们希望本书能为促进中外文化和文明的交流奉献一份绵力，让参加杭州亚运会的四海宾朋、八方来客，特别是国际友人，在亲见正向世界名城迈进的杭州的勃勃英姿的同时，也能通过这本小书进一步认识和了解中华文化，加深对于中国和杭州的印象，爱上这座文明美丽的城市！

张梦新　柏　舟

2021 年 12 月

translation. In addition, we have selected some landscape paintings of Hangzhou and the West Lake and calligraphic works through the ages as ornaments to bring out the flavor of the book. Although there is the word "ages" in the title of the book, poems selected are limited to authors born before 1900 and the works of the current generation can only be given up.

Why am I leaving Hangzhou so reluctantly?
It is the West Lake that holds me up so firmly.

For the successful publication of this book, we would like to sincerely thank the Organizing Committee of Hangzhou Asian Games for their great support; thank Zhejiang Federation of Social Sciences Circles, Hangzhou City University and Zhejiang University Press for their strong support. We would also like to thank Professors Yin Qiping and Yan Zhonghu for their meticulously rummaging through the entire English translation. We would like to express our special thanks to Academician Pan Yunhe, the former Executive Vice President of the Chinese Academy of Engineering and the former President of Zhejiang University, for kindly scripting the title of this book. And we would also like to express our thanks to Mr. Luo Weidong, the President of Hangzhou City University, for his prefaces. All these add glamor to this book.

The great poet Bai Juyi once said, "Memories of the South of Yangtze River, the most unforgettable place is Hangzhou prefecture." We hope that this book will contribute to the exchange of culture and civilization between China and abroad, so that the guests and visitors from all over the world, especially international friends, who are attending the Asian Games in Hangzhou, will witness the vigorous appearance of Hangzhou, which is becoming a world famous city, and at the same time, through this book, they will get to know and understand Chinese culture, along with a deep impression of Hangzhou and even a partiality for this beautiful city.

Zhang Mengxin　Bai Zhou
December 2021

目 录

One Hundred Poems
on the West Lake in Hangzhou
Through the Ages

Contents

南 齐

唐

宋

Southern Qi Dynasty

Tang Dynasty

Song Dynasty

Yuan Dynasty

Ming Dynasty

Qing Dynasty

近　代

Modern Times

《三潭印月》

The Moon Printed in Three Pools

南 齐

One Hundred Poems
on the West Lake in Hangzhou
Through the Ages

Southern Qi Dynasty
(479–502)

苏小小

生卒年不详，相传是南齐时钱塘名妓，年轻貌美的才女。喜欢乘油壁车出行游湖，死后葬于西湖的西泠桥侧。

苏小小歌

妾乘油壁车[1]，郎骑青骢马[2]。
何处结同心， 西陵松柏下[3]。

【注释】

1. 油壁车：车壁加有青油衣，四周有布幔的车，一般为女子所乘。
2. 青骢马：青白杂色的马。
3. 西陵：周密《武林旧事·湖山胜概》："西陵桥，又名西林桥，又名西泠桥。"西陵又称"西林""西泠"。苏小小墓在西湖孤山西北侧。

Su Xiaoxiao

(the exact dates of her birth and death are unknown) is said to be a famed courtesan from Qiantang City (now Hangzhou, Zhejiang Province) in the Southern Qi Dynasty (479—502). Well known for her impressive intellectual talent and striking beauty, she enjoyed roaming around the West Lake by a painted carriage. Died at a young age, she was buried at the side of Xiling Bridge by the West Lake in Hangzhou.

The Song of Su Xiaoxiao

I'm sitting on the painted carriage;
My lover is riding on a horse of mixed hairs.
Today, we have made a knot heart
Under the pines by the Xiling Bridge.

　　此诗最早见于《玉台新咏》。苏小小这位西湖佳人的美丽形象，通过白居易、李贺、袁宏道、袁枚等名人的诗文和民间传说变得丰满灵动。这首诗颇显南朝乐府的特色，语言质朴自然，且情意深切、纤婉缠绵，充满了对爱情的追求和渴望。至今，在西湖边苏小小栖息的慕才亭四周的柱子上，仍刻满了前人凭吊的楹联。其中一联曰："湖山此地曾埋玉，花月其人可铸金。"这是对兰心蕙质的苏小小的高度评价和叹惋。

《西湖春晓图》南宋　佚名　故宫博物院藏

Spring Dawn at the West Lake, Anonymous, Southern Song Dynasty, The Palace Museum

Comments and Tips

The earliest version of this poem is included in *Yutai Xinyong* (New Songs from the Jade Terrace). In the poem, the "heart knot" is a traditional pattern of handicraft, often employed as a symbol of love. Xiling (the west tomb) refers to Su Xiaoxiao's tomb. The beautiful image of Su Xiaoxiao, the charming lady of the West Lake, has been vitalized through folktales and compositions of Bai Juyi, Li He, Yuan Hongdao, Yuan Mei and other celebrities. This poem features considerable characteristics of Southern Dynasties' folk songs, with plain and natural expressions, and profound, delicate, and lingering feelings, fully presenting her pursuit of love. Till today, the pillars around Mucai (admiring talent) Pavilion, where Su Xiaoxiao rested by the West Lake once, are carved with memorial couplets from the past generations, one of which claims: "A piece of beautiful jade was once buried in the lake and hills here; beautiful as a flower and bright as the moon, she deserves a statue of gold." It is a high praise and a sigh of regret for Su Xiaoxiao, who was impressively charming and talented.

双峰插云

Twin Peaks Piercing into Clouds

唐

One Hundred Poems
on the West Lake in Hangzhou
Through the Ages

Tang Dynasty
(618–907)

宋之问

（约656—713），名少连，字延清，汾州（今山西汾阳）人。唐高宗上元二年（675）进士。诗与沈佺期齐名，时称"沈宋"。有《宋之问集》。

灵隐寺 [1]

鹫岭郁苕峣 [2]，龙宫锁寂寥 [3]。

楼观沧海日，　门对浙江潮。

桂子月中落，　天香云外飘。

扪萝登塔远 [4]，刳木取泉遥 [5]。

霜薄花更发，　冰轻叶未凋。

夙龄尚遐异 [6]，搜对涤烦嚣。

待入天台路，　看余度石桥 [7]。

【注释】

1. 灵隐寺：位于杭州西湖西部的飞来峰旁，背靠北高峰。始建于东晋咸和元年（326），至今已有近1700年的历史。东晋咸和元年，印度高僧慧理来杭，见此地山峰奇秀，就住下来筹建灵隐寺。
2. 鹫岭：灵鹫山，这里指灵隐寺前的飞来峰。
3. 龙宫：传说中海龙王的宫殿，此指灵隐寺。
4. 扪（mén）：摸，这里是攀的意思。
5. 刳（kū）：刻，挖。
6. 夙龄：少年，早年。
7. 石桥：此处特指浙江省天台山的名胜石梁。

Song Zhiwen

(c.656—713), a native of Fenzhou (now Fenyang, Shanxi Province). He was a jinshi (a successful candidate passes the highest level of the Chinese imperial examinations) in the second year of the Emperor Tang Gaozong's Shangyuan Period (675). There exists *The Collection of Song Zhiwen*.

Lingyin Temple

Feilai Peak is towering, with vegetation verdant.

The Buddhist temple is solemn and silent.

The sunrise over the sea can be seen from the tower;

And by the door, one can hear the tide on Qiantang River.

From the moonlight seems to fall the osmanthus.

From beyond the clouds floats the fragrance of flower

I climb vines to ascend the distant pagoda.

And make a ladle to fetch from afar the spring water.

After the first frost, the mountain flowers are still bright.

Although there is thin ice, the leaves have not withered yet.

When I was young, I liked to travel far to pursue wonder;

I also liked to search for clever couplets to get rid of uproar.

I will continue my journey south to climb Tiantai Mountain.

There I will cross the Stone Bridge to seek youth fountain.

山水未深鱼鸟少此生

逃难李福唐栖雅三公

陕流上稿朱等桥小结

卢寓和靖诗意

甲寅三月其昌画

元時倪云林王师明皆

補此诗意惟黄子久

未之见此川其画为此

玄宰书法

辛卯中秋月

【阅读提示】

杭州灵隐寺是中国佛教禅宗的十大名刹之一。这首诗首两句写灵隐寺飞来峰山势的高峻和佛殿的空寂，第三至六句写登楼之所见，后面八句则写诗人游览灵隐寺时，寻幽探胜的情趣和感想。"楼观沧海日，门对浙江潮"两句，对仗工整，景象壮阔，最为脍炙人口，有传说乃是当时出家在灵隐寺的著名诗人骆宾王所作。

《林和靖诗意图》

明　董其昌　故宫博物院藏

Poetic Contemplation of Lin Hejing, Dong Qichang, Ming Dynasty, The Palace Museum

Comments and Tips

Lingyin Temple in Hangzhou is one of the ten most famous Buddhist Zen temples in China. Feilai (Flying from Afar) Peak in front of the temple is said to have flown from India, hence the name. The "Stone Bridge" refers specifically to the famous stone beam in Tiantai Mountain, Zhejiang Province. The first two lines of the poem are about the steepness of Feilai Peak and the deserted stillness of the Buddhist temple. The third to the sixth lines are about what the poet saw when he climbed up the building. The last eight lines are about the poet's interest in exploring and seeking the secluded attractions and his consequent response when he visited Lingyin Temple. The two lines, "The sunrise over the sea can be seen from the tower; and by the door, one can hear the tide on Qiantang River", are most popular for their neat lines and magnificent scenery. It is said that these two lines were written by Luo Binwang, a famous poet who was then a monk at Lingyin Temple.

孟浩然

（689—740），襄州襄阳（今属湖北）人，世称孟襄阳。早年隐居鹿门山。年四十，游京师，应进士不第。后为荆州从事，因疽发而卒。工诗，善写山水景色，与王维齐名，并称"王孟"。有《孟浩然集》。

与杭州薛司户登樟亭楼作 [1]

水楼一登眺， 半出青林高。

帟幕英僚敞 [2]，芳筵下客叨 [3]。

山藏伯禹穴 [4]，城压伍胥涛 [5]。

今日观溟涨， 垂纶学钓鳌 [6]。

【注释】

1. 司户：官名，掌管地方的户口、钱粮、财物等。唐制，在县一级称司户。樟亭：杭州古时的观潮胜地。明代田汝成《西湖游览志》："浙江亭，古之樟亭也。"今已废。

2. 帟（yì）幕：小帐幕。

3. 下客：此指下等的宾客。作者自谦之词。叨（tāo）：食，吃，品尝的意思。

4. 伯禹穴：相传为夏代开国之主大禹的葬地。在今浙江绍兴的会稽山。

5. 伍胥涛：春秋末期吴国大夫伍子胥。他因受谗被吴王赐死，传说死后化为潮神。

6. 钓鳌：比喻抱负远大或举止豪迈。

Meng Haoran

(689—740), a native of Xiangyang (now in Hubei Province). His early years were spent in seclusion in Mount Lumen. At the age of forty, he travelled to the capital and failed the Jinshi examination. By the end of his life, he worked briefly as an official in Jingzhou and died of gangrene soon. He was celebrated as a fine poet excelling at landscape topics. He and Wang Wei, another major landscape poet, were jointly known as Wang-Meng. There exists *The Collection of Meng Haoran*.

Climbing Zhangting Tower in Hangzhou

Climbing the waterfront platform and looking far away,

From a high place a panoramic view of the forest can be seen someway.

My friend has opened his tent to set up a feast

For me, an inferior guest, to taste.

High on a mountain is hidden the tomb of the Great Yu,

The city of Hangzhou chokes the angry tides of Wu Zixu.

Today, I watched the sea tide rising,

Which has aroused my desire to go for the huge turtle fishing.

【阅读提示】

　　中国民间观潮的习俗始于汉魏，盛于唐宋，历经 2000 余年，至今不废，而杭州的钱江大潮更为世之奇观。这首诗写诗人登樟亭远眺之所见所感。前半首写登楼之所见，以及对主人的盛情款待表示自己的感谢和宾主宴饮之欢愉情景。值得注意的是后半首，作者逸兴遄飞，浮想联翩，想到了那为民治水的大禹和忠而被谤、为国身死的伍子胥，所以内心涌现欲"垂纶学钓鳌"的无限豪情。全诗情景相生，寓情于景，无愧杜甫称赞："（孟浩然）清诗句句尽堪传。"

《月夜看潮图》南宋　李嵩　台北故宫博物院藏

Watching the Tide on a Moonlit Night, Li Song, Southern Song Dynasty, Taipei Palace Museum

Comments and Tips

The Chinese custom of tide watching began in the Han and Wei dynasties and flourished in the Tang and Song dynasties, and has continued for more than 2,000 years. Zhangting Tower was formerly a tide-watching spot in Hangzhou. This poem is about how the poet responded to the bird's-eye view he got having ascended Zhangting Tower. The first half of the poem describes the panoramic view, expresses the poet's gratitude to the host for his hospitality and displays the pleasant experience of drinking with his host. In the second half of the poem, the poet's thoughts are of the Great Yu, who tamed the flood for people's sake, and Wu Zixu, who was slandered for his loyalty and died for his country. Consequently, his heart is filled with the lofty ambition of "fishing for the huge sea turtle". The whole poem is a combination of scenes and emotions, which facilitate each other. Du Fu once praised Meng Haoran's poetry, saying that "every line can be recited".

王昌龄

（约698—756），字少伯，京兆长安（今陕西西安）人。开元十五年（727）进士，曾贬官江宁丞、龙标尉，故世称"王江宁"或"王龙标"。工诗，尤长七绝，以边塞诗《出塞》《从军行》等知名。有《王昌龄集》。

浣纱女

钱塘江畔是谁家，江上女儿全胜花。
吴王在时不得出，今日公然来浣纱¹。

【注释】

1. 浣纱：洗涤棉纱或衣服等。

【阅读提示】

　　这是一首七绝。首两句以"胜花"的比喻赞美了钱塘女儿的美丽，而后两句则通过"吴王在时不得出，今日公然来浣纱"的对比，对荒淫的吴王进行了鞭挞与讽刺，而歌颂了唐代的世事清平。诗歌于叙事中寄寓了感慨，言简意深，耐人寻味，颇得温柔敦厚之体。

Wang Changling

(c.698—756), a native of Chang'an (now Xi'an, Shaanxi Province). He was a jinshi in the 15th year of Kaiyuan period (727), and was relegated to the post of county chancellor of Jiangning (now Jiangning District, Nanjing) and county lieutenant of Longbiao (now Qianyang County, Hunan Province). Wang was a major poet best known for his frontier poetry. There exists *The Collection of Wang Changling*.

The Laundry Women

Whose daughters are by Qiantang River?

The beauty of its maidens completely outdid the flowers.

They would have been locked in the palace of the King of Wu in the years early.

But now they have come to the riverside to wash silk clothes undisguisedly.

Comments and Tips

The first two lines of this poem praise the beauty of Qiantang's maidens with the metaphor of "outdid the flowers". The following two lines present a comparison scolding and satirizing the lascivious King of Wu, while praising the peace and relaxation people enjoyed in the Tang Dynasty. A sigh of relief can be sensed in the narrative, which offers this seemingly plain poem a meaningful implication in a way that is gentle and generous.

李 白

（701—762），字太白，号青莲居士，祖籍陇西成纪（今甘肃静宁西南）。天宝初供奉翰林。为权贵所谗，不到两年被迫辞官离京。安史之乱中，因曾入永王李璘幕府而受牵累，流放夜郎。中途遇赦东归。李白是伟大的浪漫主义诗人，诗风雄健豪放，想象力丰富，语言清新俊逸，被称为"诗仙"。与杜甫齐名诗坛，并称"李杜"。有《李太白集》。

与从侄杭州刺史良游天竺寺 [1]

挂席凌蓬丘 [2]，观涛憩樟楼。

三山动逸兴 [3]，五马同遨游 [4]。

天竺森在眼， 松风飒惊秋。

览云测变化， 弄水穷清幽。

叠嶂隔遥海， 当轩写归流。

诗成傲云月， 佳趣满吴洲 [5]。

【注释】

1. 从侄：堂房侄儿。刺史：州级最高行政长官。天竺寺：创建于晋代咸和年间的古寺。现有上天竺、中天竺、下天竺，此指下天竺寺。

2. 挂席：挂帆。蓬丘：传说中的蓬莱山。

3. 三山：传说中海上的蓬莱、方丈、瀛洲三座神山。

4. 五马：古代州郡刺史、太守的座驾可用五匹马拉，此指刺史李良。

5. 吴洲：泛指吴地的洲渚。杭州在春秋时曾属吴国。

Li Bai

(701—762), a poet whose family originated from Chengji (now the southwest of Jingning, Gansu Province). At the beginning of Tianbao period, he was summoned to serve at the Royal Academy of Arts. Slandered by the power, Li Bai was forced to resign and left the capital in less than two years. After the An-Shi Rebellion, he was exiled to Yelang because of his involvement with Li Lin, the Prince of Yong (the title of Li Lin) and then was pardoned on his way of the exile and returned. Li Bai was a great romantic poet with a robust and bold poetic style and known as the "poet-immortal". He and Du Fu were jointly known as Li-Du. There exists *The Collection of Li Taibai* (Li Bai's courtesy name).

Visiting Tianzhu Temple with My Nephew

Sailing on the waves to visit Penglai Island.

Climbing up the tower to see the Qiantang tide.

I want to visit the three immortal hills on the sea.

A five-horse caravan took him and me to the mountain free.

At a glance, Tianzhu Temple is hidden in the forests high,

The pine trees are soughing when autumn breeze sweeps by.

The changing of clouds can measure the changes in the world.

Indulging in the landscape, one can enjoy the secluded mood.

Although there are mountains between here and the ocean.

Sitting by the window, I can see the river flowing into the horizon.

My poems can stand proud of the moon and cloud.

The realm of Wu and Yue is full of interest all around.

【阅读提示】

　　这是一首古体诗，作于开元二十七年（739）秋。其时，李白的堂房侄儿李良任杭州刺史，而李白正漫游越中。全诗写了游览天竺寺的逸兴和欢会吟诗的愉悦。比喻、拟人、借代、夸张等手法的运用，使得全篇气势酣畅，逸兴遄飞，俊逸豪放；而"诗成傲云月"，尤显李白豪爽不羁的个性与奇思雄才。

《禹航胜迹图》册（十八之八《天竺香市》）清　佚名　杭州西湖博物馆藏

A Great Gathering of Buddhist Pilgrims in Tianzhu Temple in the album of *Spots Traversed by the Great Yu*, Anonymous, Qing Dynasty, West Lake Museum of Hangzhou

Comments and Tips

This poem was written in the autumn of the 27th year of Kaiyuan period (739) while Li Bai was traveling in Yuezhong (now the northeast of Zhejiang Province). Li Liang, Li Bai's fraternal nephew, was then the prefectural governor of Hangzhou. This poem presents Li Bai's high spirits of visiting Tianzhu Temple and his pleasure in reciting poems at the happy gathering. It also shows Li Bai's bold and unrestrained personality and his brilliant conceits and amazing gift as a poet.

白居易

（772—846），字乐天，号香山居士。祖籍太原，后迁居下邽（今陕西渭南）。贞元十六年（800）举进士，曾任翰林学士，官至刑部尚书。长庆二年（822）任杭州刺史，筑堤捍钱塘湖，溉田千顷。他是杜甫之后又一杰出的现实主义大诗人，所作诗、词、乐府等内容丰富，风格多样，语言通俗。有《白氏长庆集》。

春题湖上

湖上春来似画图，乱峰围绕水平铺。

松排山面千重翠，月点波心一颗珠。

碧毯线头抽早稻，青罗裙带展新蒲。

未能抛得杭州去，一半勾留是此湖。

【阅读提示】

　　白居易于长庆四年（824）五月从杭州刺史任满上调，这首七律是他离杭前所作。前三联写景，通过碧绿的湖水、青翠的群山、如绿色地毯的稻田和似少女青罗裙带的新蒲，描绘了一幅青葱满眼的西湖春景图。而尾联以不舍意作结，表达了对杭州深深的留恋。全诗写景生动，比喻精妙，融情于景，情景交融，结尾尤有余情。

Bai Juyi

(772—846), born to a family originated from Taiyuan, Shanxi Province. He was a jinshi in the 16th year of Zhenyuan period (800) and was promoted to the post of the royal secretary later. At one time he held the post of Minister of Punishments (an ancient Chinese official position that united the public prosecutor and the judiciary). In the second year of Changqing period (822), he served as the prefectural governor of Hangzhou and built embankments to defend Qiantang Lake (now the West Lake), irrigating thousands of hectares. He was another great poet of realism after Du Fu, and his poetry is rich in content, diverse in genre and style, and popular in language. There exist Bai's Changqing Collection (which was composed during the Changqing period) and other works.

Spring Scenery of the West Lake

The West Lake in spring is as beautiful as a picture.
A group of jagged peaks are around the lake and the lake is like a mirror.
Pine forest covering the slopes dyes the hills overlapping green;
Reflected in water, the moon is like a pearl in the lake center upside down
    hanging.
The early rice has been eared, like thread on a green carpet in display.
As a belt of the blue skirt, the newly born rushes embellish the lake bay.
Why am I reluctant to leave Hangzhou so seriously?
It is the West Lake that holds me up so firmly.

Comments and Tips

Bai Juyi was promoted from his post as the prefectural governor of Hangzhou in May of the fourth year of Changqing period (824), and this poem was written before he left the city. The first three couplets depict the spring scenery of the West Lake. The last couplet reveals how much he would love to stay in Hangzhou. The whole poem is vivid, with exquisite metaphors and a combination of feelings with scenes. The ending part is particularly sentimental.

钱塘湖春行 [1]

孤山寺北贾亭西 [2]，水面初平云脚低。

几处早莺争暖树， 谁家新燕啄春泥。

乱花渐欲迷人眼， 浅草才能没马蹄。

最爱湖东行不足， 绿杨阴里白沙堤 [3]。

【注释】

1. 钱塘湖：西湖旧名。
2. 孤山：在西湖的里湖与外湖之间，因与其他山不相连接，所以称"孤山"。贾亭：
   唐贞元间，贾全任杭州刺史时于西湖建亭，人称"贾亭""贾公亭"。今已不存。
3. 白沙堤：即今白堤。该堤在唐以前就有，后来为纪念白居易而改称白堤。

【阅读提示】

　　这首七律就像一篇短小精妙的春日西湖游记。诗人从孤山、贾亭起行，一路观赏莺歌燕舞、鲜花绿草，直到在白沙堤的绿荫下休憩。全诗以平易恬淡、清新自然的语言，生动形象地描绘了西湖春意盎然的美丽景色，抒写了闲适愉悦之情。真如王若虚所评："乐天之诗，情致曲尽，入人肝脾，随物赋形，所在充满。"（见《滹南诗话》）

Walking by Qiantang Lake in Spring

From Gushan Temple to Jia Pavilion, along the lake I was walking,

The lake was as clean and quiet as a mirror after the rain, and there were
    low clouds floating.

On my way, there were early waking warblers fighting for the branches
    sunny,

And new coming swallows carried spring soil in the mouth, nesting busy.

On roadsides I was dazzled by the colourful flowers in a mass,

And the horse hooves were just buried in the spring grass.

My favorite place to walk is on the lake's east bank,

Where the Baisha Embankment is covered in shade of green willow rank.

Comments and Tips

This poem resembles a brief and delicate travelogue of the West Lake in springtime. Qiantang Lake is the dated name of the West Lake. Gushan is located between the inner lake and the outer lake of the West Lake and is not connected with any other hills, hence the name Gushan (the Isolated Hill). Jia Pavilion was built by the West Lake by Jia Quan, who was the governor of Hangzhou during Zhenyuan period of Tang Dynasty. It was known as Jiagong Ting (Lord Jia's Pavilion) but no longer exists today. The poet started his journey from Gushan and Jia Pavilion, and enjoyed the birds singing and dancing as well as colourful flowers and green grass all the way until he rested under the shade of green trees of Baisha (white sand) embankment. The poem vividly depicts the lovely spring scenery of the West Lake and expresses the feelings of relaxation and pleasure in plain, peaceful, fresh and natural language.

杭州春望

望海楼明照曙霞， 护江堤白踏晴沙。

涛声夜入伍员庙¹，柳色春藏苏小家。

红袖织绫夸柿蒂²，青旗沽酒趁梨花³。

谁开湖寺西南路， 草绿裙腰一道斜⁴。

【注释】

1. 伍员庙：杭州有伍公山与吴山连接。山顶原有伍子胥庙，俗称"伍公庙"或"伍
   员庙"，祭祀春秋时期吴国大夫伍子胥，山由此得名。
2. 柿蒂：杭州出柿，蒂花者尤佳。此指绫的花纹图案像柿蒂。
3. 沽：买。杭俗酿酒，趁梨花盛开时将酒酿好，号为"梨花春"。
4. 末两句白居易自注云："孤山寺路在湖洲中，草绿时，望如裙腰。"

【阅读提示】

　　这首七律写杭州春望。首联写登望海楼观朝霞灿烂，阳光下江堤白沙明亮耀眼。颔联写夜潮的汹涌澎湃和秦楼楚馆的温柔妩媚，上句悲壮，下句妩媚，相反相成。颈联转而写所见杭城之特产柿蒂绫和梨花春酒。尾联则见望中之西湖，孤山寺路在湖洲中，恰如一条翠绿的裙腰。全诗八句皆写春望，特别是中间两联对仗工整，结句又比喻新奇，结足春意，自尔不俗。

Looking at the Spring Scenery of Hangzhou from Afar

Looking at the sea from upstairs, the morning glow reflects the building
    red and bright;

Walking on the riverbank, the sun shines the beach snow white.

At night, spreads into Wu Zixu's temple, the wave sounds from the river;

In the morning, the smoke-like willows are hazy, where Su Xiaoxiao's
    boudoir was hidden ever.

Wearing brocade costumes, the best you will praise the persimmon stalk
    pattern;

When pear blossoms are in full bloom, travelers drink wine at a tavern.

There is a causeway to the southwest of the temple, but who built it?

You can see from a distance, floating obliquely on the water a green skirt belt.

Comments and Tips

This poem depicts what the poet observed in the springtime of Hangzhou. Wu
Zixu's Temple, commonly known as Wugong Temple (temple of Lord Wu) or
Wu Yuan (his name) Temple, was originally located on top of Wugong Hill in
Hangzhou, which is connected with Wu Hill. The first couplet is about enjoying
the morning glow at sea from upstairs, and the bright white sand of the river
bank in the sunshine, while the second couplet mentions the surging tide at night
and the gentle charm of the courtesan's place, resulting in a parallel of solemn
magnificence and lovely tenderness, which are opposite yet complementary. The
focus of the following couplet shifts to the persimmon stalk patterned brocade and
pear-blossom-spring wine, two specialties of Hangzhou. The last couplet displays
the West Lake view, with the causeway connecting Gushan Temple and islands in
the lake looking like a green skirt belt. All the eight lines of the poem are about the
spring view, and the parallel structures of the middle two couplets are especially
neat and tidy. The concluding couplet offers an unusually novel conceit and
reveals completely the exuberance of the springtime in a particularly original way.

忆江南¹（三首其一）

江南好，风景旧曾谙²。

日出江花红胜火，春来江水绿如蓝³，能不忆江南。

忆江南（三首其二）

江南忆，最忆是杭州。

山寺月中寻桂子⁴，郡亭枕上看潮头⁵，何日更重游。

【注释】

1. 忆江南：唐教坊曲名。《乐府诗集》云："'忆江南'一名'望江南'，因白氏词，后遂改名'江南好'。至晚唐五代，成为词牌名。"
2. 谙（ān）：熟悉。
3. 绿如蓝：绿得比蓝还要绿。如，用法犹"于"，有胜过的意思。蓝，蓝草，其叶可制青绿染料。
4. 桂子：桂花。白居易《东城桂》诗自注："旧说杭州天竺寺每岁中秋有月桂子堕。"
5. 郡亭：古之樟亭，旧为观潮胜地。一说是唐代杭州刺史衙门里的虚白亭。

【阅读提示】

　　白居易久住西北，来到江南，感受最深的自然是那一江碧绿的春水。在第一首中，作者通过日出时"红胜火"的江花和"绿如蓝"的江水，写出了他眼中的江南春景。词中景物异色相衬，色彩明丽，让人耳目一新。第二首则通过"山寺月中寻桂子"和"郡亭枕上看潮头"这两个极有代表性的景观，让人感受杭州的美景奇观，从而心驰神往，心中长忆。

Yijiangnan (the First of Three)

The beauty of the South of Yangtze River,

I have experienced its scenery.

At sunrise, the flowers on the river bank are like fire burning brightly.

In spring the river water is green in its blue colour pretty.

How can I not miss Jiangnan deeply?

Yijiangnan (the Second of Three)

Memories of the South of Yangtze River,

The most unforgettable place is Hangzhou prefecture.

In the moonlight, I wandered around the temple following the fragrance of
osmanthus flower.

Lying in the county pavilion, I could see the rising tide on Qiantang River.

When will I be able to revisit this area?

Comments and Tips

The title "Yijiangnan" means "recalling Jiangnan, the South of Yangtze River".
It was renamed "Jiangnanhao" (the Beauty of the South of Yangtze River) after
these ci poems by Bai Juyi. It became the title of a settled pattern of ci in late Tang
Dynasty (late 9th century) and the Five Dynasties (early 10th century). The first
poem depicts the spring scenery of Jiangnan. It offers a refreshing presentation of
the impressive contrast between vibrant colours of the scenery. The second poem,
however, presents two representative scenes, the fragrant osmanthus flowers
of the temple in the moonlight and the rising tide of Qiantang River. Fascinated
readers therefore would long for the amazing scenery and spectacular views of
Hangzhou and keep the views in heart.

元　稹

（779—831），字微之，河南洛阳人。贞元九年（793）以明经登第。长庆二年（822）拜相，大和三年（829）为尚书左丞。元稹与白居易为至交，同倡新乐府运动，共创"元白体"，世称"元白"。有《元氏长庆集》。

代杭民答乐天

翠幕笼斜日，　朱衣俨别楚[1]。

管弦凄欲罢，　城郭望依然。

路溢新城市，　农开旧废田。

春坊幸无事[2]，何惜借三年[3]！

【注释】

1. 朱衣：唐代刺史等四品、五品官穿红袍。此指刺史。俨：庄重。
2. 春坊：太子宫官署名。白居易杭州刺史任满授太子左庶子，属春坊。
3. 借三年：唐代地方官一任为三年。

Yuan Zhen

(779—831), a native of Luoyang, Henan Province. He was a Jinshi in the ninth year of Zhenyuan period (793). In the second year of Changqing period (822), he was briefly appointed as Deputy Minister of the Cabinet. Yuan Zhen and Bai Juyi were very close friends and elaborated together on the advocacy of the New Yuefu (a new genre of ancient poetry) movement. They were known jointly as Yuan-Bai and their poetry featured the Yuan-Bai Style. There exists *Yuan's Changqing Collection*.

To Bai Juyi on Behalf of Hangzhou People

The sun slanting westward is enveloped in the blue dome,

The red official uniform made the farewell banquet look solemn.

The sad orchestral music will end,

But only the tall walls still stand.

In the new urban area, many roads have been expanded.

Outside the town, countless fields have been reclaimed and cultivated.

That the Prince's Palace is peaceful, it is fortunate.

To serve in Hangzhou for another three years, why would you hesitate?

唐

【阅读提示】

　　白居易于长庆四年（824）卸任杭州刺史，元稹时任浙东观察使，这首诗是他代杭州百姓酬答白居易的。首两句交代了别宴的时间、地点、人物与情由。帷幕笼罩了西斜的落日，刺史白居易身穿红色官服庄重地在别宴与为他送行的杭州士民相见。三、四句用"管弦凄欲罢"，表明主客双方都充满了离情别绪，内心悲伤，只有视野中的城郭还是依然如故。后四句则说，道路已经直通到了新城的郊外，昔日荒芜的农田也开垦种上了庄稼。这说明白居易为杭州百姓做了很多好事。所以末两句说他前去赴任的春坊署无甚要事，何不再在杭州当三年刺史以造福百姓。全诗以淡语写深情，既表现了杭州士民对白居易的感谢，也表现了他们对白居易政绩的高度肯定以及挽留之情。

Comments and Tips

Bai Juyi left his post as the governor of Hangzhou in the fourth year of Changqing period (824). Yuan Zhen was then the governor of Eastern Zhejiang Province, and this poem is his reply to Bai Juyi on behalf of the locals of Hangzhou. The first two lines give the time, place, characters and context of the farewell banquet. The third and fourth lines of the poem mention the sad orchestral music and indicate that both the hosts and the guest were filled with sadness at that parting moment. In the last four lines, the poet spoke in the voice of the locals, referring to the cases of contributions made by Bai Juyi to the locals. The poem implies profound sentiments in seemingly casual words, showing the locals' gratitude to Bai Juyi as well as how grateful they felt for his merits and how much they would like him to stay.

《西湖风景图》册
（二十四之二《苏堤春晓》）
清 佚名 故宫博物院藏

Su Causeway at Spring Dawn in the album of
Scenery of the West Lake, Anonymous, Qing
Dynasty, The Palace Museum

张 祜

（约785—约852），字承吉，贝州清河（今河北清河）人。性耿介不容物，数受召幕府，辄自劾去。爱丹阳，晚年筑室隐居以终。以咏史诗及宫词著名。有《张承吉文集》。

题杭州孤山寺

楼台耸碧岑，一径入湖心。

不雨山长润，无云水自阴。

断桥荒藓涩，空院落花深。

犹忆西窗月，钟声在北林。

【阅读提示】

　　这首五律写杭州孤山寺。首两句写寺楼高耸，寺路直入湖心。中间四句描写山寺内外景色，语似平淡，却属对精切工巧，非熟悉其景者不能道。"断桥"即今白堤东头第一桥。本名宝祐桥，也称"段家桥"，自唐朝始称"断桥"。末两句追忆西窗明月和北林钟声，意在言外，令人神往。《唐诗成法》甚至评曰："足令后人搁笔。"

Zhang Hu

(c.785 — c.852), a native of Qinghe (now in Hebei Province), was upright and honest, innocent and impartial. After he was frequently recruited by the Governor Office, he was marginalized and eventually resigned and left. He liked living in the Danyang County, (now in Jiangsu Province), and then he lived in seclusion there until he died. He was famous for his historical poems and palace-style poetry. There exists *The Collection of Zhang Hu.*

Gushan Temple in Hangzhou

The tower stands high on the green peak,

A causeway goes straight into the middle of the lake.

No need for rain, the hills are always verdant,

Without white clouds, the lake looks more pleasant.

The Broken Bridge is covered with moss and unfrequented.

Full with fallen flowers, the courtyard is empty and desolated.

I remember a bright moon hanging outside the west window still,

Which accompanied by the bell sound from the forest of north hill.

Comments and Tips

This poem is about Gushan Temple in Hangzhou. The first two lines depict the towering temple and its path toward the center of the lake. The next four lines talk about the landscape inside and outside the temple in plain language but the words and expressions parallel with each other neatly. The Broken Bridge mentioned in the fifth line is now the first bridge on the eastern border of Bai Causeway. In the last two lines, the poet memorized the moon outside the window when he stayed in the temple that night, and the bell ringing through the woods nearby. What he described has some meaning beyond words and fires the reader's imagination.

李 贺

（790—816），字长吉，福昌（今河南宜阳县西）人。唐宗室后裔。七岁能辞章，为韩愈、皇甫湜所重。因避家讳，被迫不得应进士试。其诗辞尚奇诡，善驰骋想象，创造出新奇瑰丽的诗境。卒年仅二十六岁。有《昌谷集》。

苏小小墓

幽兰露，　如啼眼 [1]。

无物结同心，烟花不堪剪 [2]。

草如茵，　松如盖。

风为裳，　水为佩。

油壁车，　夕相待。

冷翠烛 [3]，劳光彩。

西陵下，　风吹雨。

【注释】

1. 啼眼：泪眼。

2. 烟花：旧时为妓女的代称。此处双关，也指墓地里艳丽的花朵。

3. 翠烛：磷火。

Li He

(790—816), a native of Fuchang (now west of Yiyang, Henan Province). He was a descendant of the imperial family of Tang Dynasty. He could write such good pieces of prose and verse at the age of 7 that he was fully appreciated by the esteemed poets Han Yu and Huangfu Shi. Because of the name clash (as his father's name has the same pronunciation as the word of Jinshi), he was forced to quit this exam. He used a very peculiar and unique language in his poems, with free and rich imagination, creating a novel and magnificent poetic world. He only died at the age of 27. There exists *The Collection of Changgu* (the name of his hometown).

Su Xiaoxiao's Tomb

The dews on the orchid are her sad teardrops.

There is no more token to tie the heart knot,

And the misted flowers on the grave one could not bear to cut off.

The pine tree is an umbrella; the green grass is a carpet.

The breeze is her garment; the water is her jade pendant.

She is in a painted carriage, waiting by the lake every night.

The cold phosphorescence flashed with a sad, dark light.

Her soul is under the western grave,

Plaintive as breeze,

Sorrowful as drizzle.

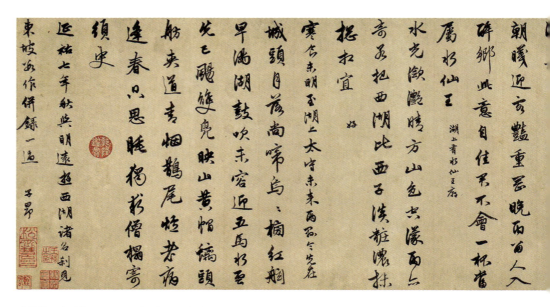

《苏轼西湖诗》元 赵孟頫 台北故宫博物院藏

Su Shi's Poems on the West Lake, Zhao Mengfu, Yuan Dynasty, Taipei Palace Museum

【阅读提示】

　　李贺这首诗写苏小小墓，通篇充满了丰富的想象和生动形象的比喻，通过幽兰、啼眼、烟花、磷火、风雨等意象，刻画了飘忽轻盈、若隐若现的苏小小鬼魂的形象和深幽凄清的意境，寄寓了对苏小小这位美丽善良却芳年早逝的才女的哀痛。在诗人心中，苏小小就是西湖里一个美丽的精灵。这种与众不同的描绘，体现了李贺诗歌浓郁的浪漫主义特色。

夜泛西湖

新月生魄迹未安　终破五六渐成圆
桓令夜吐艳如半璧　游人隐向三更看
特奇明的人争谁料得看到
三更向阑月渐落景
龙西起时
苍龙已起斗牛横　东方苍角昇长庚
渔人收筒及未晓　舡过帷
看苍蒲声
旅箔无边水茫茫　芦花夜闹沉沉露
香渐见荧明生远寺　更待月
黑看湖光
湖光非鬼亦非仙　风恬浪静光
满川须臾两三　入寺去就视不

Comments and Tips

This poem is about Su Xiaoxiao's tomb. The whole verse has rich imagination and vivid metaphors. The images of orchids, teardrops, misted flowers, phosphorescence, breeze and drizzle, all present the drifting and gleaming soul of Su Xiaoxiao, as well as create an air of melancholy. The poet lamented the death of this talented and kind young beauty. In his eyes, Su Xiaoxiao was a beautiful fairy of the West Lake. The poem is a good example of romantic features in a distinctive "Li He Style".

方　干

（约809—约888），字雄飞，新定（今属浙江）人。大和中，姚合出守金、杭二州，方干携卷投谒，深受叹赏。后举进士不第，遂隐会稽之镜湖。卒后门人私谥曰"玄英先生"。明人辑有《玄英集》。

叙钱塘异胜

暖景融融寒景清，　越台风送晓钟声[1]。
四郊远火烧烟月，　一道惊波撼郡城。
夜雪未知东岸绿，　春风犹放半江晴。
谢公吟处依稀在[2]，千古无人继盛名。

【注释】

1. 越台：越王台。在今浙江绍兴种山（今府山），相传为春秋时越王勾践登临之处。
2. 谢公：谢灵运，山水诗派的开创者。

Fang Gan

(c.809—c.888), a native of Xinding (now in Zhejiang Province). He was deeply admired for his outstanding literary attainments. He failed in the Jinshi examination, and then settled beside the Mirror Lake in Kuaiji County (now in Shaoxing County of Zhejiang Province). After his death, he was named "Master Xuanying"(It means winter, referring to one's failure life) by his own disciples. *The Collection of Xuanying* was then compiled in the Ming Dynasty.

About the Wonders of Qiantang

Warm scenery harmonious, cold scenery clear, distinct scenery in four
    seasons.
The morning breeze blows across the King Yue's Terrace, sending the bell
    tolls.
The moon is stained by the campfires and smoke in countryside terrains.
The Qiantang tide surges up a white ribbon, shaking the city walls.
It snows suddenly at night, but who knows that the east bank is full of
    green;
The spring breeze blowing, it is sunny half the river and misty rain half the
    other.
The place where Xie Lingyun chanted poems is faintly seen,
But who will continue his reputation, centuries later.

《西湖十景图》南宋　叶肖岩　台北故宫博物院藏

Ten Scenes of the West Lake, Ye Xiaoyan, Southern Song Dynasty, Taipei Palace Museum

【 阅读提示 】

　　方干此诗叙钱塘异胜。前面六句皆写实景，境界开阔，颇为大气。特别是中间两联对仗工整，既有对"远火烧烟月""惊波撼郡城"的壮观描绘，也有对"夜雪……东岸绿""春风……半江晴"的细腻刻画，可谓"气格清迥，意度闲远，于晚唐纤靡俚俗之中，独能自振"（见《四库全书总目》）。最后借对谢灵运之后无人能继盛名的感叹，含蓄表露出自己欲努力延续盛名的志向。

Comments and Tips

This poem is about the unique wonders of Qiantang (now Hangzhou). The first six lines depict the realistic view of its significance and broadness. Particularly, the couplets in the middle are in antithetical neat form. The last lines express his regret that after Xie Lingyun (the ancestor of Chinese landscape poetry in the Eastern Jin Dynasty), no one could win the same high reputation as him, implicitly revealing the ambition to be as renowned as Xie Lingyun.

皮日休

（约 838—约 883），字逸少，后改袭美，自号鹿门子，襄阳（今属湖北）人。咸通八年（867）进士，曾任著作郎、太常博士。诗文与陆龟蒙齐名，世称"皮陆"。有《皮子文薮》。

天竺寺八月十五日夜桂子

玉颗珊珊下月轮¹，殿前拾得露华新。
至今不会天中事， 应是嫦娥掷与人。

【注释】

1. 玉颗：玉珠，喻桂花。珊珊：轻盈、美好的样子。

【阅读提示】

　　这首七绝是诗人中进士一年后游杭州时所作，正是意气风发之时，所以诗中充满丰富的想象。将月宫珊珊飘落的玉珠般的桂花拾在手中，桂花露水未干，芳香宜人，那应该是月宫中的嫦娥抛向人间的吧。这种巧妙的联想，让诗作平添了几分活泼和灵动。

Pi Rixiu

(c.838 — c.883), a native of Xiangyang (now in Hubei Province). He became a Jinshi in the 8th year of Xiantong Period (867). He served as a senior civil servant in the court. His poetry and prose were on par with those of Lu Guimeng, and they were known as "Pi-Lu". There exists *The Collection Works of Pizi* (his elegant name).

Enjoying Osmanthus at Tianzhu Temple on Mid-Autumn Night

Like the jade crumbs scattering from the Moon Palace,
In front of the hall still is retained osmanthus fragrance.
No one knows what has happened in the sky yet?
It should be mascot that Chang'e threw to human race.

Comments and Tips

This poem was created a year after the poet became a Jinshi, when he travelled around Hangzhou. As he was in high feather at that time, this poem was rich in imagination. The osmanthus, like jade crumbs, slowly floated down from the moon, when held in the hand, still wet with dew, and pleasant with fragrance. They were sprinkled by the goddess Chang'e from the Moon Palace. What a brilliantly conceived association, which makes the poem more vivid and lively.

罗　隐

（833—910），字昭谏，新城（今浙江富阳）人。本名横，因十举进士不第，遂改名隐。光启三年（887），镇海军节度使钱镠表其为钱塘令，后迁节度判官、给事中等职。工诗文，其诗颇有讽刺现实之作；其杂文《谗书》，皆抗争愤激之言。清人辑有《罗昭谏集》。

钱塘江潮

怒声汹汹势悠悠，罗刹江边地欲浮[1]。

漫道往来存大信，也知反覆向平流。

狂抛巨浸疑无底，猛过西陵似有头[2]。

至竟朝昏谁主掌？好骑赪鲤问阳侯[3]。

【注释】

1. 罗刹江：钱塘江别名，因江中有罗刹石得名。

2. 西陵：此指西兴，在今杭州市滨江区。

3. 赪（chēng）鲤：赤色鲤鱼。传说中仙人所骑的神鱼。阳侯：传说中的波涛之神，借指波涛。《楚辞·九章·哀郢》："凌阳侯之泛滥兮，忽翱翔之焉薄。"马茂元注："阳侯，大波之神，这里用作波涛的代称。"

Luo Yin

(833—910), a native of Xincheng (now Fuyang District, Zhejiang Province). Since he failed many times in the Jinshi examinations, he changed his name to Luo Yin ("Yin" implies his decision to live a mundane life without taking any qualification exams for the court). In the 3rd year of Guangqi Period (887), Qian Liu, the military commissioner in the outlying prefecture of Zhenhai (now in northern Zhejiang Province and southern Jiangsu Province), appointed Luo Yin the Commander of Qiantang County. Luo Yin was later transferred to a position as an official to assist the military commissioner. He made outstanding contributions to poetry and prose. He satirized the reality in most of his poems. There exists *The Collection of Luo Yin*.

Qiantang River Tide

Fierce and boundless is the tides of anger,

The land is floating on both sides of the river.

The spring tide has always a flood season,

And after rising, to calm the tide will return.

When the tides come, it seems to throw out all the water from seas;

Until passing Xiling, its fierce momentum will not cease.

Who is in control of the law of the tide?

To inquire the god of waves, only a red carp can I ride.

【阅读提示】

　　此诗为罗隐在钱镠（五代十国时期吴越国创建者）手下为官时所作。起首两句就先声夺人，形象地描绘了钱塘江潮怒涛汹涌的浩大声势，使得江边的大地都仿佛随之沉浮。中间四句写潮水往来自有汛期，有涨也有落。大潮好似带来无尽的海水，但只要过了西陵，势头就会趋于平缓。结尾两句则发出诘问：究竟是谁在主掌潮涨、潮落的规律？我只好骑着传说中的赤色大鲤鱼，去向大波之神求教。诗歌将现实的描写与神话传说相结合，诗笔峻拔，婉畅可咏。

《钱塘秋潮图》南宋　夏圭（传）　苏州博物馆藏

Autumn Tides in Qiantang River, Xia Gui(to be decided), Southern Song Dynasty, Suzhou Museum

Comments and Tips

Luo Yin wrote the poem when he worked for Qian Liu (the founder of Wuyue State in Five dynasties and Ten states). The first two lines are very eye-catching by portraying a scene of angry torrents rolling thunderously to flood the riverside land. The four lines in the middle part tell the law of tidal seasons. The high tides were draining into the town with an inexhaustible supply of power, but when passing Xiling (now Xixing in Binjiang District of Hangzhou), they gently calmed down. In the last lines, the poet asked who was the real master of the tide? In the end, the poet had to ride on the legendary big red carp, surfing on the waves to seek the answer from the river god. The poem combines the local myth with the visible scenery in a forceful language and catchy rhythm.

《苏堤春晓》

Spring Dawn at Su Causeway

One Hundred Poems
on the West Lake in Hangzhou
Through the Ages

Song Dynasty
(960–1279)

潘 阆

（？—1009），字逍遥，自号逍遥子，大名（今属河北）人。太宗至道元年（995），以能诗受召见，赐进士及第，授国子四门助教。后坐王继恩狱，亡命潜逃。真宗时，任为滁州参军。其诗清劲洒脱而落落有致，王禹偁、苏轼皆称赏之。有《逍遥集》。

忆余杭[1]（十首其四）

长忆西湖，尽日凭阑楼上望。
三三两两钓鱼舟，岛屿正清秋。

笛声依约芦花里，白鸟成行忽惊起。
别来闲整钓鱼竿，思入水云寒。

【注释】

1. 忆余杭：词牌名，潘阆的自度曲。有《忆余杭》十首词，因回忆杭州诸胜而得名。每首词都以"长忆"开头，是宋词中最早的组词。

Pan Lang

(?—1009) was a native of Daming (now in Hebei Province). In the first year of Emperor Taizong's Zhidao Period (995), Pan was summoned to court for his fame as a poet. He was qualified as a Jinshi and was then appointed assistant professor of Guozijian (the Imperial Academy). In Emperor Zhenzong's reign, he was appointed military counsellor of Chuzhou. His poems were so fresh and vigorous, free and at ease with grace that he received great commendation from Wang Yucheng and Su Shi. There exists *The Collection of Master Xiaoyao* (Master Free and Easy, his art name).

Yiyuhang (the Fourth of Ten)

I often recall the West Lake,

Where I used to lean on the railing upstairs while awake,

Watching two or three fishing boats floating on the water awry.

It was in autumn and the island in the lake brightly caught my eye.

A clear sound of the flute seemed to come from the reed,

Startling a group of egrets flying in a high speed.

Since I left Hangzhou, I always like to go fishing by the water,

To immerse my thoughts into water-cloud and make it purer.

【 阅读提示 】

　　词，文体名。按谱填写，可合乐歌唱，是盛于宋的一种诗体。亦称"诗余""长短句"。"忆余杭"：潘阆自度曲，共十首，此为其四。这首词回忆秋天西湖的美丽风光：渔舟漂荡，笛声悠扬，白鸟飞翔，动静相宜，有声有色。最后则寄托了作者的逍遥自得、欲超尘出世的想法。通首寓情于景，情景交融，用笔淡炼，表现了作者对西湖深深的眷恋。

《西湖图》清　关槐　台北故宫博物院藏

The West Lake, Guan Huai, Qing Dynasty, Taipei Palace Museum

Comments and Tips

Ci, a Chinese literary genre of lyric poetry that began in the Tang and flourished in the Song, following certain poetic patterns based upon definitive musical tunes associated with a particular title, also known as Shiyu (another form of ci poetry) or Changduanju (lines of irregular lengths, another name of ci poetry). Originally, they were written to be sung to a tune of that title, with a set pattern of rhyme and tempo. Yiyuhang (Memories of Yuhang): the title of a pattern of ci composed by Pan Lang himself. This piece of ci here recalled the beautiful scenery of the West Lake in autumn. The ending lines present the poet's being content with his status of being free and easy and his transcendental mind. The emotion and scenery are perfectly blended here with a light and refined touch, showing his lingering nostalgia for the West Lake.

忆余杭（十首其十）

长忆观潮，满郭人争江上望。

来疑沧海尽成空，万面鼓声中。

弄涛儿向涛头立，手把红旗旗不湿。

别来几向梦中看，梦觉尚心寒。

【 阅读提示 】

　　这首词回忆了钱塘观潮的壮丽景象。农历八月十八，是钱塘江潮汛的高潮，该词首写宋时杭州万人空巷，士民皆前往江边观潮的盛况；继写大潮的波澜壮阔，生动形象地描写了钱江潮的汹涌澎湃、惊天动地。而"弄涛儿"两句，则叙写了弄潮健儿英勇搏击风浪的大无畏精神和履险如夷的不凡身手。最后则通过钱江观潮的情景频频入梦和梦醒时的心有余悸，深化了钱江潮的雄伟和壮阔。全词纯用白描，但想象丰富，描写极为生动传神。

Yiyuhang (the Tenth of Ten)

I often recall the sight of the Qiantang tide,

When people all over the city rushed up the riverside,

To see if all the sea water was pouring into the river course.

Suddenly, thousands of drums were beaten, shaking the sky hoarse.

But you could see the surfers standing on the top of the tides as a set,

Holding the red flags and keeping them not wet.

Ever since I left Hangzhou, this scene has always appeared in my dream,

And when I wake up it still scares me that I deem.

Comments and Tips

This ci poem recalls the splendour of tidal bore watching. The 18th day of the eighth month of the Chinese lunar calendar coincides with the climax of Qiantang River's spring tidal bore. This ci poem here begins with the impressive moment of Hangzhou locals flooding to the riverside for bore watching in the Song Dynasty, followed by a vivid description of the spectacular waves of the surging tides of the billowy Qiantang River. The two lines involving "surfers" bring to life their valor and expertise. Finally, the magnificence of the Qiantang tide are reinforced by the poet's recurring dreams of the tide watching and the haunting fear and excitement when the poet awakened. The whole piece offers merely a plain presentation of the scene, but the imagination is rich and the description is extremely vivid and subtle.

林 逋

（967—1028），钱塘（今浙江杭州）人，字君复。早岁游江淮间，后归杭州，隐居西湖孤山二十年。种梅养鹤，终身不仕，也不婚娶，故时称"梅妻鹤子"。善行书，喜为诗，风格淡远。卒，仁宗赐谥"和靖"（不刚不柔曰和；柔德安众曰靖）。有《和靖诗集》。

山园小梅

众芳摇落独暄妍[1]，占尽风情向小园。

疏影横斜水清浅，暗香浮动月黄昏。

霜禽欲下先偷眼，粉蝶如知合断魂。

幸有微吟可相狎，不须檀板共金尊[2]。

【注释】

1. 暄妍：明媚美丽。
2. 檀板：演唱时用以打拍子的檀木拍板。

【阅读提示】

本诗首联写梅花盛开在百花凋零的寒冬，所以能独占风情。颔联写了梅花的气质和风韵，不但写出了梅枝疏影横斜的姿态，更刻画出其暗香浮动的神韵。颈联则借霜禽"偷眼"和粉蝶"断魂"的拟人手法，衬托出作者爱梅之深。尾联直抒胸臆，借咏梅抒发了自己澄澹高逸的情怀。全诗写梅、咏梅、赞梅、爱梅，浑然一体，而这凌霜傲雪的寒梅，也俨然是作者人格的化身。其中"疏影横斜水清浅，暗香浮动月黄昏"两句，最为脍炙人口，成为千古传诵的名句。

Lin Bu

(967—1028) was a native of Qiantang City (now Hangzhou, Zhejiang Province). He travelled to Jiangsu and Anhui in his early years. When he returned home at Hangzhou, Lin lived in recluse for 20 years on the Isolated Hill by the West Lake. He had never been an official or married. He planted Chinese plum trees and raised cranes, and was therefore known as having "plum wife and crane sons". His poems share a seemingly indifferent and remote style. When he died, Emperor Renzong bestowed the posthumous title of "Hejing" (harmony and calmness) on him. There exists *The Collected Poems of Hejing*.

Plum Blossoms in the Garden

You open in the season when all the other flowers fall,
And you have a unique style in this garden.
Your slanting shadow in the clear shallow water;
Your fragrance is floating in the air when the moon hangs in heaven.
White birds returning to the forest can't help taking a peek at you.
If butterflies know you are so beautiful, they will be smitten.
Fortunately, I have poetry to accompany you,
So why do I need music and wine as a perfect fusion?

Comments and Tips

The first couplet of this poem describes plum blossoms bloom in the cold winter with unique elegant appearance when all other flowers have faded. The second couplet is about the essential quality and charm of the blossoms. The personifying metaphors involving birds and butterflies in the following couplet reveal how affectionate the poet was towards plum blossoms. The last couplet expresses his ideals of transcendental purity and grace by means of eulogizing plum blossoms. The descriptions and chants of plum blossoms in this poem mingle with praises and affection, revealing the fact that the poet identified himself with the proud plum blossoms triumphing over frost and snow. The two lines involving slanting shadow and floating fragrance of the plum trees are the most popular and have been famous for thousands of years.

《湖上诗》南宋　赵昀　大都会博物馆藏

A Poem on the West Lake, Zhao Yun, Southern Song Dynasty, The Metropolitan Museum of Art

《林和靖探梅图》南宋　马远　出光美术馆藏

Lin Hejing Viewing Plum Blossoms, Ma Yuan, Southern Song Dynasty, Idemitsu Museum of Arts

北山晚望

晚来山北景，图画亦应非。

村路飘黄叶，人家湿翠微[1]。

樵当云外见，僧向水边归。

一曲谁横笛，蒹葭白鸟飞[2]。

【注释】

1. 翠微：青绿的山色。
2. 蒹葭：芦苇。

【阅读提示】

　　这首诗描写了北山傍晚宁静幽美、连图画也难以描绘的景色。你看，村边的小路上飘落着黄叶，青绿色的山气弥漫山村。远处山上的樵夫在云雾中若隐若现，寺庙中的僧人也正汲水归来。笛声悠扬，惊飞了芦苇丛中的白鸟。这种以动写静的方法，更衬托出山间的宁静。诗人正是通过对这种"诗中有画，画中有诗"的色彩斑斓秋景的描绘，巧妙地抒写了自己对山居的喜爱和隐逸之情。

Looking at the North Hill at Dusk

Looking at the scenery of North Hill at dusk,

No picture can compare with its beautiful nature.

Yellow leaves are falling along the roadside of the cottage,

And behind the bamboo the courtyard has an elegant feature.

You can meet woodcutters in the cloudy hill,

And monks return to the monastery at leisure.

Who is playing the music with a clear and bright flute,

Startling the egrets to fly from reed by the water?

Comments and Tips

The poem displays the peaceful and secluded scenery of North Hill at dusk, which can hardly be depicted even by means of pictures. The poet skillfully expressed his love for dwelling in a mountain in seclusion by the depiction of the colourful autumn scenes with a "picturesque poem" or a "poetic picture".

宋

长相思[1]

吴山青，越山青，两岸青山相送迎，谁知离别情？

君泪盈，妾泪盈，罗带同心结未成[2]，江边潮已平。

【注释】

1. 长相思：乐府《杂曲歌辞》名，内容多写男女或友朋久别思念之情。也为唐教坊曲名，后用为词牌。
2. 罗带同心：古代男女定情时，常用丝绸锦带打成心结，赠送对方作为信物，以示彼此"同心"。

【阅读提示】

　　这首词的上片起句用吴山、越山（杭州有吴山，无越山，"越山"是虚指）起兴，并借青山的无情，反衬主人公内心的离愁别恨。下片则借一女子的口吻，抒写了她"罗带同心结未成"的悲伤。词作采用了《诗经》以来民歌中常用的重复吟咏的手法，回环往复，有一唱三叹之妙。兼之语言质朴清新，使得这首词更声情并茂，名副其实，成为情深韵美的名篇。

Changxiangsi

Wu Hill is green; Yue Hill is green.

They seem to say farewell and meet again.

But who knows the feelings of parting?

There are tears in your eyes and tears in my eyes;

We can't tie a ribbon into a co-heart knot.

On the river bank has subsided quietly the tides.

Comments and Tips

Changxiangsi (Long Lasting Remembrance): a folk-song-style form of poetry which is mostly about the nostalgia for a long-lost love or friend. It was also used as the title of a song of Jiaofang (the royal institute for court entertainment) in the Tang Dynasty, and later employed as a Cipai (a particular pattern of ci poetry). The first half of this ci poem is introduced by the two hills of Wu and Yue (the latter does not exist in real life), and reflects the main character's innermost sadness at departure in contrast to the indifference of the hills. In the latter half, a woman's tone of voice is employed to express the sadness of unfulfilled love. This ci poem adopts the technique of repetitive chanting commonly used in folk songs since *The Book of Songs,* echoing unutterable pathos. It has become a famous piece with intense feelings and pleasant rhythm that comfort perfectly well with the title.

柳 永

（约987—约1053），初名三变，字耆卿，崇安（今福建武夷山）人。景祐年间进士，曾任屯田员外郎，世称"柳屯田"。他是北宋最早专力写词的作家，其词多写市井生活和羁旅行役，善用俚词俗语。有《乐章集》。

望海潮 [1]

东南形胜，三吴都会 [2]，钱塘自古繁华。

烟柳画桥，风帘翠幕，参差十万人家 [3]。

云树绕堤沙，怒涛卷霜雪，天堑无涯。

市列珠玑，户盈罗绮，竞豪奢。

Liu Yong

(c.987—c.1053) was a native of Chong'an, (now Wuyishan, Fujian Province). He was a Jinshi in Jingyou Period. In the Northern Song Dynasty, he was the first poet devoting himself to the writing of ci poems. Liu found subject matters in travels, labour services and vulgar life. His poetry utilized much colloquial language. There exists *Yuezhang Ji* (a collection of poetry with music).

Wanghaichao

Located in the southeast with beautiful mountains and rivers

And being the metropolis of Wuyue State,

Since ancient times, Qiantang has been a city prosperous.

Willows floating like smoke are covering the painted bridges,

And the breeze is gently opening the green curtains.

The jagged houses are visible, where live thousands of residence.

Along the river embankment, big trees surround;

When the tide comes, rolling up the snow-white waves,

Qiantang River is like a natural barrier and you can't see its bound.

There are jewellery shops all over the streets,

And every family is full of silks and satins,

Competing each other with luxury and treats.

重湖叠巘清嘉 [4]，有三秋桂子，十里荷花。

羌管弄晴，菱歌泛夜，嬉嬉钓叟莲娃。

千骑拥高牙 [5]，乘醉听箫鼓，吟赏烟霞。

异日图将好景，归去凤池夸 [6]。

【注释】

1. 望海潮：词牌名，乃柳永首创。双调，一百零七字，平韵。
2. 三吴：旧指吴兴、钱塘、会稽三郡。一说指吴兴、吴郡、会稽三郡。
3. 参差：大约。
4. 叠巘：重叠的山峰。
5. 骑：骑兵。牙：牙旗。
6. 凤池：凤凰池，此处指代朝廷。

【阅读提示】

这是一首用词写的"杭州赋"。上片起句总写杭州为东南形胜、三吴都会，接着从都市繁华、钱江壮阔、市民殷富三个方面写杭州的重要与富庶。而下片从湖山美景、四时风光、昼夜笙歌、老少同乐四个角度专门描写西湖。全词用铺叙手法，融写景、叙事、抒情于一体，且画面优美，词语典雅，乃歌咏杭州的名作。

A lake is inside the lake and hills outside the hills, which makes a
　　landscape place.
Not only osmanthus fragrance is drifting everywhere in autumn,
But lotuses are blooming in summer on lake surface.
On sunny days, the flute tune blows into the clouds from the reeds;
At night the songs of collecting water caltrops are heard in the lake,
Mixed with the laughter of the old fishing man and the girls picking lotus
　　seeds.
A team of honour guards is passing by, surrounding a huge flag imposing.
And the senior official is listening to the music while drunk,
Enjoying the colourful clouds above the lake and poems praising.
In the coming days, you will paint this beautiful scenery;
To present it in the Forbidden Garden and win praises surely.

Comments and Tips

Wanghaichao (Watching the Sea Tide from Distance), a pattern of ci poetry, could
be regarded as a "fu" (a Chinese literary genre of rhymed prose) of Hangzhou
presented by means of ci poetry. The first half offers a general introduction to
the grand city of Hangzhou, displaying its importance and affluence from three
aspects: the prosperity of the city, the magnificence of Qiantang River, and the
wealth of citizens. The latter half focuses on the West Lake from four perspectives:
the beauties of the lake and hills, the scenery of four seasons, playing and
singing by day and night, and the joy of people of all ages. The entire work uses
narrative techniques, integrating scenery, narration and lyricism. This ci poem is
famous as a masterpiece eulogizing Hangzhou with graceful pictures presented
in elegant language.

范仲淹

（989—1052），字希文，吴县（今江苏苏州）人。大中祥符八年（1015）进士。庆历三年（1043），入为枢密副使、参知政事。皇祐元年（1049）任杭州知州。工诗文及词，有《范文正公文集》。

寄西湖林处士[1]

萧索绕家云， 清歌独隐沦。
巢由不愿仕[2]，尧舜岂遗人[3]。
一水无涯静， 群峰满眼春。
何当伴闲逸， 尝酒过诸邻。

【注释】

1. 林处士：宋时隐居西湖的林逋。
2. 巢由：巢父和许由的并称。相传为尧时的隐士，尧欲让位于二人，二人皆不受。因用以指隐居不仕者。
3. 尧舜：唐尧和虞舜的并称。古史传说中的贤明君主。

【阅读提示】

　　这首诗是时任杭州知州的范仲淹写给林逋的。首联以萧索的居住环境，反衬林逋清歌独居的高洁；颔联以巢父和许由的不仕，比喻林逋的高逸；颈联再以对比的手法，赞美林逋"一水无涯静"和"群峰满眼春"的心境与幽逸之情；尾联则直接表明了自己欲与林处士相伴为邻的愿望。全诗起承转合层次分明，反衬、对比等手法的运用，更加深了诗人对林逋隐居不仕高尚志趣的赞赏，也表达出自己对隐逸生活的向往。

Fan Zhongyan

(989 — 1052) was a native of Wu County (now Suzhou, Jiangsu Province). He was a Jinshi in the eighth year of Dazhongxiangfu Period (1015). In the third year of Qingli Period (1043), he was appointed the Deputy Military Commissioner and then Chancellor of the government. In the first year of Huangyou Period (1049), he became the governor of Hangzhou. He was an expert in prose, poetry and ci. There exists *The Collection of Fan Wenzhenggong* (his posthumous title).

To Recluse Lin Bu of the West Lake

The house is surrounded by white clouds and looks desolate;

The chanting voice suggests that there is a hermit living in the garden.

In ancient times, Chao and You refused to join the court as an official;

How could there be a non-appointee in the times of Yao and Shun?

The lake is open and it seems extraordinarily secluded.

Encircled by the hills, there enters a spring view.

When can I be with you, a man of leisure?

I will come to visit and get drunk with you.

Comments and Tips

This poem was dedicated to Lin Bu when Fan Zhongyan was the governor of Hangzhou. The first couplet displays the desolate living environment in contrast to the loftiness of Lin Bu. The second couplet employs the allusion to Chaofu and Xu You (i. e. Chao You, two legendary hermits who refused Emperor Yao's offer of his crown) to present Lin Bu's nobleness and preference to freedom. The following couplet uses a contrast of the secluded lake and the hills with a lively spring view to praise Lin Bu's peaceful state of mind and leisurely feeling in solitude. The ending couplet directly expresses his desire to be with Lin Bu as a neighbor. The poem is well-structured, and the use of contrast reinforces the poet's appreciation of Lin Bu's noble ambition to live in seclusion, and expresses his own longing for a life of seclusion.

和运使舍人观潮 [1]（二首其一）

何处潮偏盛？钱塘无与俦 [2]。

谁能问天意，独此见涛头？

海浦吞来尽，江城打欲浮。

势雄驱岛屿，声怒战貔貅 [3]。

万叠云才起，千寻练不收。

长风方破浪，一气自横秋。

高岸惊先裂，群源怯倒流。

腾凌大鲸化，浩荡六鳌游 [4]。

北客观犹惧，吴儿弄弗忧。

子胥忠义者，无覆巨川舟！

【注释】

1. 运使舍人：运使的亲随。
2. 俦：相比。
3. 貔貅（pí xiū）：传说中的一种猛兽。
4. 六鳌：神话传说中负载海上仙山的六只巨龟。

Rewarding a Friend for Watching the Tide (the First of Two)

In vast China where is the most violent tide?

Only the Qiantang River tide is unparalleledly typified.

Who can understand the will of the heaven?

Why does the Qiantang tide have such a unique momentum?

As if swallowing up all the water in the bay,

The tide is going to beat the city floating away.

Its power can drive the islands in the Sea East;

Its momentum can surpass the fantastic beast.

When the tide comes, the wind rises and clouds surge over,

Like thousands of troops and horses galloping against the river.

Long wind can blow thousands of miles of waves broken,

The autumn air crossing, you can't distinguish between earth and heaven.

The tide washes down the high embankment;

Many tributaries are fed back by the torrent.

Like the incarnation of a giant whale, the waves are undulating.

The tide is vast, as if there were six great turtles swimming.

Tourists from the north will feel panic when they see this sight.

However, the local tide riders are not afraid to stand on the tide.

Besides, Wu Zixu is a man loyal and righteous.

He will not capsize the boats on the river dangerous.

《钱塘观潮图》南宋　李嵩　故宫博物院藏

Watching Qiantang Tides, Li Song, Southern Song Dynasty, The Palace Museum

【阅读提示】

　　范仲淹写有两首《和运使舍人观潮》,此为其一。诗歌以设问句式开篇,赞美了钱江大潮乃天下无与伦比,是只此独见的奇观。继而从潮水浪头之汹涌澎湃、声音之惊天动地、巨浪之前赴后继、气势之宏伟壮美、怒涛之崩崖裂岸,具体形象地描绘了钱江大潮,其波澜壮阔,可让大鲸飞空,让神话传说中负载海上仙山的六只巨龟畅游。这壮伟的景象,足以让北方的客人胆战心惊,而健硕的吴儿却还能表演弄潮。最后诗人赞美伍子胥是忠义之人,其怒涛不会翻覆巨舟,显示了作者对民生的关切。全诗写景生动传神,比喻、夸张和神话传说的运用,更渲染烘托了钱江潮的惊心动魄和壮观。

Comments and Tips

The poem begins with a rhetoric question. Then it vividly depicts the momentum of the spring tide of Qiantang River, by using the myth of six giant turtles (legendary large sea turtles carrying five sacred hills at sea swimming at will). Finally, the poet praised Wu Zixu (a senior official of Wu State in the late Spring and Autumn Period, who was ordered by his King to commit suicide for slander. Legend has it that he was incarnated as the tide god after death.) The poem offers a vivid and lively depiction of the views with the use of metaphor, exaggeration and allusion.

曾　巩

（1019—1083），字子固，南丰（今属江西）人，世称"南丰先生"。嘉祐二年（1057）进士。少有文名，为欧阳修所赏识。能诗，尤擅散文，为"唐宋八大家"之一。有《元丰类稿》。

钱塘上元夜祥符寺陪咨臣郎中丈燕席 [1]

月明如昼露叶浓，　锦帐名郎笑语同。
金地夜寒消美酒，　玉人春困倚东风。
红云灯火浮沧海，　碧水楼台浸远空。
白发蹉跎欢意少 [2]，强颜犹入少年丛。

【注释】

1. 上元：正月十五是上元节，又称"元宵节"，这一天民间有观灯的习俗。咨臣郎中：宋朝礼部郎中的别称。丈：古代对老年男子的尊称。
2. 蹉跎：时间虚度。

【阅读提示】

正月十五，杭州城的花灯自是美不胜收。此诗首联即写元宵夜的盛况，满城灯火通明，士女同乐，热闹非凡。颔联、颈联继写宴席的美酒歌舞，特别是"红云灯火浮沧海，碧水楼台浸远空"两句，对仗工整，描写夸张，写灯会的火树银花和舞榭歌台的灯火映照天空，极言满城灯火之盛。然而在尾联作者却突发感喟：自己"白发蹉跎欢意少"，只是"强颜犹入少年丛"。这种前后有巨大反差的反跌手法的运用，深化了诗歌的内涵，令人深思。

Zeng Gong

(1019—1083) was a native of Nanfeng (now in Jiangxi Province). He was a Jinshi in the second year of Jiayou Period (1057). He was known as a talented author since an early age and received commendation from Ouyang Xiu. As a fine poet, Zeng was also acclaimed as an expert in prose and was ranked as one of the Eight Great Prose Masters of the Tang and Song Dynasties. There exists *Yuanfeng Leigao* (classified scripts composed in Yuanfeng Period).

Accompanying Officials to the Lantern Festival Banquet

The full moon illuminated the dewdrops on the leaves glittering;
The officials in the tent were laughing and talking.
It was a cold night at the Buddhist temple, a good pastime in drinking;
The beauties looked mentally weary in the east wind blowing.
The lights reflected the clouds red, and the city seemed on the sea to swing;
By the water the buildings looked as if they were in the night sky floating.
The white-haired man seldom had a happy time in his whole being,
But he was like an old boy tonight, reluctantly frolicking.

Comments and Tips

The first couplet of this poem displays the festivities at the Lantern Festival night. The following two couplets move on to focus on fine wine and excellent performance of the banquet. The two lines about the "red clouds" and "emerald water" are neat in structure with exaggerated descriptions, speaking highly of the floweriness of the city lights. However, in the last couplet, the poet unexpectedly sighed that as an unaccomplished old man, he was merely forcing himself to join the young. This sharp contrast conveys a profound connotation of the poem and makes people ponder.

王安石

（1021—1086），字介甫，号半山，临川（今江西抚州）人。庆历二年（1042）进士，神宗时任参知政事，后两度为宰相。他执政后积极变法革新，曾封荆国公，世称"王荆公"。其在诗、词、散文上都有很高成就，为"唐宋八大家"之一。其诗词风格雄健峭拔，其散文简洁峻切。有《临川集》。

游杭州圣果寺 [1]

登高见山水，身在水中央。
下视楼台处，空多树木苍。
浮云连海气，落日动湖光。
偶坐吹横笛，残声入富阳 [2]。

【注释】

1. 圣果寺：位于杭州凤凰山。
2. 富阳：浙江省杭州市辖区，位于杭州市西南。

Wang Anshi

(1021—1086) was a native of Linchuan (now Fuzhou, Jiangxi Province). He was a Jinshi in the second year of Qingli Period (1042). He served as Chancellor of the government during the reign of Emperor Shenzong, and then twice as the Prime Minister. During his service, he was active in reforms. He was conferred the title of the Duke of Jing. His poetry and prose were all highly accomplished, and was ranked among the Eight Great Prose Masters of Tang and Song Dynasties for his majestic and creatively sharp style. There exists *The Collection of Linchuan* (the alias of Wang Anshi).

A Visit to Shengguo Temple in Hangzhou

Climbing high and overlooking the water and hill,

It is as if I were standing in the lake still.

At the bottom of the hill the buildings and pavilions

Are mostly hidden among the dense woods from high visions.

From the sea the puffy clouds are coming;

In the lake is tossed the afterglow of the sun setting.

We are sitting opposite each other and have a flute to play;

Its sound is drifting to the direction of Fuyang far away.

《万松金阙图卷》南宋　赵伯骕　故宫博物院藏

Golden Pavilion in Pine Forest, Zhao Bosu, Southern Song Dynasty, The Palace Museum

【阅读提示】

　　圣果寺，又名"胜果寺"，原称"崇圣寺"，位于杭州凤凰山上。《名胜志》记载："万松岭在凤山门外，折而西南，有圣果寺。唐乾宁间，无著禅师建。" 诗歌情景相融，前两联写登高所见，描写了圣果寺幽静旷然之态。颈联"浮云连海气，落日动湖光"，写出了西湖水天一色、浑然一体的壮丽景色，对仗精工，气象恢宏，展现了诗人广阔的诗情与胸怀。尾联以笛声结景，景中含情，余韵悠长。

Comments and Tips

Shengguo Temple is located on the Phoenix Hill in Hangzhou. Emotions and the scenery are blended in this poem, with the first two couplets describing what the poet saw when he was ascending the hill, displaying the seclusion of Shengguo Temple. The following couplet depicts the magnificent scenery of the West Lake where the water and the sky merged in one colour. The refined parallel structure and grand style reveal the author's poetic loftiness and broad mind. The last couplet concludes with the sound of a flute, where sentiments are revealed in the views with lingering echoes. Fuyang is a district of Hangzhou, Zhejiang Province, located in the southwest of the city.

登飞来峰[1]

飞来山上千寻塔[2]，闻说鸡鸣见日升。

不畏浮云遮望眼， 自缘身在最高层。

【注释】

1. 飞来峰：在杭州灵隐寺前。
2. 千寻：寻，古时长度单位，八尺为一寻。千寻，形容极高。

【阅读提示】

　　飞来峰在今杭州灵隐寺前。皇祐二年（1050）夏，诗人在鄞县（今浙江宁波鄞州区）知县任满回江西临川故里，途经杭州，访灵隐寺登飞来峰，写下了这首千古传诵的佳作。"不畏浮云遮望眼，自缘身在最高层"，景中寓理，却流畅自然，从中可以感受到杰出的政治家、改革家王安石的壮志豪情。诗歌始终洋溢着昂扬向上的精神，展现了诗人广阔的胸襟抱负。

Climbing Feilai Peak

On Feilai Peak there stands high a pagoda;
The rising sun can be seen when crows the rooster.
Not afraid of my view obscured by the puffy clouds,
Because I am standing on the highest level of the tower.

Comments and Tips

Feilai Peak (Flying Peak) is located in front of today's Lingyin Temple by the West Lake of Hangzhou. In the summer of the second year of Emperor Renzong's Huangyou Period (1050), the poet returned to his hometown of Linchuan, Jiangxi Province, after serving as governor of Yin County (now Ningbo, Zhejiang Province). Passing by Hangzhou, he visited Lingyin Temple and ascended Feilai Peak, the result of which is this poem, a masterpiece recited by generations of readers. The poem offered an argument through the description of scenery in an easy and natural way, revealing Wang Anshi's ambition as a great statesman and political reformer.

苏　轼

（1037—1101），字子瞻，号东坡居士，眉州眉山（今属四川）人。与父苏洵、弟苏辙并称"三苏"。嘉祐二年（1057）进士，曾于熙宁四年（1071）和元祐四年（1089）分别任杭州通判、知州。发动百姓疏浚西湖，并取葑泥筑堤，"苏堤"因此而来。苏轼是一位文学艺术大师，为"唐宋八大家"之一。其散文汪洋恣肆、平易晓畅；诗歌奔放灵动，被誉为"诗神"；词豪迈劲拔，开豪放词风，与辛弃疾并称"苏辛"；书画造诣也很高。有《苏东坡全集》。

望湖楼醉书[1]（五首其一）

黑云翻墨未遮山，白雨跳珠乱入船。
卷地风来忽吹散，望湖楼下水如天。

【注释】

1. 望湖楼：古楼名。五代时吴越王钱俶所建，在杭州西湖边。

Su Shi

(1037－1101) was a native of Meishan (formerly known as Meizhou now in Sichuan Province). Su Shi, his father Su Xun and his younger brother Su Zhe were revered as Three Su. He was a Jinshi in the second year of Jiayou Period (1057), served as the magistrate of Hangzhou in the fourth year of Xining Period (1071) and then the governor in the fourth year of Yuanyou Period (1089). He mobilized the people to dredge the West Lake and took the sludge to build a dike across the lake, which was named after him and known as Su Di (Su Causeway). Su Shi was a master of literature and art. His achievements in prose made him one of the Eight Great Prose Masters of Tang and Song Dynasties. His poetry was so spirited and dynamic that he was known as a "poetry god". His initiated a new style of ci poetry which was mighty and unrestrained. He and Xin Qiji, another most acclaimed poet of this style, were known as Su-Xin. Su Shi also had high attainments in painting and calligraphy. There exists *The Complete Works of Su Dongpo* (his art name).

Drunk and Chanting Poems on Wanghu Building (the First of Five)

The sky was surging with black clouds, but hills appeared in cloud gaps;
Suddenly fell white rain, and into the boat jumped the water drops.
A gust of wind whistled close to the ground, blowing the clouds away;
Below Wanghu Building the lake surface became as clear as the sky again.

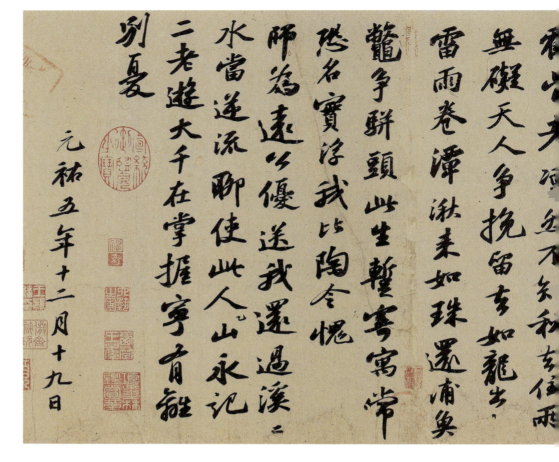

《次辩才韵诗帖》北宋　苏轼　台北故宫博物院藏

Poems Used the Rhymes of Biancai's, Su Shi, Northern Song Dynasty, Taipei Palace Museum

【阅读提示】

　　这首七绝作于熙宁五年（1072）。首句写黑云翻滚，次句写暴雨骤降，第三句写风过雨停，第四句写湖水涨溢。全诗就像一个画面和结构清晰精彩的短视频，云、雨、风、水，接得紧又转得快，正如夏日雷雨的骤起骤停。诗中暴雨击打湖面、溅起的水珠蹦跳入船的画面，让人印象尤深。

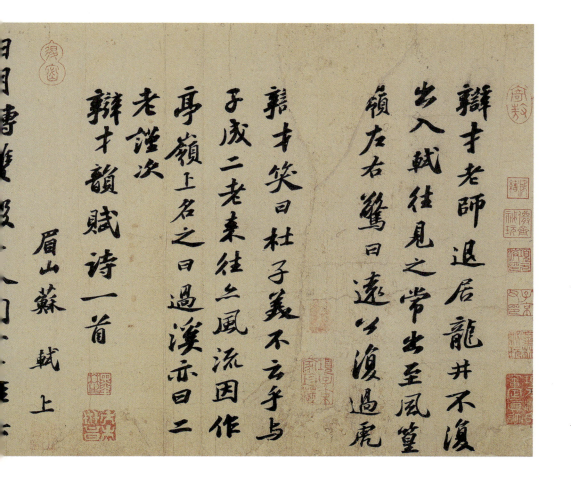

Comments and Tips

Wanghu Building was built by Qian Chu, the King of Wuyue State during the period of Five Dynasties, and is located by the West Lake of Hangzhou. The whole poem resembles a short video with high definition images and amazing frames, where clouds, rain, wind and water are connected tightly and shift quickly, just like the sudden start and stop of a summer thunderstorm. The poem is particularly impressive because of the image of the rainstorm hitting the lake surface and the splashing water droplets jumping into the boat like ten thousand pearls.

饮湖上初晴后雨（二首其二）

水光潋滟晴方好，山色空蒙雨亦奇。
欲把西湖比西子，淡妆浓抹总相宜。

【阅读提示】

　　此诗首两句写西湖湖光山色之美，无论是晴空下的波光潋滟，还是雨天中的山色空蒙，都是美好奇妙的。而后两句则用了一个贴切而又巧妙的比喻：西湖就像那美女西施，无论是浓妆艳抹，还是淡扫蛾眉，都是最美的。苏轼的这一比喻具有极强的概括性，可谓妙手偶得的神来之笔，前人甚至有"除却淡妆浓抹句，更将何语比西湖"的赞叹。因为苏轼此诗，杭州人也称西湖为"西子湖"。

Drinking on the Lake When It Cleared Up and Then Rained Again (the Second of Two)

Under the sun, the water is glittering and beautiful;

In the rain, the hills are hazy, misty, and wonderful.

To compare the West Lake to Xishi, the ancient beauty,

Any makeup would be suitable, light or heavy.

Comments and Tips

The first two lines of this poem display the amazing beauty of the West Lake's natural views, be it the sparkling waves under the clear sky or the misty hills in the rainy day. The second two lines employ an apt and ingenious simile relating the West Lake and Xishi, the charming lady, who was always most beautiful with either light or heavy make-up. This simile reveals the very essence of the unique charm of the West Lake and has been long regarded as a divine stroke accomplished by a stroke of genius, so much so that it is claimed that the lines are unparalleled when the West Lake is the target of comparison. Locals of Hangzhou also call the West Lake "Xizi (i. e. Xishi) Lake" because of this poem.

有美堂暴雨 ¹

游人脚底一声雷，　满座顽云拨不开。

天外黑风吹海立，　浙东飞雨过江来。

十分潋滟金樽凸，　千杖敲铿羯鼓催 ²。

唤起谪仙泉洒面 ³，倒倾鲛室泻琼瑰 ⁴。

【注释】

1. 有美堂：在西湖东南面的吴山上，系嘉祐二年（1057）杭州知州梅挚所建。宋
   仁宗赠梅挚诗有"地有吴山美，东南第一州"之句，因而取名"有美堂"。
2. 敲铿：敲击，喻鼓声。羯鼓：唐代从西域传入的乐器，其声尤擅急促鸣烈。此处
   借急促的鼓声形容暴雨之骤密。
3. 谪仙：李白。
4. 鲛室：海中鲛人居住之地，传说鲛人的眼泪会化成珍珠。琼瑰：泛指珠玉。

【阅读提示】

　　这首七律作于熙宁六年（1073）秋。开头两句写置身吴山绝顶的有美堂，却
听一声惊雷炸响脚下，满座颓云。三、四句写狂风呼啸、暴雨骤至，雄峻奇杰，气
势夺人。五、六句写大雨中的西湖，水面涨溢，就像一樽十分满溢的金杯；而暴雨
声宛如千槌击鼓，急促铿锵，震人心魄。最后说这场暴雨若唤醒了醉酒中的李白，
他必定能源源不断地写出琼瑰般的佳词丽句，就像海面倾覆，倒出无数鲛人眼泪化
成的珍珠一样。全诗充满奇思妙想，快捷的节奏和宏大的气势，亦如诗中的风雨，
来如雷霆，去如飘风，挥洒自如，而且从中又展现了诗人豪放不羁的个性，确实令
人赞叹。

A Rainstorm at Youmei Hall

A loud thunder seemed to tremble under the guests' feet.

Thick clouds could not be dispersed in the luxurious fete.

The wind carried dark clouds, blowing the sea water upright;

A rainstorm struck across Qiantang River and made everyone in fright.

The West Lake was full of rainwater, like a bowl golden;

The raindrops hit the water and the trees as drums beaten.

I really wanted to wake up Li Bai with the flying spring, thus

Let him see all the jade pearls being poured out of the Crystal Palace.

Comments and Tips

Youmei Hall is located on Wu Hill to the southeast of the West Lake, built by Mei Zhi, the then governor of Hangzhou, in the second year of Jiayou Period (1057). This poem was composed in the autumn of the sixth year of Xining Period (1073). The first two lines are about visiting Youmei Hall on the top of Wu Hill, when a sudden thunderbolt exploded at foot, leaving the room haunted by dark clouds. The third and fourth lines display the imposing and breathtaking scene of a howling wind and unexpected rainstorm. The following two lines depict the West Lake in the heavy rain with the water rising and overflowing accompanying the shocking sound of the rainstorm. In the end, the poem claimed that if the rainstorm awakened the drunk poet Li Bai, he could contribute marvellous lines non-stop. This admirable poem is filled with amazing conceits, fast rhythm and grand momentum, revealing the poet's bold and unrestrained personality.

江神子·湖上与张先同赋时闻弹筝 [1]

凤凰山下雨初晴 [2]。

水风清，晚霞明。

一朵芙蕖 [3]，开过尚盈盈。

何处飞来双白鹭，如有意，慕娉婷 [4]。

忽闻江上弄哀筝。

苦含情，遣谁听。

烟敛云收，依约是湘灵 [5]。

欲待曲终寻问取，人不见，数峰青。

【注释】

1. 江神子：词牌名，又名"江城子""水晶帘"等。起于晚唐五代，始见于《花间集》韦庄词：原为单调，七句五平韵；后演变为双调，上下阕都是七句五平韵。
2. 凤凰山：在杭州西湖南面。
3. 芙蕖：荷花。
4. 娉婷：姿态美好貌。
5. 湘灵：相传尧帝之女娥皇、女英死于湘江，遂为湘水女神。

Jiangshenzi: Hearing the Zither When Writing a Poem with Zhang Xian on the Lake

The rain has just cleared up at the bottom of the Phoenix Hill.

The wind is clear on the water,

And the sunset is bright still.

A lotus flower blooming

With a crystal of grooming.

A pair of egrets fly here,

As if to appreciate it,

Charming and delicate.

Suddenly, from the river I hear the sound of zither playing.

The music contains sadness,

To whom it expresses a hidden feeling.

Gradually, the mists on river clear,

As if Goddesses of Xiang River appear.

When the music is over I want to visit them,

But they have already gone,

Only a few green peaks stand on.

《西湖图》南宋　李嵩　上海博物馆

The West Lake, Li Song, Southern Song Dynasty, Shanghai Museum

【阅读提示】

　　这首词系苏轼在杭州通判任上与词人朋友张先同游西湖时所作。据《墨庄漫录》卷一载：东坡在杭时，一日游西湖，遇一彩舟渐前，靓妆数人，中有一人尤丽，方鼓瑟，风韵娴雅。曲未终，翩然而逝。东坡戏作长短句云云。此词上片写雨后初晴的西湖美景，用了比喻和拟人手法。下片则写美女鼓筝，通过"哀筝""苦含情"和湘灵的传说，表现了筝声的哀怨。最后化用了唐代钱起《湘灵鼓瑟》诗"曲终人不见，江上数峰青"句意，给人言尽意无穷的感觉，令人久久回味。

Comments and Tips

Jiangshenzi (Tune of River Goddess): a pattern of ci poetry. According to record, Su Shi once visited the West Lake when he was in Hangzhou and met a decorated boat approaching, on which he spotted a woman particularly beautiful among her nicely dressed companions. She was playing "zheng" (a Chinese name of zither, a stringed instrument) in elegant style and swiftly flew away, leaving the music unfinished, upon which Su Shi playfully made this ci. The first half depicts the beautiful scenery of the West Lake after the rain, employing metaphor and personification. The latter half is about a beautiful woman playing zheng, whose mournful sound is revealed by mentioning the bitter love and the legend of Xiangling (Goddesses of Xiang River). In the end, Su borrowed the last lines of the poem of "Xiangling Playing Se (a stringed instrument)" by Qian Qi (a famous poet by the end of the golden age of Tang Dynasty), with an endless echo of his thoughts.

八声甘州·寄参寥子 [1]

有情风、万里卷潮来，无情送潮归。

问钱塘江上，西兴浦口 [2]，几度斜晖？

不用思量今古，俯仰昔人非。

谁似东坡老，白首忘机 [3]。

记取西湖西畔，正春山好处，空翠烟霏。

算诗人相得，如我与君稀。

约他年、东还海道，愿谢公、雅志莫相违 [4]。

西州路，不应回首，为我沾衣。

【注释】

1. 八声甘州：词牌名，又名"甘州""潇潇雨"等。"甘州"本唐代大曲名，因上下阕八韵，故名"八声甘州"。双调八平韵，共有七体。苏轼此词共九十七字。
   参寥子：宋僧道潜的别号，苏轼诗友。
2. 西兴：在今杭州市滨江区。
3. 忘机：消除机巧之心。
4. 谢公：东晋名臣谢安。

Bashengganzhou: To Monk Canliao Zi

When I came, my mood was like a tide rolled up by a fierce wind.

When I go, I will follow the ebb tide with a calm state of mind.

Have you ever remembered that at the Xixing ferry or on Qiantang River,

How many times you and I have enjoyed the sunset together?

No need to think about the changes between past and present.

Things have been different in an instant;

I don't want to be bound by conventional patterns like a bird in a cage,

Till my gray-haired age.

How can we forget the most beautiful time of spring,

On the western shore of the West Lake

The hills are green and the fog is floating.

Confidant among poets, like you and me,

How many can there be?

One day I will retire along the eastern route;

It is the ideal Xie An failed to accomplish that I will retrieve.

You will not look back and cry for me under the Xizhou Gate;

Don't let the tears wet your sleeve.

苏轼此词作于元祐六年（1091），自杭州知州召为翰林学士承旨。这首词开头几句将风拟人化，借物言情，引出作者对人世沧桑的感慨，并表明自己的恬静忘机、淡泊功利。下片先是回忆与参寥子的亲密交往和知己深情，然后反用谢安死后，其外甥羊昙为之痛哭的典故，嘱咐参寥子要牢记谢安雅志，切勿为两人的分别落泪伤心。该词表现了苏轼与参寥子的深情厚谊，也表现了作者"白首忘机"的积极旷达的人生态度。清末著名词评家陈廷焯在《白雨斋词话》中赞曰："寄伊郁于豪宕，坡老所以为高。"

Comments and Tips

Bashengganzhou (Eight Rhymes of Ganzhou): A pattern of ci poetry. "Ganzhou" is the name of a grand song of eight rhymes in the Tang Dynasty, hence the title. Monk Canliao Zi was a poet friend of Su Shi's. This ci poem was composed in the sixth year of Yuanyou Period (1091), when Su was summoned from his post as the governor of Hangzhou to an official who drafted edicts for the Emperor. The first few lines lead to the poet's sentimental response to the vicissitudes of the human world, indicating his indifference to earthly fame. In the latter half, the poet recalled his intimate friendship with Monk Canliao Zi, and then reversely employed the allusion to Xie An's (the famous official of Eastern Jin Dynasty) death, enjoining Can Liao zi to never shed tears for their separation. This ci poem reveals the deep friendship between them, as well as the poet's positive and open-minded attitude towards life.

黄庭坚

（1045—1105），字鲁直，号山谷道人、涪翁，洪州分宁（今江西修水）人。治平四年（1067）举进士，为《神宗实录》检讨官，迁著作佐郎。他出于苏轼门下，为"苏门四学士"之首。以诗负盛名，为"江西诗派"宗祖。有《山谷集》。

钱塘旧游

薄宦飘然笑漫郎[1]，瑟洲花草弄幽芳。

莫教景物添春色， 转觉山川是异乡。

南北峰岩空入梦[2]，短长亭舍自相望[3]。

湖边山寺清明后， 相见兰开禊水香[4]。

【注释】

1. 漫郎：唐朝诗人元结。后也借指放浪形骸、不守世俗检束的文人。

2. 南北峰岩：指杭州的南高峰和北高峰。

3. 短长亭：古时设在城外大道旁的亭舍，常作为送行饯别处。十里一长亭，五里一短亭。

4. 兰开禊水：指兰亭修禊。古时三月初三，人们欢聚水滨洗濯，以消除不祥。东晋永和九年（353）三月，王羲之与友人雅集于兰亭，并写下《兰亭集序》，传为美谈。

Huang Tingjian

(1045—1105) was a native of Fenning, Hongzhou (now Xiushui, Jiangxi Province). Qualified as a Jinshi in the fourth year of Zhiping Period (1067), Huang was appointed the editor of *Shenzong Shilu* (the official records of the former Emperor Shenzong's reign), and then promoted to the position of the assistant of the official composer of national documents. He was a disciple of Su Shi and was the head of the "Four Scholars of the Su School". He was highly acclaimed for his poems and was the patriarch of the "Jiangxi School of Poetry". There exists *The Collection of Shangu* (his art name being "the Daoist Shangu").

Memories of Visiting Hangzhou

With a humble official position, I am often ridiculed by people,

And can only fiddle with flowers on the deserted shore of the river.

Don't add the spring breath to the scenery in front of me,

Which makes me feel that I am in a distant continent.

The towering north and south peaks often enter my dreams;

In my mind the scenes of the farewell at the long pavilion always linger.

Remembering that after the Qingming Festival that year, we went to the temple

By the lake, we had a gathering together in the Lanting elegant.

【阅读提示】

　　这首七律首联写诗人自己官职卑微，飘然一身，为放浪形骸、不守世俗检束的文人所笑，只能在萧瑟的江洲采摘幽兰。颔联承上，表现了为宦异乡的悲凉，所以说出了"莫教景物添春色"这样违背常理之语，因为他乡的美景，不仅触景伤情，还增添游子的思乡思亲之情。颈联转而回想曾在杭州与友人同游的情景，但是现在那南北峰岩只有梦中才能见到，送别时的长亭、短亭也徒增感伤。"空""自"两字，凸显了诗人的孤寂。尾联更以回忆昔日与友人在清明后修禊雅集的欢聚与今日别离后的孤苦寂寞形成反差。全诗感情的醇厚沉郁，炼字炼句，表现了孤身宦游内心的孤独，以及对与志同道合朋友的深情和思念。

Comments and Tips

The first couplet of this poem mentions how humble and lonely the poet felt. The second couplet continues to reveal his dismal mood serving as a minor official in a place far away from home. The third couplet shifts to recall the moments he visited Hangzhou with friends. What's more, the last couplet presents a contrast between the joyful and graceful gathering with friends after the Qingming Festival and the solitude and misery after the farewell today. The mellow and melancholy sentiment and refined diction of this poem display his loneliness and how much he loved and missed his like-minded friends.

《梅竹聚禽图》北宋　赵佶

台北故宫博物院藏

Birds Gathering in Plum and Bamboo Forest,

Zhao Ji, Northern Song Dynasty,

Taipei Palace Museum

《西湖柳艇图》南宋　夏珪　台北故宫博物院藏

Boats by the Willow Bank of the West Lake, Xia Gui, Southern Song Dynasty, Taipei Palace Museum

周邦彦

（1056—1121），字美成，号清真居士，钱塘人。宋徽宗时为徽猷阁待制，提举大晟府（皇家音乐机构）。精通音律，能自度曲。其词上承温庭筠、柳永之风，下开吴文英、史达祖一派，时誉甚高。有《片玉词》。

苏幕遮[1]

燎沉香[2]，消溽暑[3]。
鸟雀呼晴，侵晓窥檐语。
叶上初阳干宿雨，
水面清圆[4]，一一风荷举[5]。

故乡遥，何日去？
家住吴门[6]，久作长安旅[7]。
五月渔郎相忆否？
小楫轻舟，梦入芙蓉浦[8]。

【注释】

1. 苏幕遮：唐教坊曲名，后用为词牌，又名"古调歌""云雾敛"等。双调六十二字。

2. 燎：细焚。沉香：一种名贵香料。

3. 溽（rù）暑：闷热潮湿的暑气。

4. 清圆：形容荷叶清润而圆正。

5. 一一风荷举：意谓荷叶在晨风中一一挺立，犹如被擎举着。

6. 吴门：作者乃钱塘人，钱塘古属吴郡，故称之。

7. 长安：此处借指汴京。

8. 芙蓉浦：有荷花的水边，此指杭州西湖。

Zhou Bangyan

(1056—1121) was a native of Qiantang (now Hangzhou, Zhejiang Province). He served as the editorial review officer of the national library and later the director of the national academy of music research. He was a master of music, and was able to compose his own songs. His works of ci were highly acclaimed at that time. There exists *The Pianyu Collection* (the collection of pieces of jade), which is also known as *The Collection of Qingzhen* (his art name).

Sumuzhe

Light the incense
To reduce the humid heat of summer.
Birds chirp and call for clear sky at dawn,
And under the eaves I can hear their whisper.
The early sun has dried the raindrops on the leaves of lotus;
They are smooth and round on the water,
The breeze is blowing, and they are twisting like dancers.

My hometown is so far away, when can I go back?
My family is in south of Yangtze River,
But in Chang'an, for a long time, I have been a sojourner.
The Dragon Boat Festival is coming;
Whether my relatives are also missing me, I wonder?
In dream, I paddled a small boat
To enter again the lotus cluster.

这首词上片写景，写盛夏朝阳下的新荷，没有用那些为人常用之语，而只写了"叶上初阳干宿雨，水面清圆，一一风荷举"，却让人耳目一新，故近代诗词评论家王国维在他的《人间词话》中称"此真能得荷之神理者"。下片写思乡之情和归乡之梦。全词语意精新，词韵清蔚，从实写到梦境，过渡极为自然，风格清新淡雅。

《疏荷沙鸟图》南宋　佚名　故宫博物院藏

Sparse Lotuses and wagtail, Anonymous, Southern Song Dynasty, The Palace Museum

Comments and Tips

Sumuzhe (Song of Waterbag Dance): the name of the court music in the Tang Dynasty, which was first introduced from the Western Regions and later used as a pattern of ci poetry. The first half of this ci poem displays a scene of fresh lotus leaves under the sunrise in the height of summer. It presents the refreshing image of lovely round leaves of lotuses stretching out in the breeze. The latter half is about homesickness. The whole piece of ci has a fresh and tasteful style, offering an exact and refreshing choice of words as well as elegant rhyme.

张元幹

张元幹（1091—约1170），字仲宗，号芦川老隐，长乐（今福建福州）人。宋室南渡后，他因力主抗金，受到打击和排斥。他的词风格豪迈，部分作品对投降派进行了揭露与谴责。张元幹与张孝祥一起号称南宋初期"词坛双璧"。有《芦川归来集》《芦川词》。

八声甘州·西湖有感寄刘晞颜 [1]

记当年共饮，醉画船、摇碧罥花钿 [2]。

问苍颜华发，烟蓑雨笠，何事重来。

看尽人情物态，冷眼只堪咍。

赖有西湖在，洗我尘埃。

Zhang Yuangan

(1091 — c.1170) was a native of Changle (now Fuzhou, Fujian Province). After the royal household of Song Dynasty escaped to the south, he suffered attack and repulsion for his advocating to fight against the invasion of the Kingdom of Jin. His works of ci were bold and powerful, some of which exposed and condemned the surrenderors. There exist *The Collection of the Return of Luchuan* (his art name) and *Ci of Luchuan*.

Bashengganzhou: To My Friend When I Am on the West Lake

I remember when we were drinking on the West Lake;

The boat cut across the lake and formed two ripples,

Like on a woman's hair the flower hairpins crystal.

Asking the white-haired man,

"You are wearing the coir raincoat and the bamboo hat,

What makes you visit the West Lake again?"

"I have seen through the human sentiments in the world,

And can only smile at everything with a calm eye.

Fortunately, the West Lake is still clean,

Which could wash away the dust on my body thereby.

夜久波光山色，间淡妆浓抹，冰鉴云开³。

更潮头千丈，江海两崔嵬⁴。

晓凉生、荷香扑面，洒天边、风露逼襟怀。

谁同赏，通宵无寐，斜月低回。

【注释】

1. 刘晞颜，丹徒（今属江苏镇江）人，政和五年（1115）进士，终尚书郎，张元幹好友。

2. 罥（juàn）：挂。

3. 冰鉴：代指月。

4. 崔嵬：高耸貌；高大貌。

【阅读提示】

　　张元幹夜游西湖，寄调《八声甘州》，向友人抒发感怀。上阕从回忆写起，由昔及今，表达了阅尽人世的苍凉心态。下阕则笔法宕开，状西湖夜色，以西湖景洗经年尘埃，寄托词人的高洁情怀。词人生逢乱世，将家国之痛、人世坎坷与怀思友人一并打揉，融入这西湖盛景之中，情思哀婉，境界空阔，情调高远。

The lake and hills at night,

with makeup heavy or light,

And breaking through the clouds the moon bright.

There is also the Qiantang tide,

The great spectacle of river and sea.

It is getting cooler at dawn;

The scent of lotuses rushes towards the face

And the breeze and dew of autumn

Are blowing from the sky into my bosom.

I stay awake all night;

Who will come to enjoy with me?

The moon is gradually dropping in a western trace.

Comments and Tips

Zhang Yuangan once visited the West Lake at night and composed this ci poem to share his feelings with Liu Xiyan, his friend. The first half starts from memories all through his life, revealing the bleak mood of a soul that had experienced many vicissitudes. In the latter half, the view is extended to the night scene of the West Lake, which washes away the dust of the years, expressing the poet's lofty sentiments. Born in troubled times, the poet combined the pain of his family and country, frustrations of life and thoughts of his friends into the spectacular view of the West Lake, featuring a gentle pathos, a broad mind and a lofty tone.

陆　游

（1125—1210），字务观，晚号放翁，越州山阴（今浙江绍兴）人。早年试礼部，因得罪秦桧而被黜免，后赐进士出身。曾官朝议大夫、礼部郎中。其立志"扫胡尘""靖国难"，但屡受投降派打击，壮志难酬。诗风激昂悲壮，雄浑奔放，与尤袤、杨万里、范成大并称为"南宋四大家"。有《渭南文集》《剑南诗稿》等。

临安春雨初霁 [1]

世味年来薄似纱，　谁令骑马客京华。

小楼一夜听春雨，　深巷明朝卖杏花。

矮纸斜行闲作草 [2]，晴窗细乳戏分茶 [3]。

素衣莫起风尘叹，　犹及清明可到家。

【注释】

1. 霁（jì）：雨后转晴。
2. 矮纸：短纸。
3. 分茶：宋元时煎茶之法。注汤后用箸搅茶乳，使茶汤波纹幻变成种种形状。

Lu You

(1125–1210) was a native of Shanyin, Yuezhou (now Shaoxing, Zhejiang Province). In his early years, Lu passed the metropolitan qualification exam during Emperor Gaozong's reign, but was deposed for offending Qin Hui (a notorious bureaucrat traitor). He was granted the qualification only when the successive Emperor Xiaozong came to reign. He served as a court official and then an assistant of the Minister of Rites. His ambition was to resist the enemy and save the country. However, repeatedly attacked by the surrenderists, he never managed to achieve the great aspirations. His poetry was so impassioned, majestic and powerful that he was known as one of the Four Great Poets of Southern Song Dynasty. There exist *Collected Works of Weinan* (south of Wei River) and *The Poem Collection in Jiannan* (the south of Jiange, now Sichuan Province).

Spring Rain Over in Lin'an City

Recently, the ways of the world are as thin as gauze;

To ride to the capital and stay as a guest, who sent me?

I listened to the sound of spring rain on a small building all night long.

Tomorrow morning, there will be people selling apricot blossoms in the
     deep alley.

Spread out the paper to write cursive script askew,

And in front of the sunny window, I will boil water, make and taste tea.

Don't complain that the dust on the way will stain my white clothes;

There is still time to return to my hometown at the Qingming Festival
     truly.

【 阅读提示 】

淳熙十三年（1186）春，作者被起用为严州（今建德及其周边诸县）知州，赶赴临安（今杭州）听候召见，暂住在西湖边的客舍里，写下了这首脍炙人口的佳作。明丽的春光与闲适的情境之下隐含着诗人壮志难酬的惆怅与百无聊赖。"小楼一夜听春雨，深巷明朝卖杏花"，让杏花、烟雨成了江南的典型物象，在淡淡的春光之下，深藏的却是因国事家愁而一夜无眠之人。"作草"用张芝的典故，暗喻国家正是多事之秋，诗人却只能无事以草书消遣。"分茶"句与"作草"句对仗精工，同样看似呈现闲情，却隐喻着诗人的自嘲与心中浓浓郁结的悲愤。尾联之中，诗人反用陆机"素衣化为缁"之典，自我解嘲。诗歌以相较轻盈的笔调呈现了一个一以贯之又别开生面的陆游的形象。

Comments and Tips

This universally acclaimed poem was composed when Lu You was waiting for the emperor's summons at an inn by the West Lake. Between the lines filled with the splendid beauty of spring scenery and leisurely mood was the poet's disconsolation and boredom because his lofty ideal failed. The metaphor of writing cursive script implies that the country was suffering, while the poet could only waste his time with cursive writing. The lines involving tea making and cursive writing offer seemingly easy feelings, leaking out the poet's innermost grief and self-deprecation. In the last couplet, the poet tries to console himself. The poem presents a consistent yet unusual image of Lu You with a relatively light touch.

《腊嘴桐子图》南宋　佚名　上海博物馆藏

Hawfinch Sitting on a Paulownia Tree, Anonymous, Southern Song Dynasty, Shanghai Museum

西湖春游

灵隐前，天竺后¹，鬼削神剜作岩岫。

冷泉亭中一樽酒²，一日可敌千年寿。

清明后，上巳前， 千红百紫争妖妍。

冬冬鼓声鞠场边³，秋千一蹴如登仙。

人生得意须年少， 白发龙钟空自笑。

君不见灞亭耐事故将军⁴，醉尉怒诃如不闻。

【注释】

1. 灵隐前，天竺后：《咸淳临安志》："灵隐、天竺两山，由一门而入。陆羽记云：'南天竹，北灵隐。'"
2. 冷泉亭：在灵隐飞来峰下。
3. 鞠（jū）场：古代蹴鞠的场地。蹴鞠是我国古代的一种踢球游戏。
4. 灞亭耐事故将军：《史记·李将军列传》："（李广）尝夜从一骑出，从人田间饮。还至霸陵亭。霸陵尉醉，呵止广。广骑曰：'故李将军。'尉曰：'今将军尚不得夜行，何乃故也！'止广宿亭下。"

【阅读提示】

　　诗歌首先记录了陆游在临安的生活场景，他游灵隐、天竺，赏美景，有时也在那冷泉亭中酌一樽美酒。春光正好时，百花争艳，蹴鞠场也热闹非凡。然而这热闹动人的场景，在诗歌的最后两句中急转直下，由喜转悲，表达了诗人渴望为国效力有所作为，到头来不过是枉度人生"白发龙钟空自笑"。尾句借用了李广在灞陵受辱的典故，表达了诗人壮志难酬的无奈与对奸佞之臣的讽刺。

Visiting the West Lake in Spring

In front of Lingyin Temple and behind Tianzhu Temple,

There stands a rocky peak, shaped as if by ghosts but towering.

Drinking a glass of wine in the Cold Spring Pavilion,

One day seems to me a thousand years living.

After the Qingming Festival and before the Shangsi Day,

Hundreds of flowers are fully blooming.

The thumping drums sound from the cuju field;

Swinging up, like fairies in the sky flying.

Life should be proud when you are young.

When with your hair white, you can only be in vain laughing.

Don't you know that General Li Guang, who was so tolerant,

When faced with such an angry rebuke,

He acted as if he didn't hear the drunken lieutenant.

Comments and Tips

This poem begins with a record of Lu You's life in Lin'an, where he visited the temples of Lingyin and Tianzhu, enjoying the fabulous views and drinking wine at times in the Cold Spring Pavilion. However, this lively and attractive scene takes a sharp turn from happiness to sadness in the last two couplets of the poem. The last line expresses the poet's helplessness resulting from unfulfilled aspirations and his sarcasm against the treacherous courtiers, employing an allusion to Li Guang's humiliation at Baling. According to "General Li's Biography" of *Shiji* (Records of the Grand Historian), one night Li Guang went out with a squire and drank in the field. When he came back to Baling Pavilion, the officer on duty was drunk and stopped him rudely. The squire said, "This is the former General Li." The officer scolded, "Even the present general is not allowed to ride at night, let alone a former one!" Thus Li Guang was stopped and had to spend the night in the pavilion.

杨万里

（1127—1206），字廷秀，号诚斋，吉州吉水（今属江西）人。绍兴二十四年（1154）进士，曾任国子监博士、太子侍读、秘书监、宝谟阁学士等职。一生作诗两万多首，语言浅近自然、清新活泼而富有幽默情趣，人称"诚斋体"。有《诚斋集》。

晓出净慈送林子方（二首其二）[1]

毕竟西湖六月中，风光不与四时同。
接天莲叶无穷碧，映日荷花别样红。

【注释】

1. 净慈：净慈寺，在西湖南岸南屏山慧日峰下，与灵隐寺齐名。

【阅读提示】

林子方是杨万里的知己好友，其时，林子方欣然往福州任知州，杨万里则写下此诗，劝友人不要离开杭州。全诗没有直接叙说友谊，更没有直接规劝，而是通过对六月西湖美景的描绘赞美，表达立场观念，寄寓对友人的眷恋。这首诗歌以其朴实清新的造语、流畅自然的叙述、真实浓郁的情感，抓取了六月西湖最为动人的景色，因此也成了西湖诗歌中脍炙人口的典范佳作。

Yang Wanli

(1127 — 1206) was a native of Jishui (now in Jiangxi Province). He was qualified as a Jinshi in the 24th year of Shaoxing Period (1154). Yang served as professor of Guozijian and was promoted to other posts for scholars. During his lifetime, Yang composed over 20,000 poems with plain, fresh and lively language and a pleasant sense of humor, which is known as "Chengzhai (his art name) style". There exists *The Collection of Chengzhai*.

Farewell to Lin Zifang from Jingci Temple in the Early Morning (the Second of Two)

After all, it is the West Lake in summer prime,

But her unique charm is different from other seasons or time.

The lake is covered with endless emerald green lotus leaves;

Under the sunshine the lotus flowers' colour appears sublime.

Comments and Tips

Yang Wanli composed this poem to advise Lin Zifang, a close friend of his, not to leave Hangzhou when Lin was happy to go to Fuzhou as governor. The poem does not directly relate friendship, nor does it directly advise, but expresses the poet's standpoint and reluctance to let his friend go by admiring description of the West Lake's beauty in high summer. With its plain and fresh language, smooth and natural narration, and true and intense emotions, this poem captures the most impressive scenery of the West Lake in high summer and has become a popular masterpiece among poems about the West Lake.

同君俞季永步至普济寺晚泛西湖以归得四绝句（四首其二）

烟艇横斜柳港湾，　云山出没柳行间。

登山得似游湖好 [1]，却是湖心看尽山。

【注释】

1. 得似：怎似，哪似。

【阅读提示】

　　诗人与友人夜晚泛舟西湖之上，生发诗兴，写下了四首绝句。这首是其中的第二首，记录了云山出没、烟艇横斜的西湖美景，笔调轻盈，意境朦胧，心境愉悦。后两句直抒胸臆，晓畅通达，通过将登山与游湖比较，突出了西湖的观景视野，山水相映，景色美不胜收。

Walking to Puji Temple, Boating on the Lake in Evening, and Returning to Write (the Second of Four)

The boats in the misty waves lie askew through willow bay;

The peaks appear and disappear through the willows with floating white cloud.

How could it be as nice to climb hills now as on the lake to play?

In the middle of the lake, you can enjoy the scenery of peaks crowd.

Comments and Tips

Four poems are inspired by the night-boating experience of the poet and his friends on the West Lake, the second of which is this poem here. The poem features a light tone, a hazy mood and a delighted state of mind. The last two lines are straightforward and broad-minded, highlighting the scenic view of the West Lake by comparing hill climbing with lake cruising. The fabulous scenery of hills and water reflecting each other is simply beyond words.

朱淑真

（约1135—约1180），号幽栖居士，钱塘人。其父曾在浙西做官，家境优裕。幼即聪慧，博通经史，能文善画，尤工诗词，是宋代著名才女，但婚姻不幸。有《断肠词》《断肠诗集》。

清平乐·夏日游湖 [1]

恼烟撩露，留我须臾住 [2]。
携手藕花湖上路，一霎黄梅细雨。

娇痴不怕人猜，和衣睡倒人怀。
最是分携时候，归来懒傍妆台。

【注释】

1. 清平乐：词牌名。双调四十六字，前段仄韵，后段平韵。
2. 须臾：片刻，短时间。

Zhu Shuzhen

(c.1135—c.1180) was a native of Qiantang. Her father was an official in western Zhejiang, and her family was well-off. Zhu was intelligent at an early age; she was well versed in the traditional Chinese confucian classics and history. She was a famous talented woman in the Song Dynasty, an expert at writing and painting, and especially excelled at poetry. However, she suffered an unhappy marriage, hence the titles of her collections *The Broken Heart Ci* and *Poems of the Broken Heart.*

Qingpingyue: Summer Wandering by the West Lake

The smoke was annoying; the dew was moistening.

the scene kept my steps a moment stopping.

With my lover hand in hand we walked

On the lakeside road full of lotuses, its drizzle stalked.

My feelings of love are not afraid of people's gossiping,

And I slept in his arms with the clothes I was wearing.

The saddest thing is the time when we part;

I do not do the makeup after returning with a longing heart.

《荷香清夏图》南宋　马麟　辽宁省博物馆藏

Lotus Fragrance in Summer Breeze, Ma Lin, Southern Song Dynasty, Liaoning Provincial Museum

【阅读提示】

　　朱淑真是宋代著名的才女，留下了众多的诗词，这些作品大多反映了其细腻的情思与爱情、婚姻生活。这首词记述的是一次与恋人同游西湖的经历，上片交代背景，因一霎黄梅细雨，二人驻足共赏，烟雨茫茫，增添一份朦胧的情趣。下片则具体到人物情态，描写了躲雨时"和衣睡倒人怀"的大胆举动，叙说了与恋人分别后"归来懒傍妆台"的忧愁。该词刻画了一个大胆追爱的女子形象，艺术表现生动；读者通过此词，更能理解朱淑真在包办婚姻中的情感苦闷。

Comments and Tips

Qingpingyue (Pure and Serene Music): a pattern of ci poetry. This ci poem by Zhu Shuzhen recounts a trip to the West Lake with her love. The first half gives the context of a brief drizzle, which enables the two to pause and enjoy the scene. The latter half shifts to the specific posture of the characters, as well as her sorrow after departing from her love. This ci poem portrays a woman boldly pursuing love with a vivid artistic expression, enabling readers to better understand Zhu Shuzhen's emotional distress in the arranged marriage.

辛弃疾

（1140—1207），字幼安，号稼轩，历城（今山东济南）人。绍兴三十一年（1161）参加抗金义军，为掌书记。后南归，官至江西安抚使、湖南安抚使、福建安抚使等。受投降派打击落职。嘉泰三年（1203）起用，任浙东安抚使、镇江知府，但不久又遭排斥。辛弃疾是南宋伟大的爱国词人，发展了苏轼开创的豪放词，与苏轼并称"苏辛"。词风以豪放沉郁为主，兼有明快、婉约、清新之特点。有《稼轩长短句》。

念奴娇·西湖和人韵 [1]

晚风吹雨，战新荷、声乱明珠苍璧。
谁把香奁收宝镜，云锦红涵湖碧。
飞鸟翻空，游鱼吹浪，惯趁笙歌席。
坐中豪气，看公一饮千石 [2]。

Xin Qiji

(1140－1207) was a native of Licheng (now Jinan, Shandong Province). In the thirty-first year of Shaoxing Period (1161), he joined the northern anti-Jin army. Later, he returned to the south, and served as the governors of Jiangxi, Hunan and Fujian in succession before he was removed from office as a result of attacks from the surrenderors. Since the third year of Jiatai Period (1203), he was reappointed and then dismissed again. Xin Qiji was a great patriotic ci poet of Southern Song Dynasty, who developed the bold and powerful style initiated by Su Shi. They were therefore jointly known as Su-Xin. There exists *The Collection of Jiaxuan's Changduanju* (Jiaxuan: Xin Qiji's art name; Changduanju: another name of ci).

Niannujiao: Visiting the West Lake and Rhyming with Friends

The evening wind blew a shower,

Sprinkling on the lotus leaves,

And splashing water droplets like pearls falling on the jade salver.

Who put the treasure mirror into the cosmetic case?

Let the red clouds and the lotus flowers soak in the blue water.

Birds flying in the air, fish wandering in the waves,

They have long been accustomed to the singing and banquet of visitor.

The lofty ambitions at the banquet, I really want to see

How can you drink a thousand glasses of liquor?

遥想处士风流³，鹤随人去，老作飞仙伯。

茅舍疏篱今在否，松竹已非畴昔。

欲说当年，望湖楼下，水与云宽窄。

醉中休问，断肠桃叶消息⁴。

【注释】

1. 念奴娇：词牌名，又名"百字令""酹江月""大江东去"等。调名取自唐代歌
   妓念奴之名，其调高亢，豪杰之士喜用之。
2. 石：古代计量单位，十斗为一石。
3. 处士：指隐士林逋。
4. 桃叶：晋王献之爱妾名。代指心爱女子。

【阅读提示】

　　这是辛弃疾早年吟咏西湖的一首词作。大约作于乾道六年或七年（1170 或
1171），其时，辛弃疾在临安任司农寺主簿。此词题为"和人韵"，当是聚会时有
感而作的和词作品。上片写景，模山范水，从新荷雨声、晚照湖光、飞鸟游鱼等描
写西湖的美景与生机，然后引出歌席宴饮。下片写情，在湖光山色中追忆西湖著名
隐士林逋，"桃叶消息"寄寓着一段伤离情事。这首词虽是辛弃疾早年作品，未能
充分体现稼轩词风貌，但写景言情自然妥帖。

Lin Hejing, the elegant hermit,

He and his white crane have already ascended

And become immortal in Nature.

Are the cottage and fence of his day still there?

The pine trees and bamboos are not what they used to be now either.

With emotion back then, looking down from Wanghu Building,

The sky and water merge in the same colour.

I am already drunk, and don't ask again,

How I long to have you back, my fair lover!

Comments and Tips

Niannujiao (Singing-girl Niannu's Charm): a pattern of ci poetry. This ci poem was composed in Xin Qiji's early years in around the sixth or seventh year of Qiandao Period (1170 or 1171), when Xin served in Lin'an as an official of the Court of National Granaries. The first half of this ci poem describes the scenery, displaying the hills and the water, presenting the beauty and vibrancy of the West Lake. The latter half is about emotions. The poet recalled Lin Bu, a famous hermit of the West Lake, in the scenery of the lake and the hills, and a sad love affair the poet himself had. As a ci poem composed in Xin Qiji's early years, it does not fully reveal his style, but the scenery and emotions are still presented naturally and properly.

刘 过

（1154—1206），吉州太和（今江西泰和）人，字改之，号龙洲道人。生平以功业自许，究心古今治乱之道。终身未仕，漫游江、浙、湘、鄂一带，与陆游、辛弃疾、陈亮等友善。工词，多感慨时事之作。词风与辛弃疾相近，抒发抗金抱负，狂逸俊致，与刘克庄、刘辰翁享有"辛派三刘"之誉，又与刘仙伦合称为"庐陵二布衣"。有《龙洲集》《龙洲词》。

沁园春·寄辛承旨。时承旨招，不赴[1]

斗酒彘肩[2]，风雨渡江，岂不快哉。

被香山居士[3]，约林和靖，与东坡老，驾勒吾回。

坡谓西湖[4]，正如西子，浓抹淡妆临镜台。

二公者，皆掉头不顾，只管衔杯。

Liu Guo

(1154—1206) was a native of Taihe, Jizhou (now Taihe, Jiangxi Province). During his lifetime, he never doubted that he could make great achievements in politics, and concentrated on the study of how dynasties of different generations managed to bring peace to the country. However, he never served in the government, but travelled along Jiangsu, Zhejiang, Hunan and Hubei. He made good friends with poets Lu You, Xin Qiji, Chen Liang and others. He excelled at ci poems; most of his works are about current affairs of his time. The style of his ci is similar to that of Xin Qiji, which is wild and smart, expressing his ambition to fight against Jin Kingdom. There exist *The Collection of Longzhou* (his art name being "Longzhou the Taoist") and *The Collection of Longzhou's Ci*.

Qinyuanchun: To Xin Qiji (Xin invited me but I couldn't go)

A whole jar of wine and a whole ham, it is so delightful that in a storm I
    will cross Qiantang River.
But I was forced to come back because of Bai Juyi, Lin Hejing and Su
    Dongpo, those great writers.
Su said, the West Lake is so beautiful, whether with heavy or light makeup,
    she is just like Xizi in the mirror.
But the two, Bai and Lin, did not look up, only drinking wine with
    laughter.

白云天竺飞来⁵。

图画里、峥嵘楼观开。

爱东西双涧，纵横水绕，两峰南北，高下云堆。

逋曰不然⁶，暗香浮动，争似孤山先探梅。

须晴去，访稼轩未晚，且此徘徊。

【注释】

1. 沁园春：词牌名。"沁园"为东汉明帝女沁水公主所有，建初二年（77）被窦宪所夺。后泛称公主的园林为"沁园"。辛承旨：指辛弃疾，辛弃疾曾被任命为枢密都承旨，但未受命而卒，刘过比辛弃疾早一年逝世，故"承旨"当为后人所加。《宋六十名家词》载题序作："风雪中欲诣稼轩，久寓湖上，未能一往，因赋此词以自解。"

2. 斗酒彘肩：《史记·项羽本纪》："项王曰：'壮士，赐之卮酒。'则与斗卮酒。哙拜谢，起，立而饮之。项王曰：'赐之彘肩。'则与一生彘肩。樊哙覆其盾于地，加彘肩上，拔剑切而啖之。"

3. 香山居士：唐代诗人白居易晚号香山居士。

4. "坡谓"三句：苏轼《饮湖上初晴后雨》："欲把西湖比西子，淡妆浓抹总相宜。"

5. "白云"六句：白居易题咏杭州，有诗《西湖晚归回望孤山寺赠诸客》"楼殿参差倚夕阳"，《春题湖上》"湖上春来似画图"，《寄韬光禅师》"东涧水流西涧水，南山云起北山云"等。

6. "逋曰"三句：林逋《山园小梅》："疏影横斜水清浅，暗香浮动月黄昏。"

【阅读提示】

　　刘过与辛弃疾交往颇深，稼轩"得之大喜，致馈数百千，竟邀之去，馆燕弥月"，后世传为佳话。此词为刘过辞稼轩之邀而作，诗人创造性地化用前人成句入对话体，融写景、抒情、叙事、议论为一体，形成了气势豪迈、逸趣横生的审美效果。开篇三句，用樊哙事，起势豪放。正欲成行，被白居易、林逋、苏轼三人拉回，借三人咏杭佳句，写出游杭州一事。稼轩之约，不如等晴天再赴。就章法而言，此词打破了上下分片的限制，配合内容上跨越时空的巧思，显示出词人艺术上的匠心独运，体现了词人狂放不羁的个性与迅捷过人的才情。

Go to the Flying Peak in Tianzhu, said Bai, where it is like an unfolding
    picture scroll with temples towering over the valley timber.

There are also double streams of east and west winding around,

And the two peaks of north and south emerging in cloud layer.

No, no. Lin said, let's go to Isolated Hill to enjoy the plum blossoms first,
    it is now the season floating the fragrance of flower.

It will not be too late to visit Mr. Jiaxuan until the weather is clear.

Let's take a moment by the West Lake to appreciate her glamor.

Comments and Tips

Qinyuanchun (Spring in Princess's Garden): a pattern of ci poetry. The close
relationship between Liu Guo and Xin Qiji remains legendary for later generations.
This ci poem was composed as a refusal to Xin's invitation to visit. Presenting
a style of dialogue, the poet creatively employed lines of his predecessors,
integrating landscapes, emotions, narrative and discussion into one, resulting in
an aesthetic effect with impressive momentum and fun. The opening lines offer
a bold start. Then the poet mentioned that when he was about to leave for the
invitation, Bai Juyi, Lin Bu and Su Shi pulled him back, and thus introduced the
plan of visiting Hangzhou by borrowing the three poets' great lines about the city.
Naturally it would be a wiser choice to wait for a sunny day to visit Jiaxuan (Xin's
art name). In terms of structure, this ci poem breaks the limits of the traditional
two halves. With the clever presentation of the content crossing time and space, it
reveals the poet's artistic ingenuity, reflecting his wild and uninhibited personality
as well as quick and overwhelming talents.

姜 夔

（约 1155—1209），字尧章，号白石道人，饶州鄱阳（今属江西）人。南宋文学家、音乐家。往来鄂、赣、皖、苏、浙间，与当时诗人、词客交游，卒于杭州。善音律，精鉴赏，工翰墨，能自度曲，是继苏轼之后又一难得的艺术全才。其词清空峭拔，被清初浙西词派奉为圭臬。有《白石道人歌曲》《白石道人诗集》等。

鹧鸪天·正月十一日观灯 [1]

巷陌风光纵赏时， 笼纱未出马先嘶 [2]。
白头居士无呵殿 [3]，只有乘肩小女随。

花满市，月侵衣， 少年情事老来悲。
沙河塘上春寒浅 [4]，看了游人缓缓归。

【注释】

1. 鹧鸪天：词牌名，又名"思佳客""醉梅花"等。双调五十五字，前段四句三平韵，后段五句三平韵。
2. 笼纱：纱笼，用绢纱作外罩的灯笼。
3. 呵殿：古代官员出行，仪卫前呵后殿，喝令行人让道。此处指仪仗队伍或随从人员。
4. 沙河塘：地名，在钱塘南五里。

Jiang Kui

(c.1155—1209) was a native of Poyang, Raozhou (now Jiangxi Province). He was a litterateur and musician of Southern Song Dynasty. He travelled among Hubei, Jiangxi, Anhui, Jiangsu and Zhejiang, made friends with poets at that time, and died in Hangzhou. He was an excellent musician, connoisseur and an expert in writing, calligraphy and painting. He could compose music by himself. He was an other versatile artist after Su Shi. His ci poems give a sense of lofty clearness and steep power, which are regarded as the textbook model by poets of Western Zhejiang Ci School in the early Qing Dynasty. There exist *Songs of Baishi Taoist* (Jiang's art name) and *Poetry of Baishi Taoist* and so on.

Zhegutian: Viewing the Lantern Festival on the 11th Day of the First Lunar Month

Watching the Lantern Festival in the lanes filled with coloured light;
Before the lanterns were taken out of the house the horse neighed outside.
There was no entourage around me, an old fellow;
Only my youngest daughter sitting on my shoulders follow.

The streets were full of lanterns, and the moonlight reflected on my robe of
    cotton.
It was full of joy in my youth but much sadness in my present situation.
With the slight chill in the early spring, on the riverbank, the sightseers
Who had finished watching the Lantern Festival were slowly returning to
    their shelters.

正月十一日观灯，南宋临安元夕节前常有试灯预赏之事。这首词写观灯时节之情境与词人之心境。上片采用对比手法，将贵族出行"笼纱未出马先嘶"的繁华盛大与白头居士"无呵殿""只有乘肩小女随"的寂寥清苦做对比，反映了统治阶级的奢侈腐朽和文人志士的清贫孤寂，抒发了词人的自嘲与激愤。下片起句承接上片的繁华，再引出自身情事，以乐景衬哀情。夜深灯尽，春寒浅浅，繁华散去，词人仿佛抽身在外，看游人缓缓归去，只留清冷悲凉之感。此词表面上描写灯会之景，实际上却借节日的热闹抒发漂泊江湖的羁旅困顿之情与情事难觅的遗憾悲凉，令人生出无限感慨。

Comments and Tips

Zhegutian (Partridges Singing in the Sky): a pattern of ci poetry. This ci poem reveals the view of the festival and the poet's state of mind. The first half presents a contrast between the prosperity and grandeur of noblemen's trip and the loneliness and poverty of the grey-haired "old fellow", expressing the poet's self-deprecation and irritation. The second half continues to cescribe the prosperity of the previous half, and then introduces the personal feelings of the poet himself. The poet took a seemingly remote and irrelevant position and watched the visitors slowly return, leaving only a desolate and dismal touch. This ci poem uses the festivity to express the emotional feeling of being adrift in the world and the regret and sadness at the loss of the youthful joys, which fills readers with emotion.

《群鱼戏藻图》南宋 佚名   故宫博物院藏

Fish Playing in Algae, Anonymous, Southern Song Dynasty, The Palace Museum

吴文英

（约1212—约1272），字君特，号梦窗、觉翁，四明（今浙江宁波）人。一生未第，游幕终身。往来江浙间，游踪所至，多有题咏。知音律，能自度曲，词名极重。有《梦窗词集》。

丑奴儿慢·双清楼 [1]

空濛乍敛，波影帘花晴乱。

正西子、梳妆楼上，镜舞青鸾 [2]。

润逼风襟，满湖山色入阑干。

天虚鸣籁，云多易雨，长带秋寒。

遥望翠凹，隔江时见，越女低鬟。

算堪羡、烟沙白鹭，暮往朝还。

歌管重城，醉花春梦半香残。

乘风邀月，持杯对影，云海人间。

【注释】

1. 丑奴儿慢：词牌名。一名"采桑子慢"，辛弃疾词名"丑奴儿近"。双调九十字，前后段各九句五平韵。双清楼：在杭州钱塘门外。
2. 镜舞青鸾：《太平御览》引南朝宋范泰《鸾鸟诗》序："昔罽宾王结罝峻卯之山，获一鸾鸟，王甚爱之，欲其鸣而不致也。乃饰以金樊，飨以珍羞。对之愈戚，三年不鸣。夫人曰：'尝闻鸟见其类而后鸣，何不悬镜以映之！'王从其意。鸾睹形悲鸣，哀响中霄，一奋而绝。"后即以"青鸾"借指妆镜。

Wu Wenying

(c.1212—c.1272) was a native of Siming (now Ningbo, Zhejiang Province). Never succeeded in the imperial examinations, he spent his entire life as a counselor. He travelled between Jiangsu and Zhejiang, and left many poems wherever he went. He knew the rhythms of music and was able to create his own pattern of ci poetry, and was especially esteemed as a great poet of ci. There exists *The Collection of Mengchuang's Ci* (Mengchuang: Wu's art name).

Chounu'erman: Shuangqing Building

The rain and fog on the lake has just dissipated,

And under the sun, the waves are shining and dazzling.

Just like the beauty Xishi in her dressing room,

In front of a phoenix-engraved mirror dancing.

The moist air flows through the clothes,

And the lake and hills rush into the wooden rail together.

In the sky there is a pipe playing,

And dark clouds gather as if it is going to rain,

Making people feel the autumn chilling.

The green cols look like a young girl of the Yue region,

Shy with her head bowed

On the other side of the river.

What is enviable is the egrets that come and go every morning and evening

On the smoke island and sandbar.

In the prosperous city, people spend their lives

In drunken dreams, singing and dancing.

I want to ride the wind,

Holding a glass of wine to invite the moon and my shadow,

Between the clouds and the earth wandering and drinking.

【阅读提示】

西湖天下景，杭人无时不游，南宋时杭谚谓西湖为"销金锅儿"，也留下了文人墨客们众多觞咏佳作。吴文英此词铺陈水色山光，为西湖作了明媚的写照，同时亦抒发了词人高朗的襟怀。上片以"西子""鸾镜"作比，言西湖水色之美；下片写遥望山野，以"烟沙白鹭"表达了词人对自由生活的向往，更引出下句"醉花春梦半香残"，直接描写都城的歌舞升平，讽刺世人的醉生梦死。结尾"乘风邀月，持杯对影"写出了词人的孤独感与对精神超脱的无限渴望。这首词作，笔轻意远，不似吴文英常见之严丽，却亦是思想和艺术俱佳的作品。

Comments and Tips

Chounu'erman (Slow Tune of the Ugly Slave), a pattern of ci poetry. This ci poem by Wu Wenying presents a bright picture of the West Lake with the charm of its water and hills, and at the same time expresses his lofty state of mind. The first half describes the beauty of the lake water; the second half presents a distant view of the hills and reveals the poet's longing for freedom, which leads to a direct description of the carefree singing and dancing in the capital city in order to satirize people's befuddled way of life as if drunk or in a cream. The ending line reveals the poet's loneliness and his infinite longing for spiritual transcendence. This ci poem offers profound connotations with a seemingly light touch, which does not comply with Wu's usual style of regularity and lofty grace. Still it has been regarded as a masterly piece of work that achieves thinking and artistic perfection.

陈人杰

（1218—1243），一名经国，字刚父，号龟峰，长乐（今福建福州）人。二十多岁时游历江淮，曾在杭州居住。词仅存《沁园春》三十一首，多抒写忧时报国之情，用调方式为两宋罕见。有《龟峰词》。

沁园春·咏西湖酒楼

南北战争，惟有西湖，长如太平。

看高楼倚郭，云边矗栋，小亭连苑，波上飞甍。

太守风流，游人欢畅，气象迩来都斩新。

秋千外，剩钗骈玉燕，酒列金鲸¹。

人生。

乐事良辰。

况莺燕声中长是晴。

正风嘶宝马，软红不动，烟分彩鹢²，澄碧无声。

倚柳分题，藉花传令³，满眼繁华无限情。

谁知道，有种梅处士，贫里看春。

【注释】

1. 金鲸：比喻容量大的华美盛酒器。
2. 彩鹢：古代常在船头上画鹢，着以彩色，因以彩鹢借指船。
3. 分题、传令：指宴饮时作诗、行酒令，泛指诗酒饮宴。

Chen Renjie

(1218 – 1243) was a native of Changle (now Fuzhou, Fujian Province). He travelled to the areas of Yangtze and Huai Rivers in his twenties and once lived in Hangzhou. There are only 31 ci poems of Qinyuanchun, which are mostly an expression of concern for the country at the time, and the use of tone is rare in the Song Dynasty. There exists *The Collection of Ci by Guifeng* (Chen's art name).

Qinyuanchun: In a Restaurant by the West Lake

While China is engaged in a south-north warfare,

For a long time only the West Lake is in a peaceful and tranquil air.

At a glance, standing against the city wall upright in the sky are the tall
buildings;

Pavilions connect the gardens into one piece, and the galleries by the pool
are full of cornices towering.

The mayor is arty, the visitors are happy,

And the fashion has taken on a new look recently.

Outside the swing are a pair of jade hairpins on the beauty's head, and
gorgeous wine vessels for luxurious feasting.

Life is always longing for a time happy and gay.

Even the birds are always singing on a sunny day.

The singing and dancing remains the same; the stallions neigh with the
wind shrill.

The colourful boats dot and the water is clear, green, and still.

Among willows and flowers people poetry writing and drink.

Their eyes are full of pride prosperous.

Who grows plum blossoms in Isolated Hill?

No one knows that Lin Hejing in the lanes of the poor is visiting spring.

　　南宋以来，家国动荡，但唯有西湖依旧安宁太平。此词首句，便对歌舞沉醉、偏安一隅的南宋王朝给予无情的讽刺，寓含无限感慨。接下来，分别从高楼亭苑、官宦游人、诗酒宴饮等方面，铺陈西湖之繁华与世人之美梦沉酣，借此揭露南宋君臣"西湖歌舞几时休"的奢靡生活。尾句笔锋一转，引出西湖著名隐士林逋，与先前铺陈形成鲜明对比，表达了词人高洁的精神追求。

《捕鱼图》南宋　夏圭（传）　大都会博物馆藏

Fishing, Xia Gui (to be decided), Southern Song Dynasty, The Metropolitan Museum of Art

Comments and Tips

Since the establishment of Southern Song Dynasty, families and the country had been suffering from turmoil and unrest. Ironically, the West Lake still enjoyed peace and tranquility. The first line of this ci poem gives a deep sigh and relentless satire on the Southern Song Dynasty, whose government was intoxicated by singing and dancing and precarious peace. Then it presents the prosperity of the West Lake and describes how people abandoned themselves to fancy dreams from the aspects of high buildings and pavilions, officials and tourists, poetry and wine banquets, etc., thus exposing the extravagant life of Southern Song emperors and their officials. The last line shifts to Lin Bu, the famous recluse of the West Lake, to offer a contrast with the previous description and expresses the poet's noble spiritual pursuit.

张　矩

生卒年不详，字成子，号梅深。乃布衣词客，与周密、陈允平、毛珝等人交游唱酬，其词以《应天长》西湖组词最为著名。周密在他的组词《木兰花慢》的序中写道："张成子（张矩）尝赋《应天长》十阕，夸余曰：是古今词家未能道者。"《校辑宋金元词》收其今存《梅渊词》一卷。

应天长·平湖秋月 [1]

候蛩探暝 [2]，书雁寄寒，西风暗剪绡织。

报道凤城催钥 [3]，笙歌散无迹。

冰轮驾 [4]，天纬逼。

渐款引、素娥游历 [5]。

夜妆靓，独展菱花，淡绚秋色。

Zhang Ju

(the exact date of his birth and death unknown) was a common ci poet without any titles. He had several cronies such as Zhou Mi, Chen Yunping and Mao Xu, and they found pleasure in exchanging poems. His best-known work is the West Lake ci poems, which are ten pieces of "Yingtianchang" (Song of Following the Mandate of Heaven). Zhou Mi wrote in the preface of his ci poems of "Mulanhuaman" (Slow Tune of Magnolias) that "Zhang Ju, who had composed ten pieces of 'Yingtianchang', once boasted to me that no one else through the ages could compete with his ci poems." There exists Zhang Ju's *The Ci Collection of Meiyuan* (another art title for Zhang Ju).

Yingtianchang: Autumn Moon over the Calm Lake

Autumn cicadas hastening the dusk approaching;

Wild geese flying south through the clouds convey the news of autumn;

The cold west wind is like scissors, your tulle clothes cutting.

Informing that the city gate will be closed,

And it's time to disperse singing and dancing.

The bright moon rises into the vault of heaven and is surrounded by the
    stars,

Which attracts Chang'e to travel in the sky, lingering.

She has beautiful night makeup, with diamond pattern decorations,

And gorgeous autumn colours flickering.

人在涌金楼[6]，漏迥绳低，光重袖香滴。

笑语又惊栖鹊，南飞傍林阒[7]。

孤山影，波共碧。

向此际、隐逋如识。

梦仙游，倚遍霓裳[8]，何处闻笛。

【注释】

1. 应天长：词牌名。此调有令词和慢词，令词始于五代韦庄，慢词始于北宋柳永。张矩写有《应天长》十首，乃为"西湖十景"所作。平湖秋月：西湖十景之一。南宋时并无固定景址，康熙三十八年（1699），康熙游西湖，御书"平湖秋月"匾额，从此景点固定。如今的平湖秋月景点位于白堤西端，背依孤山，面临外湖。

2. 蛩（qióng）：蟋蟀。

3. 凤城：京城。此指南宋都城杭州。

4. 冰轮：月亮。

5. 素娥：嫦娥的别称，亦用作月亮的代称。

6. 涌金楼：北宋政和六年至七年（1116—1117），杭州当时的知州徐铸所建，楼旁有涌金池。后几经重建，现在的涌金楼位于杭州南山路"西湖天地"景点内。

7. 阒（qù）：形容寂静，没有声音。

8. 霓裳：《霓裳羽衣曲》的略称，为唐代著名舞曲。开元中，河西节度使杨敬述进献《婆罗门曲》，此曲经唐玄宗润色并制歌词，后改名为"霓裳羽衣曲"。传说有唐玄宗游月宫密记仙乐而作之说，诗人常援引入诗，本词亦用此意。

The moon watchers sit on the Surging Gold Building,

Seeing the stars shifting and the Milky Way hanging low.

From the fragrant silk sleeve the clear light dripping.

The laughter startles the magpies out of the forest;

To south direction they are flying.

The distant shadow of Isolated Hill

In the water light jumping.

I think back then, Lin Bu, who lived in seclusion,

Had also seen the same thing.

Entering into the fairyland like a dream, so close to the cloud clothes.

At this time I hear somewhere a flute playing.

张矩的《应天长》十首，是最早的"西湖十景"词。这首《平湖秋月》，紧扣"秋""月""平湖"落笔。上片首句通过探暝的蟋蟀、传书的大雁和西风，点出时值秋天。次句通过城门催关、笙歌散去，说明夜已较晚。这时月轮驾临，星星高挂，嫦娥仙子姗姗来迟，她夜妆靓丽，令人惊艳。"独展菱花"既是写嫦娥，也是比喻西湖水面波平如镜。下片转写在平湖秋月对面的涌金楼上看到的景象。虽然更漏已残，但是笙歌未休，舞袖香滴，已栖湖边的鸟鹊被笑语惊起，南飞到静寂的林间。孤山倒映在湖中，隐居的林逋似乎也出来赏月。恍惚似梦间与飞仙遨游，倚遍霓裳，不知何处闻笛。词人写了西湖边观月的美景，更生动描摹了此时飘然欲仙的感受。全词境界高洁，平淡中见精巧，把月下之西湖写得淡雅幽渺，有声有色，恍若仙境。

Comments and Tips

Zhang Ju's "Yingtianchang" (Song of Following the Mandate of Heaven) is the earliest ci version about "Ten Views of the West Lake". "Autumn Moon over the Calm Lake", one of the ci poems, focuses on the images of "autumn", "moon" and "the Calm Lake". In the first line, the images of cicadas, wild geese and the cold west wind demonstrate the season of autumn. The second line indicates the darkness of the night, as the city gate closes and the party ends, the moon and stars appear, among which, the goddess Chang'e approaches. The next stanza introduces the scene seen from the "Surging Gold Building". Even in the darkness, laughter and songs are still heard and seen everywhere, startling a flock of magpies to fly. The familiar scene might have attracted the recluse Lin Bu to enjoy the moonlight in the shadow of the Isolated Hill. It becomes an illusion of wandering in a fairyland. This ci poem is written in plain language, but full of fantastic ingenuity. Its noble spirit can be sensed throughout the verse. It also gives readers a dreamy impression that the West Lake in the moonlight is particularly ethereal and elegant, like the vivid fairyland.

周　密

（1232—约1298），字公谨，号草窗、弁阳老人等，原籍山东济南，后徙吴兴（今浙江湖州）。宋末，曾为临安府幕属，又为义乌令。宋亡不仕，居杭州。工诗词，善画。有《洲渔笛谱》《草窗韵语》《武林旧事》《齐东野语》《癸辛杂识》等，又选南宋词人佳作编为《绝妙好词》。

木兰花慢·南屏晚钟 [1]

疏钟敲暝色，正远树、绿愔愔。

看渡水僧归，投林鸟聚，烟冷秋屏。

孤云。

渐沈雁影，尚残箫、倦鼓别游人。

宫柳栖鸦未稳，露梢已挂疏星。

重城。

Zhou Mi

(1232 — c.1298) was born in Jinan (now in Shandong Province) and later moved to Wuxing (now in Zhejiang Province). In Li Zong's Period, he served as the staffer (an assistant to a ranking official) of Lin'an prefecture, and later as the Commander of Yiwu County. After the collapse of Southern Song Dynasty, Zhou Mi stopped serving as an official and settled in Hangzhou. He was good at poetry writing and painting. His works include *Caochuang* (an art name of the author) *Lyrics*. He selected the good works of ci writers in the Southern Song Dynasty and compiled them into the book *Excellent Ci*.

Mulanhuaman: Evening Bell Ringing from Nanping Hill

The sound of sparse bells came in the night;

The trees in the distance were dark and green.

There are monks returning from crossing the water,

The lodging birds flying into the forest,

And the cooking smoke dotting the South Hill screen.

The lonely cloud is silent, the wild geese are flying away,

And the sound of flute and drums in the night

Is urging the travelers to return, chop-chop!

The crows flying on the willow have not yet entered the nest;

A few stars hang in the night sky outside the dew-covered treetop.

There is a city outside the city,

禁鼓催更。

罗袖怯、暮寒轻。

想绮疏空掩，鸾绡黦锦，鱼钥收银²。

兰灯。

伴人夜语，怕香消、漏永著温存。

犹忆回廊待月，画阑倚遍桐阴。

【注释】

1. 木兰花慢：词牌名。宋柳永《乐章集》注"高平调"。双调一百零一字，前段十句五平韵，后段十句七平韵。南屏晚钟：《西湖志》载："南屏山在净慈寺右，兴教寺之后，正对苏堤。寺钟初动，山谷皆应，逾时乃息。盖兹山隆起，内多空穴，故传声独远。"
2. 鱼钥：鱼形的锁。

【阅读提示】

　　南屏山，在西湖南岸，正对苏堤，因山势高耸、内多空穴，所以寺钟初动时，山谷响应，传声甚远，形成了著名的西湖十景之一"南屏晚钟"。周密此词，寄调《木兰花慢》，题咏南屏晚钟。"疏钟"至"烟冷秋屏"句，铺陈破题，写西湖晚景，僧归鸟聚，暮色苍茫，情调清冷。"尚残箫、倦鼓别游人"写罢游欲归，而此时已将入夜，"露梢已挂疏星"。下片接写归后闺中情思，虽与"南屏晚钟"之题无涉，但用语清丽雅致，言情婉转动人，亦是佳制。

And the drums of the curfew announce the deep night.

It is no longer warm enough wearing a thin silk shirt,

For the chill of autumn twilight.

Imagine that in the carved window,

There is a beauty in cloud pattern brocade skirt,

And the embroidered door will open slightly.

Under the lamp painted with orchids, we talk to each other at night;

Being afraid that the fragrance will dissipate about love we are narrating.

I still remember my date in the winding corridor,

Under the tree shade leaning against the railing.

Comments and Tips

"Mulanhuaman" (Slow Tune of Magnolias) is a pattern of ci poetry. Nanping Hill rests on the southern bank of the West Lake, right facing Su Causeway. As the hill itself is high, with lots of caves and cavities inside, sounds of a bell made here reach afar. Hence one of the "Ten Views of the West Lake" is entitled "Evening Bell Ringing from Nanping Hill". The first two lines point out the title of the poem and illustrate a picture of the evening lake view in a cold silence, the monks returning and the birds flying back in the deepening dusk. Then in the following lines, it depicts the sentimental love story in the boudoir. The words selected are elegant and exquisite, in a very sincere and touching tone. The whole work can rank as a quality piece.

叶绍翁

生卒年不详，南宋中期诗人，字嗣宗，号靖逸，处州龙泉（今属浙江）人。其学出于叶适，与真德秀友善。诗属江湖诗派。有《四朝闻见录》《靖逸小稿》。

题鄂王墓 [1]

万古知心只老天，英雄堪恨复堪怜。

如公少缓须臾死，此虏安能八十年。

漠漠凝尘空偃月，堂堂遗像在凌烟 [2]。

早知埋骨西湖路，悔不鸱夷理钓船 [3]。

【注释】

1. 鄂王墓：在杭州西湖边栖霞岭下。宋宁宗时，追封岳飞为鄂王。
2. 凌烟：凌烟阁。封建王朝为表彰功臣而建造的绘有功臣画像的高阁，以唐太宗贞观十七年（643）画功臣像于凌烟阁之事最为著名。
3. 鸱夷：指范蠡，自号鸱夷子皮，晚年功成身退，泛舟五湖。

Ye Shaoweng

(whose birth and death dates were unclear) was born in Longquan (now in Zhejiang Province). He was a poet in the mid-Southern Song Dynasty. His poetry belongs to the Jianghu (outside officialdom) School. His works include *Things Heard and Seen in the Reigns of Four Emperors* and *The Collection of Jingyi* (the author's art name).

Tomb of Yue Fei

Only heaven knows the good and evil of the hearts of all ages,

And the fate of heroes even more makes people feel sad and pity.

If Yue Fei had not been framed and killed,

How could the Jin regime in northern China have lasted for years eighty?

Obscures the light of the moon the misty dust;

Sits in Lingyan Pavilion the great effigy.

Had he known that he would eventually bury his remains by the West Lake,

He would regret not being able to sail on the Five Lakes leisurely.

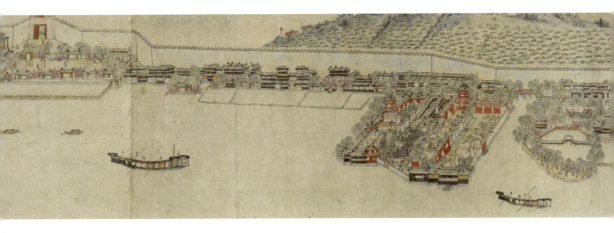

《西湖清趣图》（局部）元　佚名　弗利尔美术馆藏

The Elegance of the West Lake (Partial), Anonymous, Yuan Dynasty, Freer Gallery of Art

【阅读提示】

　　岳飞是南宋抗金名将，中国历史上著名的军事家、战略家。他挥师北伐、大败金军，金军有"撼山易，撼岳家军难"之说；在逼近故都开封时，却因奸佞迫害，以"莫须有"之罪被害，岳飞被杀成为南宋历史上的一大冤案，也成为北归无望的南宋臣子心中之伤痛。宋孝宗时，岳飞冤狱被平反，以礼改葬栖霞岭下，追谥"武穆"。这首南宋诗人叶绍翁的诗，直抒胸臆，表达了对岳飞功绩、人格的无限敬仰与缅怀，对岳飞不公遭遇的愤慨与痛惜。

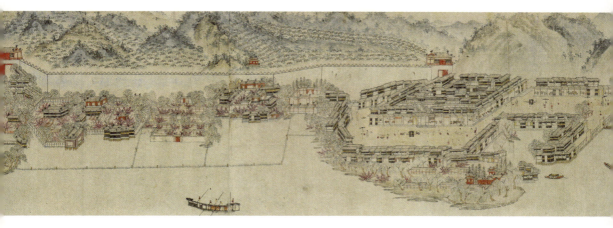

Comments and Tips

Yue Fei, a famous Chinese military general, who led Southern Song forces against the Jurchen-ruled Jin Kingdom, was also known as a great militarist and strategist. In the wars, he attempted to push northward to defeat the offensive Jin army. When his troops were approaching Kaifeng, the old capital before the fall of Northern Song Dynasty, he was persecuted, imprisoned and later executed under a groundless charge. His death was regarded as one of the unjust cases in Southern Song history, and the great loss in the hearts of those Southern Song people who were hopeless to see the recovery of their motherland. When Emperor Xiaozong rose to power, Yue Fei was cleared of wrongful charges and reburied with courtesy at the foot of Qixia Ridge. He was then granted the posthumous name Wumu ("Wumu" used here praises his outstanding military achievements in history). The poet expressed his minds directly, showing his great respect to Yue Fei's achievements and personality charm and condemning and lamenting Yue Fei's unfair sufferings.

文及翁

生卒年不详，字时学，号本心，绵州（今四川绵阳）人，徙居吴兴（今浙江湖州）。理宗宝祐元年（1253）进士，历国子司业、礼部郎官、秘书少监等职。宋亡后隐居不仕。有文集二十卷，已佚。

贺新郎·西湖 [1]

一勺西湖水。

渡江来、百年歌舞，百年酣醉。

回首洛阳花石尽 [2]，烟渺黍离之地 [3]。

更不复、新亭堕泪 [4]。

簇乐红妆摇画艇，问中流、击楫谁人是 [5]。

千古恨，几时洗。

Wen Jiweng

whose birth and death dates are unknown, was born in Mianzhou (now Mianyang in Sichuan Province) and later transferred to Wuxing (now Huzhou in Zhejiang Province). He became a Jinshi in the first year of Baoyou Period (1253) and then served as an education officer in the Imperial Academy, an official of Ministry of Rites and a vice-curator of the Imperial Library in a row. After the fall of Southern Song Dynasty, he lived in seclusion and ceased to be an official for the court. He wrote an anthology of twenty volumes but they were all lost.

Hexinlang: The West Lake

The West Lake is but a spoonful of water.

Since the Southern Crossing, a hundred years of singing and dancing,

And a hundred years of drunken race.

Looking back, the precious flowers and exotic rocks had been destroyed,

Now barren farmland is the place.

There is no one like Wang Dao who sat in the New Pavilion,

Telling the gentlemen not just tears to gleam.

Only the dancers' figures in the painted boats were seen in the music.

Where is the hero who swore in the middle of the stream?

The shame will be finally cleared but it is just a dream.

余生自负澄清志。

更有谁、磻溪未遇⁶，傅岩未起⁷。

国事如今谁倚仗，衣带一江而已。

便都道、江神堪恃。

借问孤山林处士，但掉头、笑指梅花蕊。

天下事，可知矣。

【注释】

1. 贺新郎：词牌名，又名"金缕曲"。传作以《东坡乐府》所收为最早，唯句豆平仄，与诸家颇多不合，因以《稼轩长短句》为准。此调声情沉郁苍凉，宜抒发激越情感，历来为词家所习用。

2. 洛阳花石：洛阳以园林著称，多名花奇石。宋李格非《洛阳名园记》载："天下之治乱，候于洛阳之盛衰而知；洛阳之盛衰，候于园囿之兴废而得。"此处借指汴京，以影射北宋末年宋徽宗花石纲事。

3. 黍离之地：《诗经·王风·黍离》："彼黍离离。"《毛诗序》言："《黍离》，闵宗周也。周大夫行役，至于宗周，过故宗庙宫室，尽为禾黍，闵周室之颠覆，彷徨不忍去，而作是诗也。"后多以黍离寄慨亡国之悲。

4. 新亭：又名"劳劳亭"，建于三国吴时，故址在今江苏南京。《世说新语·言语》："过江诸人，每至美日，辄相邀新亭，藉卉饮宴。周侯中坐而叹曰：'风景不殊，正自有山河之异！'皆相视流泪。唯王丞相愀然变色曰：'当共戮力王室，克复神州，何至作楚囚相对！'"

5. 中流、击楫：《晋书·祖逖传》载："（祖逖）仍将本流徙部曲百余家渡江，中流击楫而誓曰：'祖逖不能清中原而复济者，有如大江！'"

6. 磻溪：水名。在今陕西宝鸡市东南，传说为周吕尚未遇文王时垂钓处。

7. 傅岩：相传殷相傅说曾隐于傅岩，后因以泛指栖隐之士或隐逸之士。

I consider myself to have the ambition to save the country from hazards.

But if hadn't met King Zhou Wenwang,

Even Jiang Ziya and Fu Yue, the talented sages, could only look up to the

heaven to murmur.

What else could we rely on to save our country now?

There is only a dress belt of Yangtze River.

But some people said that we could rely on the River God.

I went to ask Lin Hejing, who lived in seclusion on Isolated Hill;

He just shook his head and pointed at the plum blossom, smiled and

hawed.

The future of the country

Will be on the way slipshod.

　　文及翁此词，慷慨激昂，表达了作者对国事的深刻担忧；针砭时弊，揭示了南宋王朝岌岌可危的现状；抒发忠愤，批判、讽刺了歌舞沉酣的南宋君臣和逃避现实的文人隐士。词人从首句"一勺""百年"而下，便直讧世事，后多处用典，用"新亭堕泪""中流击楫""磻溪未遇""傅岩未起"等连环设问，拓展了文本的历史空间，古今震荡，共抒黍离悲慨。最后以"天下事，可知矣"收束全篇，在极悲愤之中，又发出了无可奈何的浩叹，读来更令人扼腕沉痛。

《林和靖图》南宋　马麟　东京国立博物馆藏

Lin Hejing, Ma Lin, Southern Song Dynasty, Tokyo National Museum

Comments and Tips

Hexinlang (Congratulations to the Groom): a pattern of ci poetry. Its tone is gloomy and desolate and is suitable to express intense emotions, so it has always been used by ci poets. This ci poem, in an impassioned tone, expresses the poet's great concern about the national affairs, criticizes the maladies of the times and reveals the collapsing situation of Southern Song empire. The examples, such as the Southern Song emperor and his courtiers obsessed by singing and dancing, as well as literati and recluses escaping from reality, work as strong criticism and satire. The poet directly starts with sarcasm on the national affairs, then cites several classics to ask a series of questions in the following lines. This setting expands the historical horizon in the context, resonates with the present situation, and even delivers the deep sorrow and pain. Finally, in extreme grief and anger, the poet uttered a helpless sigh, which is even more painful to read.

林 升

生卒年不详，孝宗淳熙时人，字梦屏，平阳（今属浙江）人。明田汝成《西湖游览志余》曰："绍兴、淳熙之间，颇称康裕。君相纵逸，耽乐湖山，无复新亭之泪。士人林升者，题一绝于旅邸云……"

题临安邸[1]

山外青山楼外楼，西湖歌舞几时休。
暖风薰得游人醉，直把杭州作汴州[2]。

【注释】

1. 邸：旅店。
2. 汴州：汴京，北宋都城，今河南开封市。

【阅读提示】

这是一首家喻户晓的爱国诗歌，从诗题"题临安邸"可知，它原是作者林升写在南宋皇都临安一家旅舍壁上的"墙头诗"。诗歌以杭州的山水胜景、歌舞繁华开篇，欲抑先扬，对当权者的辛辣讽刺不留痕迹地设置在这不知"几时休"的热闹场面中。紧接其后，用自然界之"暖风"，引出偏安一隅不思收复失地的当权者，点出他们"游人"的身份，揭露他们"自醉"的丑态，又通过醉后将"杭州"当作"汴州"的对照，巧妙自然地揭示了南宋王朝的腐朽本质。诗人匠心独运，以七绝之短小体制，以不加谩骂的冷言冷语，惟妙惟肖地刻画了南宋统治者的精神状态，深刻讽刺了南宋统治者的纵情声色与荒淫腐朽，表达了自身的忧国之心与激愤之情，的确是讽刺诗中的难得佳作。

Lin Sheng

(whose birth and death dates are unknown) was born in Pingyang (now in Zhejiang Province) and active during the years of Chunxi, a period of Emperor Xiaozong's reign. According to Tian Rucheng's *West Lake Tour Annals* written in the Ming Dynasty, people lived a rich and peaceful life during the years of Shaoxing and Chunxi. Monarchs and officials there indulged in the joy of sightseeing tours, no longer remembering the pain of national disintegration. Lin Sheng, a scholar, then wrote a poem about this situation at his inn.

The Poem Written on the Wall of Lin'an Inn

There are hills beyond the hill and buildings beyond the building.
On the West Lake never ends the singing and dancing.
The warm spring breeze enchants the visitors there and here,
Who are treating today's Hangzhou as Bianzhou of yesteryear.

Comments and Tips

It's a patriotic poem, known to every Chinese household. From the title "The Poem Written on the Wall of Lin'an Inn", we know that it was once a scribbled poem on a wall of an inn in Lin'an (now Hangzhou), the imperial capital of Southern Song Dynasty. In this poem, poignant sarcasm to those in power is naturally exposed throughout "never ending indulgence". The ruling class indulged in joy and pleasure without thinking of retaking the lost territory, and was intoxicated by themselves and even mistook Hangzhou for Bianzhou (now Kaifeng in Henan Province), which was their old capital. This also reveals the corrupt nature of Southern Song Dynasty. This exquisite quatrain, in its cold words, manifests the poet's intentions to the full. It vividly represents the mental state of the Southern Song monarchs, deeply satirizes their pursuit of sensual and dissolute lives and expresses the poet's great concern about his nation and rising wrath. It's considered a classic of satirical poems.

陈允平

生卒年不详，字君衡，号西麓，四明鄞县（今浙江宁波鄞州区）人。出身官宦家庭，陈文懿孙。恭帝德祐时授沿海制置司参议官。善诗词，词学周邦彦，曾创作"西湖十咏"。有《西麓诗稿》《日湖渔唱》《西麓继周集》等。

八声甘州 · 曲院风荷 [1]

放船杨柳下，听鸣蝉、薰风小新堤。

正烟茫露蓼，飞尘酿玉，第五桥西 [2]。

遥认青罗盖底，宫女夜游池。

谁在鸳鸯浦，独棹玻璃。

Chen Yunping

(whose birth and death dates are not known) was born in an official family in Siming, Yin County (now Ningbo in Zhejiang Province). During Deyou Period (Emperor Zhao Xian's reign), he was appointed the counsellor of the Coastal Military Commission. He excelled in poetry, imitating Zhou Bangyan's style to write ci and once wrote "Ten Odes to the West Lake". There exist the collections of his poems and prose, such as *Poem Collection of Xilu* (the author's art name), *Ci Collection of Rihuyuchang* and *Collection of Xilujizhou*.

Bashengganzhou: Breeze-ruffled Lotuses at Quyuan Garden

Row the boat under the willow trees and listen to the sound of cicadas;

Across the new causeway, the warm breeze is blowing .

By Dongpu Bridge, the water plants grow luxuriantly,

And white catkins are flying just like it is snowing.

From a distance, it seems that under green umbrellas,

The palace maids by the pool are playing.

And on this wonderful waterfront,

Who is alone in the boat, rowing?

一片天机云锦，见凌波碧翠，照日胭脂。

是西湖西子，晴抹雨妆时³。

便相将无情秋思，向菰蒲深处落红衣。

醺醺里，半篙香梦，月转星移。

【注释】

1. 曲院风荷："西湖十景"之一，位于西湖西侧。明田汝成《西湖游览志》说："曲
   院，宋时取金沙涧之水造曲以酿官酒。其地多荷花，世称'曲院风荷'是也。"
2. 第五桥：指苏堤上由南向北的第五座桥，即东浦桥。
3. "是西湖"两句：化用宋苏轼《饮湖上初晴后雨》名句："欲把西湖比西子，淡
   妆浓抹总相宜。"

【阅读提示】

　　陈允平作词，学周邦彦，其词和平婉丽。这首写曲院风荷的词作，用语精妍，
绘景明丽，情调清新，寄调《八声甘州》，倒不见调中应有之感慨顿挫，应为变调
之作。词上片写寻访所见，放船杨柳下，循蝉鸣步新堤，随着词人弃船寻访的视野，
曲院风荷之景，也在读者眼前旖旎展开。"正烟荭露蓼"三句点出曲院之功用与位
置。"遥认"四句绘出遥望"曲院"之佳境。下片写游赏曲院风荷，"一片天机云锦"
数句写出傍晚曲院凌波碧翠、落霞满天的绚丽景色，用苏轼的诗歌意象，以西子作
比赞美西湖。最后，词人不舍离去，带秋思纵深夜游，"醺醺里"沉醉于美景之中。
词作细致地描绘了曲院风荷的美丽景色，洋溢着词人陶然沉醉的愉悦之情。

The lake surface is like brocade woven by the fairies,

Where you can see the green hats on the water waves,

And the bright red lotus flowers in the sunlight.

Is this the West Lake, or is it Xizi?

Whether it's sunny or rainy, the makeup is always appropriate, heavy or
    light.

I have no choice but to accompany with the ruthless thoughts

Until the lotus petals from the branches alight.

Going drunk on the boat into a dream, and not realizing

That the moon is shifting in the sky during the night.

Comments and Tips

Breeze-ruffled Lotuses at Quyuan Garden is one of the Ten Views of the West
Lake, located in the west of the lake. This ci poem has exquisite words, clear
scenery depiction and fresh tones. The first part of the ci poem portrays what
the poet had seen. Along with the poet's visit, the scenery of Quyuan Garden
exposes itself to readers. The second part marks a real visit in the garden, where
the beauty of its nightfall can be enjoyed. The metaphor of Xizi, as is adopted
from Su Shi's poetic image, is a way to compliment the West Lake. At the end
of the ci poem, the poet is immersed in the nocturnal strolls, reluctant to leave.
The ci poem depicts the superb view of the garden, and the immersive joy of the
poet.

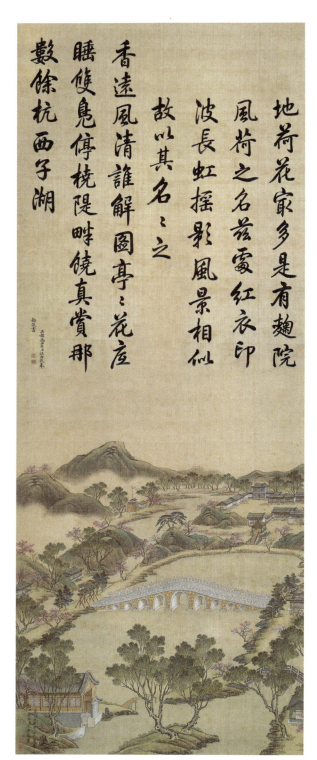

地荷花家多是有麴院
風荷之名蓋霎紅衣印
波長虹搖影風景相似
故以其名之之
香遠風清誰解圖亭亭花庭
睍睆㕙傳橈隄畔饒真賞那
數餘杭西子湖

《曲院风荷》

清　唐岱、沈源绘　汪由敦书

法国国家图书馆藏

Breeze-ruffled Lotuses at Quyuan Garden,
Painted by Tang Dai and Shen Yuan, Qing
Dynasty, written by Wang Youdun,
National Library of France

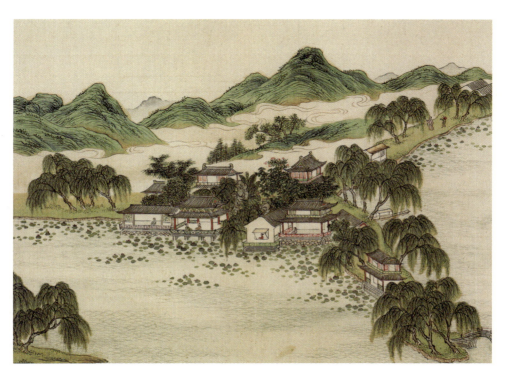

《西湖风景图》册（二十四之三《曲院风荷》）清　佚名　故宫博物院藏

Breeze-ruffled Lotuses at Quyuan Garden in the album of *Scenery of the West Lake*, Anonymous, Qing Dynasty, The Palace Museum

王 洧

生卒年不详，号仙麓，闽县（今福建福州）人。理宗宝祐四年（1256）入浙江帅幕。
事见《洞霄诗集》卷五（《洞霄诗集》是元代孟宗宝编名胜诗集，共十四卷）。

湖山十景·柳浪闻莺（十首其六）[1]

如簧巧啭最高枝[2]，苑树青归万缕丝。
玉辇不来春又老[3]，声声诉与落花知。

【注释】

1. 柳浪闻莺："西湖十景"之一，位于西湖东南岸清波门处。
2. 簧：乐器中用以发声的片状振动体。《诗·小雅·巧言》："巧言如簧，颜之厚矣。"
3. 玉辇：天子所乘之车，以玉为饰。

【阅读提示】

　　柳浪闻莺，为西湖十景之一，位于西湖东南岸清波门处，原是南宋皇家御苑，
沿湖遍植垂柳，苑中有柳浪桥。这首诗从如簧巧啭的莺声与万缕青丝的杨柳写起，
绘出了柳浪闻莺春季柳丝如帘、莺声鸣啭的动人景色。"玉辇"二句，生出惜春感
慨之情，或亦有自伤之意，写春天又要过去了，帝王的玉辇亦不再来，这婉转动人
的莺啼只能空付与落花听取了。

Wang Wei

whose birth and death dates are not known, was born in Min County (now Fuzhou in Fujian Province). He served as an advisor to the generals of Zhejiang in the 4th year of Baoyou Period (1256). His life experiences can be seen in *Collection of Dongxiao Poetry*, Vol. 5 (in Collection of Scenic Poems compiled by Meng Zongbao of Yuan Dynasty).

Ten Views of Lake and Hills: Warblers Singing in Willow Waves (the Sixth of Ten)

On the highest branches are chirping the warblers;
The willows in the garden have sprouted, drooping with hair green slender.
But until the end of spring, no one has seen His Majesty visit here;
And these warblers can only cry to the fallen flowers.

Comments and Tips

"Warblers Singing in Willow Waves", at Qingbo Gate off the southeast bank of the West Lake, is recognized as one of the Ten Views of the West Lake. It was once an imperial park in the Southern Song Dynasty, with luxuriant willows along the winding bank and a bridge named Liulang (willow waves) in between. This poem starts with the image of willows, forming a spring scene with curtain—like willow branches and softly singing warblers. Then the lines with the image of the jade chariot of the emperor convey a feeling of mourning the passing of spring, or that of self-pity. The spring is gone; the imperial jade chariot is also gone; the warblers' soft singing can only be enjoyed by the fallen petals.

文天祥

（1236—1283），字履善，又字宋瑞，号文山，吉州庐陵（今江西吉安）人，宝祐四年（1256）进士第一。元军东下时率义兵万人入卫临安。次年，任右丞相兼枢密使，出使元军议和，被拘至镇江，后逃脱。端宗即位，复拜右相兼枢密使，率兵坚持抗元。祥兴元年（1278）被俘，囚于元大都三年，屡拒威逼利诱，视死如归。临刑作《正气歌》。明代时追赐谥号"忠烈"。有《文山先生全集》。

自　叹

正月十三夜，予闻陈枢使将以十五日[1]，会伯颜于长堰[2]，予力言不可，陈枢使为尼此行[3]，予自知非不明，后卒自蹈，殊不可晓也。

长安不可诣[4]， 何故会皋亭[5]。

倦鸟非无翼， 神龟弗自灵[6]。

乾坤增感慨， 身世付飘零。

回首西湖晓， 雨余山更青。

【注释】

1. 陈枢使：时任宋朝枢密使的陈宜中。
2. 伯颜：元朝名臣，当时征伐南宋的元军统帅。长堰：长安堰，在今浙江海宁市西北。
3. 尼：停止。
4. 长安：此指长安堰。
5. 皋亭：在临安东北，今属杭州市拱墅区，南宋时为临安重要的防守要隘。
6. "神龟"句：《庄子·外物》云：宋元君梦见一神龟，说自己被渔人捕获。宋元君诏令该渔人献龟，得龟后杀之。这个故事说明神龟虽有灵性托梦给人，但却不能料到自己被人所杀。

Wen Tianxiang

(1236－1283) was born in Jizhou, Luling (now Ji'an County in Jiangxi Province). He was ranked the first in the Jinshi examination in the 4th year of Baoyou Period (1256). Next year, he served as the Prime Minister and Military Commissioner. He was later detained in Zhenjiang after going to the Yuan army to negotiate peace, but later escaped. After the accession to the throne of Emperor Duanzong, he resumed his previous positions. He led the troops to fight against the Yuan army. In the first year of Xiangxing Period (1278), he was captured by the Yuan army and imprisoned in Dadu (the capital of Yuan Dynasty, now Beijing) for three years. He faced death unflinchingly no matter how the enemy coerced and bribed him. He wrote "Song of Righteousness" before his execution. After his death, he was given the posthumous name of Zhonglie (a title of martyrs). He wrote *The Complete Works of Master Wenshan* (the author's art name).

Self Sigh

Already cannot go to Chang'an Weir, and why

Come to Gaoting to negotiate with the enemy should I?

The weary bird is not without wing,

And the turtle is no longer compelling.

The national crisis makes me feel more indignant;

In the wind my personal experience will be like a leaf floating.

The last time I look back at the West Lake in the morning;

After the rain the hills appear more verdant.

这首五律作于至元十三年（1276）。首联写自己明明劝阻陈枢使长安堰不可去，但是何故自己又会去皋亭与伯颜谈判。这里似有一种自责，但更多的是对自己为国不避艰险，前往敌营的无怨无悔。颔联把自己比作倦飞之鸟和不能料到自身死亡的神龟。颈联直抒感慨：自己悲哀的是国家衰亡（当时都城已破，宋恭帝被掳），个人壮志难酬，身世飘零。尾联说自己一夜不眠，回看故都西湖的拂晓，雨后的群山更显青翠。全诗语句沉痛，读之使人怆然，但充溢着强烈的爱国之情和坚定不移的英雄气节。

Comments and Tips

The first couplet of this poem literarily indicates self-blame, but reflects his courage to negotiate peace with the enemy troops without any regrets. The second couplet uses images of the weary bird and the turtle as metaphors for himself. The third couplet expresses his sorrow for the decline of his nation, his regret of being unable to fulfill his ambition and his personal experience of drifting around. The last couplet shows his restless night because of recalling the beauty of the West Lake. Between the lines, readers can see his deep love for his homeland and his determination to defend its integrity.

宋

仇 远

（1247—1326），字仁近，一字仁父，号山村、山村民，钱塘人。诗与白珽齐名，人称"仇白"。入元，为溧阳儒学教授，旋罢归，优游湖山以终。工诗文。有《金渊集》《山村遗集》。

凤凰山故宫

渐无南渡旧衣冠[1]，尚有西湖风雨寒。

凤鸟不来山寂寂，　鸱夷何在海漫漫[2]。

荒陵樵采官犹禁[3]，故苑烟花客自看。

惟恨余杭门外柳，　长年不了送征鞍。

【注释】

1. 南渡旧衣冠：南渡衣冠。原指西晋末天下乱，中原士族和政权南迁。西晋末晋元帝渡江定都建康（今南京）建立东晋。此指北宋末宋高宗渡江在临安建立南宋。李清照有诗云："南渡衣冠少王导，北来消息欠刘琨。"
2. 鸱夷：革囊，借指春秋时期吴国的伍子胥。伍子胥被谗致死后，吴王夫差把他的尸体装在鸱夷里投入江中。传说伍子胥死后化为潮神。
3. 荒陵：指荒废的南宋皇陵，遗址在今浙江绍兴攒宫山。1278 年，杭州被元军攻陷不久，元朝江南佛教总管杨琏真迦就率兵盗挖宋高宗、孝宗等六帝及皇后、嫔妃等的陵寝，并将尸骨抛弃遍地。

Qiu Yuan

(1247—1326) was born in Qiantang. After entering the Yuan Dynasty, he served as a teacher of Confucianism in Liyang County and soon resigned. He then travelled around mountains and waters in his later life. He was good at writing poems and prose and authored *Collection of Jinyuan* (named after a river in Liyang County) and *The Legacy of Shancun* (his courtesy name).

The Old Palace at the Foot of the Phoenix Hill

Have long disappeared the costumes since crossing the Yangtze River;

The wind and rain on the West Lake are chilling in winter.

The hill looks lonely without the phoenix flying in.

And there is no Wu Zixu but only the sea vaster.

Although the imperial tombs are deserted, lumbering is still forbidden;

In the old palace garden, the bloom is fascinating, attracting no flower admirers.

Only the willows outside Yuhang Gate still hold resentment;

Year after year, they watch marching away the soldiers.

【阅读提示】

　　这首诗咏位于杭州凤凰山的南宋故宫。首联即写南渡衣冠已成过往，昔日莺歌燕舞的西湖在风雨飘摇中已令人顿生寒意。颔联写虽然山名"凤凰"，但凤凰不来，只余青山寂寂；也不见伍子胥，只见大海波涛漫漫。颈联写宋代皇陵被盗挖后已夷为平地，但陵园上的树木仍被官府禁止砍伐；往日宫苑一片荒芜，那野花颓垣也无人观赏。尾联诗人迁怒于余杭门外的杨柳，它们已多年没有为出征之人送行了。诗歌先是运用对比，于写景、叙事中寄寓亡国之痛；而尾联移情及物的手法，更加深了对复国无望的悲凉。全诗清峻和雅，寄慨遥深。

Comments and Tips

This poem depicts the Southern Song Palace at the foot of the Phoenix Hill in Hangzhou. The poet firstly used a comparison, whose sadness of losing his motherland was conveyed in the scenery and narrat on. Then the ending line tends to show great empathy on the scene description, which boosts a desperate feeling of restoring his motherland. The whole poem is of clean and elegant form, with profound meanings.

《湖山春晓图》南宋　陈清波　故宫博物院藏

Spring Dawn at Lake and Hills, Chen Qingbo, Southern Song Dynasty, The Palace Museum

张　炎

（1248—约1320），字叔夏，号玉田、乐笑翁。祖籍秦州成纪（今甘肃天水），出生于临安，张镃曾孙，幼承家学。宋亡，潜迹不仕，漫游吴越间，晚年隐居杭州。工词，多写亡国之痛。研究声律，尤得神解。有《山中白云词》《词源》等。

高阳台·西湖春感 [1]

接叶巢莺，平波卷絮，断桥斜日归船。

能几番游，看花又是明年。

东风且伴蔷薇住，到蔷薇、春已堪怜。

更凄然。

万绿西泠，一抹荒烟。

Zhang Yan

(1248 — c.1320), whose ancestral home was Chengji in Qinzhou (now Tianshui in Gansu Province), was born in Lin'an. His knowledge was greatly originated from the influence of his family circumstance at his young age. When the Song Dynasty perished, he retired from his official life and just wandered along the Wu and Yue areas, and lived in seclusion in Hangzhou in his later years. Zhang Yan was good at writing ci, especially about lamenting over the demise of his nation. He also studied the demands on phonetics of ancient Chinese poems, obtaining a profound ingenious understanding. His works include *Ci Collection Featuring White Clouds Coiling Around Mountains* and *The Source of Ci*.

Gaoyangtai: Spring Feeling at the West Lake

In the dense forest the warblers are nesting;

Catkins floating on the lake, the sun is west slanting,

And to the Broken Bridge the boat is returning.

How many more times can I visit the West Lake?

I have to wait until next year if I want to enjoy the flowers blooming,

The east wind that accompanies the roses do not disappear in a hurry please.

When the roses are in flower, it is about the end of spring.

What is more sad is that,

Xiling Bridge was once hidden in the greenery,

Only a desolate sunset fog leaving.

当年燕子知何处，但苔深韦曲，草暗斜川²。

见说新愁，如今也到鸥边。

无心再续笙歌梦，掩重门、浅醉闲眠。

莫开帘。

怕见飞花，怕听啼鹃。

【注释】

1. 高阳台：词牌名。取战国时期楚国文人宋玉赋神女事以为名。
2. 韦曲：本在陕西长安皇子陂西，唐代韦氏世居之地。斜川：在江西都昌附近，陶潜有《游斜川》诗。"韦曲""斜川"两句以故地寓南北沦丧，因此"苔深""草暗"，更显颓败荒凉。

【阅读提示】

　　这首词系张炎于德祐元年（1275）重到西湖所作。上片起首写景，"接叶"两句词语精炼，体物工巧。继而"断桥斜日"、残春蔷薇，颇显惨淡凄迷，而上片结句当年"万绿西泠"，已成"一抹荒烟"的今昔对比，更让人触目惊心，倍感凄凉。下片"当年燕子""见说新愁"四句，用刘禹锡"旧时王谢堂前燕，飞入寻常百姓家"诗意，写家国兴亡之感。而"无心再续笙歌梦"以下五句，直写自己本想掩门闲眠，但落花啼鹃，更恼人情怀。全词写愁，写国危家亡的哀怨之情，一句接一句，一层深一层，深婉蕴藉，凄凉哀怨，极为苍凉沉郁。

Where have gone in the past the swallows nesting?

In the courtyard I can see the moss growing,

And the grass covering.

The newly added sorrows

Can only be confided to the white gulls on the lake flying.

No longer in the mood to continue the old dream of the song,

Close the door, drink and get drunk sleeping.

Don't pull the curtains aside,

I'm afraid of seeing flowers flying,

And also afraid of hearing the cuckoos crying.

Comments and Tips

"Gaoyangtai" (Song of Goddess of Wushan Mountain) is a pattern of ci poetry, taking the story of Wushan Goddess as its name. This ci was made in the first year of Deyou Period (1275), when Zhang Yan went back to visit the West Lake. The first part of the ci presents the scenery, in which the words selected are of terseness and elegance, and the images of "the Broken Bridge" in the sunset and "the roses" in the late spring portray a dim and chill scene. The last lines of the first part, on the contrary, show a contrast of "Xiling Bridge in the greenery" in the past with "a desolate sunset smoke" in the present, which are more sorrowful and desperate. In the second part, "in the past the swallows" and "the newly added sorrows" point out the lament over the demise of his nation. His feelings of infinite melancholy about losing his nation runs through the ci, which gives readers an air of forlornness and hopelessness.

《断桥残雪》

Lingering Snow on the Broken Bridge

元

One Hundred Poems
on the West Lake in Hangzhou
Through the Ages

Yuan Dynasty
(1271–1368)

关汉卿

（约1220—1300），号已斋叟，大都（今北京）人。元代戏曲作家，晚年居杭州。所作杂剧六十余种，今存十多种，《拜月亭》《窦娥冤》《救风尘》《蝴蝶梦》等尤为著名。另有散曲作品多种，现存套曲十余套、小令五十余首。与马致远、白朴、郑光祖并称"元曲四大家"。

南吕·一枝花　杭州景[1]

普天下锦绣乡，寰海内风流地。

大元朝新附国，亡宋家旧华夷。

水秀山奇，一到处堪游戏。

这答儿忔憎富贵[2]，满城中绣幕风帘，一哄地人烟辏集[3]。

Guan Hanqing

(c.1220—1300) was a native of Dadu (now Beijing). As a playwright and poet of Yuan Dynasty, he spent his later life in Hangzhou. Guan produced over 60 variety plays. Among the extant 18 variety plays, *The Pavilion of Moon-Worship*, *The Injustice to Dou E* (or *Snow in Midsummer*), *Saving the Dusty-Windy* (or *Saving the Prostitute*) and *The Butterfly Dream* are particularly popular. He also authored over 10 Taoshu (a set of verse with multiple tunes connected) and more than 40 Xiaoling (short lyrics of no more than 58 characters).

Nanlü•Yizhihua: Hangzhou View

On earth this is a beautiful place,

And also a place of grace.

It is the Yuan Dynasty's new subsidiary state,

And the perished Southern Song's old territory.

With so beautiful landscape,

Everywhere you can play.

It is so rich;

The city is full of people wealthy,

Crowded, and lively.

梁　州

百十里街衢整齐，万余家楼阁参差，并无半答儿闲田地。

松轩竹径，药圃花蹊，茶园稻陌，竹坞梅溪。

一陀儿一句诗题，行一步扇面屏帏。

西盐场便似一带琼瑶，吴山色千叠翡翠。

兀良[4]，望钱塘江万顷玻璃。

更有清溪绿水，画船儿来往闲游戏。

浙江亭紧相对，相对着险岭高峰长怪石，堪羡堪题。

Liangzhou

The streets are neat and crisscrossed for miles;

Thousands of buildings are lined up;

And there is no vacant space at all.

The pine corridors with bamboo paths;

The medicine gardens along flower trails;

The tea ridges above rice fields;

The bamboo valley hiding plum streams.

Each place has a line of a poem;

Every step is taken to change a beautiful view.

The salt piled up in the salt field is as crystalline as jade,

And the dense forest on Wu Hill is like cascading emeralds.

Then look at the vast expanse of blue waves on Qiantang River.

There are also clear streams flowing in the mountains

And boats coming and going on water.

Zhejiang Pavilion is standing on the riverside,

Relying on the towering peaks on the river bank,

It is so majestic that people admire and write poems about it.

尾

家家掩映渠流水，楼阁峥嵘出翠微。

遥望西湖暮山势，看了这壁，觑了那壁，纵有丹青下不得笔[5]。

【注释】

1. 南吕：宫调名，一枝花和梁州等均属这一宫调的曲牌。把同一宫调的若干曲子连缀起来表达同一主题，就是所谓"套数"。
2. 这答儿：这里，这地方。忒：太。
3. 一哄地：形容人多而热闹非凡的样子。
4. 兀良：元曲中语气词，用于加强语气或使音节顿宕。
5. 丹青：中国古代绘画常用之色，借指绘画。

【阅读提示】

"南吕·一枝花"套数，系关汉卿于元朝初年至杭州时所作。当时南北统一，海内初定，而杭州繁华如昔。作者以宏阔的视野、酣畅的语言，歌咏了杭州城的盛况。首段极言杭州游人如云、锦绣风流，反映了作者对杭州秀美富丽景象的赞叹与感慨。继而以赋的铺陈手法，摹写杭州的街衢景观之严整、楼阁参差之华贵、山光水色之澄净，点出其间处处如诗如画。结尾以苍茫暮色中的西湖美景收束全篇。意大利旅行家马可·波罗赞叹杭州是世界上最雄伟美丽、富庶繁华的"天城"，关汉卿的《杭州景》就是对其最好的诠释和证明。

Tail

Houses are hidden behind each other;

Day by day the water in front of the door flows;

The towering shadow of the buildings is revealed in a patch of green
  woods.

Looking at the hills in the twilight on the other side of the West Lake,

Looking at this side but also at the other side,

Even a landscape painter can't use his brush.

Comments and Tips

Nanlü · Yizhihua (a branch of flowers) is a case of Taoshu or Taoqu (a specific pattern of Sanqu poetry). It was composed when Guan Hanqing visited Hangzhou in the early years of Yuan Dynasty. At that time, the north and the south were unified, the country was just settled, and Hangzhou was as prosperous as before. The poet sang about the prosperity of the city with a broad vision and mellifluous language. The Italian traveler Marco Polo praised Hangzhou as City of Heaven, this "Hangzhou View" by Guan Hanqing of which (the finest and most splendid city in the world) serves as the best interpretation.

奥敦周卿

生卒年不详，元初女真族人，字周卿，号竹庵。奥敦是女真姓氏。其先世仕金，父奥敦保和降元后，累立战功，官至德兴府元帅。周卿本人历官怀孟路总管府判官、侍御史、河北河南道提刑按察司佥事等职。为元散曲前期作家，今存小令二首，套数三曲。

双调·蟾宫曲 [1] 西湖（二首其一）

西山雨退云收，缥缈楼台，隐隐汀洲。
湖水湖烟，画船款棹，妙舞轻讴 [2]。
野猿搦丹青画手，沙鸥看皓齿明眸 [3]。
阆苑神州 [4]，谢安曾游 [5]。
更比东山，倒大风流 [6]。

【注释】

1. 《蟾宫曲》：北曲小令。此曲又有"折桂令""天香引"等名。有十二句、十一句两体。奥敦周卿的前一首属十二句体，后一首属十一句体。
2. 款：缓。
3. 搦（nuò）：挑动，挑引。
4. 阆苑：传说中神仙居住的地方。
5. 谢安：东晋政治家、名士。淝水之战中，作为东晋主帅，大败前秦苻坚军队。
6. 倒大：无比。

Aodun Zhouqing

(the exact dates of whose birth and death unknown) was of the Jurchen in the early Yuan Dynasty, whose ancestors served the Kingdom of Jin. His father Aodun Baohe surrendered to the Yuan and was promoted as the Marshal of Dexing District for many outstanding achievements in battle. Zhouqing himself also served as a government official in many positions. As an early sanqu writer of Yuan Dynasty, his works known to contemporary readers are no more than two pieces of Xiaoling and three sets of Taoshu.

Double Tune • Chan'gongqu: The West Lake (the First of Two)

The clouds in the western hills disperse and the rain stops.

The buildings and pavilions are vaguely visible on the misty water islands.

The painted boats slowly travel on the foggy lake with songs and dances.

The monkeys tease the painter to wield his brushes,

And the gulls come to appreciate the beauty's appearance.

This place is a fairyland on earth where Xie An toured once,

But far more elegant than the East Mount where he was in recluse.

双调·蟾宫曲　西湖（二首其二）

西湖烟水茫茫，百顷风潭，十里荷香[1]。

宜雨宜晴，宜西施淡抹浓妆。

尾尾相衔画舫，尽欢声无日不笙簧[2]。

春暖花香，岁稔时康[3]。

真乃上有天堂，下有苏杭。

【注释】

1. 百顷风潭：形容西湖水域广阔。
2. 笙簧：指笙，簧是笙中之簧片。这里泛指音乐声。
3. 稔：庄稼成熟，这里指丰收。

【阅读提示】

　　《双调·蟾宫曲》为元曲中的北曲小令。元代著名的杂剧作家白朴有《木兰花慢》词，题作"覃怀北赏梅，同参政西庵杨丈，和奥敦周卿府判韵"，说明白朴与奥敦周卿有交往，并相互唱和。奥敦周卿这两首小令描写的是雨后的西湖。只见楼台缥缈，汀洲隐约，烟水茫茫。湖面缓缓行驶的画船上轻歌曼舞，音乐声、欢笑声不绝于耳。前一首中，作者用野猿逗引画家和沙鸥观赏明眸皓齿的舞姬歌女的拟人兼夸张的手法，极言西湖这一人间仙境，更绝胜"风流宰相"谢安隐居的东山。后一首中，作者化用了苏轼"欲把西湖比西子，淡妆浓抹总相宜"诗意，通过"十里荷香""春暖花香""岁稔时康"，概括了西湖的四时美景和杭州的富庶繁华，并发出"真乃上有天堂，下有苏杭"的感喟。据说，这也是"上有天堂，下有苏杭"这句民谚在现存文史资料中的最早出处。

Double Tune • Chan'gongqu: The West Lake (the Second of Two)

The lake is covered with fog and looks boundless,

Wafts over the vast lake the fragrance of lotus flowers.

Whether sunny or rainy, light or heavy make-up, the charm of Xishi it
shows.

Line up on the lake traveling are the painted boats,

And every day the lake is full of songs and dances.

Every year a peaceful harvest and everywhere full of spring flowers.

It's true that on earth there are Suzhou and Hangzhou and in sky the
Paradise.

Comments and Tips

"Double Tune · Chan'gongqu (Toad Palace Song)" is a Xiaoling of the northern qu. Bai Pu, a famous playwright of Yuan Dynasty's Zaju (a form of poetic music drama), was friends with Aodun Zhouqing and they wrote each other poems. These two pieces of Xiaoling by Aodun Zhouqing depict the West Lake after the rain. In the first piece, the poet employs the techniques of simile and hyperbole, mentioning the painter was teased by the monkeys and gulls were attracted by the charming dancers and singers, suggesting that the West Lake is a celestial realm on earth, which is even more fascinating than the East Mount where Xie An, the "Stylish Chancellor", lived in seclusion. In the second piece, the poet borrows Su Shi's lines of "To compare the West Lake to Xishi, the ancient beauty, any makeup would be suitable, light or heavy" to present the beauty of the West Lake all through the year and Hangzhou's affluence, and proclaims that "It's true that there is the Paradise in sky and Suzhou and Hangzhou on earth", which is allegedly the earliest origin of the proverb in existing literary materials.

赵孟頫

（1254—1322），字子昂，号松雪道人，吴兴（今浙江湖州）人。宋太祖赵匡胤十一世孙，累官至翰林学士承旨、荣禄大夫，谥"文敏"。博学多才，能诗善文，工书法，精绘画，擅金石。开创元代新画风，被誉为"元人冠冕"；创"赵体"书，与欧阳询、颜真卿、柳公权并称"楷书四大家"。有《松雪斋文集》《谈录》等。

钱塘怀古

东南都会帝王州， 三月莺花非旧游。
故国金人泣辞汉[1]，当年玉马去朝周[2]。
湖山靡靡今犹在， 江水茫茫只自流。
千古兴亡尽如此， 春风麦秀使人愁[3]。

【注释】

1. 金人泣辞汉：即"金铜仙人"典，李贺《金铜仙人辞汉歌并序》曰："魏明帝青龙元年八月，诏宫官牵车西取汉孝武捧露盘仙人，欲立置前殿。宫官既拆盘，仙人临载，乃潸然泪下。"故用此典喻亡国之痛。
2. 玉马去朝周：即"玉马朝周"典，《文选》李善注引《论语比考谶》："殷惑妲己玉马走。"玉马指商代贤臣微子启。纣王昏乱，启数谏不听，启乃去而朝周。此处"玉马朝周"喻自己在宋亡后仕元。
3. 麦秀：商代贵族箕子朝周途中经过故殷墟，睹宫室毁坏生黍，作《麦秀歌》，寓兴亡之感。

Zhao Mengfu

(1254—1322) was a native of Wuxing (now Huzhou, Zhejiang Province). He was a descendant of Song Dynasty's imperial family. Zhao was erudite and versatile, capable of verse and prose, and expert in calligraphy, painting and epigraphy. He created a new style of painting of Yuan Dynasty and is known as the "Crown of the Yuan". There exist collected *Works from Songxuezhai* (pine snow studio: the name of his study) and so on.

Hangzhou Nostalgia

Hangzhou is a big city in the southeast, where founded were empires;
I come here again in spring with singing birds and blooming flowers.
The gold statues wept because they were moved away;
The virtuous official also abandoned the tyrant and went to serve the Zhou
    Dynasty.
The lake and hills are still so beautiful and bright;
And the river is still flowing day and night.
Many dynasties prospered, declined, and finally perished to zero;
The spring breeze blowing green wheat makes me feel sorrow.

本诗为怀古之作。身为赵氏宗亲的赵孟頫在宋亡之后再到杭州，有感此际国祚已移、物是人非，对大宋故国深感伤悼。首联"东南都会""三月莺花"已含兴寄，但"非旧游"三字与此形成强烈反差，令人倍添伤感。颔联用"金人辞汉""玉马朝周"两个典故，巧妙关合了作者的处境。金铜仙人原为汉朝之物，暗指宋室已亡，而魏国地处北方，在这里借指元朝。殷商微子启朝周，喻自己是迫不得已而仕元。尾联用箕子经过殷墟故地，见宫室毁坏生黍，作《麦秀歌》以寄悲思。黍离、麦秀的故事，历来是诗人抒写亡国哀痛的惯用典故。作者重到杭州，面对湖山绵延不绝，江水奔流不息，不免将这一重朝代更迭之思，延伸到千古皆似的兴亡浩叹中，为诗篇注入了感今怀古的浓重愁绪。

《秀石疏林图》元　赵孟頫　故宫博物院藏

Strange Rocks in Sparse Forest, Zhao Mengfu, Yuan Dynasty, The Palace Museum

Comments and Tips

This is a nostalgic poem. As a descendant of Song Dynasty's imperial Zhao family, Zhao Mengfu visited Hangzhou again after the fall of Song Dynasty. Touched by the vicissitudes of life, he was deeply saddened by his country lost. The first couplet reveals his emotions by mentioning "a big city in the southeast" and "singing birds and blooming flowers in spring", exposing his sorrow by the sharp contrast of "I come here again". The second couplet employs two allusions of "the gold statue" removed from the palace of Han Dynasty and "the virtuous official abandoned" leaving for Zhou Dynasty, which just coincide with the poet's bitter situation. The last couplet uses the allusion of Ji Zi, who passed by the ruins of Yin court and viewed the millet growing, and wrote a poem entitled "Song of Wheat Earing" to express his sorrow. When the poet revisited Hangzhou, facing the endless stretches of the lake and hills as well as the ceaseless flow of the river, he could not help but sigh for the rise and fall of dynasties.

黄公望

（1269—1354），本姓陆，名坚，常熟（今属江苏）人。后过继永嘉（今浙江温州）黄氏为子，因改姓黄，名公望，字子久，号一峰、大痴道人。擅画山水，与吴镇、倪瓒、王蒙合称"元四家"。擅书能诗，撰有《写山水诀》，存世画作有《富春山居图》《九峰雪霁图》等。

西湖竹枝词

水仙祠前湖水深[1]，岳王坟上有猿吟[2]。
湖船女子唱歌去， 月落沧波无处寻[3]。

【注释】

1. 水仙祠：《西湖志纂》："水仙王庙本伍胥祠。胥浮尸江上，吴人称为水仙，见《越绝书》。宋时水仙祠在苏堤第四桥，名水仙王庙，后人误为水仙女神。"
2. 岳王坟：宋代抗金名将岳飞墓，在西湖栖霞岭下。
3. 沧波：碧波。

【阅读提示】

　　唐代刘禹锡据民歌改作的《竹枝词》，历代作者甚众。黄公望这首《西湖竹枝词》咏西湖景物，带有民歌浑朴真厚的特点。黄公望同样写西湖之水，只以一"深"字出之，情怀自是不同。下句岳王坟上的猿声，渲染了英烈遗迹的哀肃，进一步烘托了深沉的情思。相比千古凭吊的伟人，湖船女子的歌唱，随着月影一起隐没在碧波之中，美妙的景象再难寻觅。其间流露出的生命意识显豁地体现在了两联的映照中。

Huang Gongwang

(1269—1354) was a native of Changshu (now in Jiangsu Province). He was expert in landscape painting, calligraphy and poetry. There exist his treatise *The Secrets of Landscape Painting* and paintings *Dwelling in the Fuchun Mountains, Nine Peaks Clearing After Snow* and so on.

Bamboo Branch Lyric: The West Lake

In front of the Water God Temple, the lake is deep and serene;
Above Yue Fei's grave, the monkeys are crying and chanting.
The woman in the boat leaves with singing;
The moon jumps in the water, but she is missing.

Comments and Tips

This "Bamboo Branch Lyric: The West Lake" by Huang Gongwang describes the scenery of the West Lake with simplicity and profoundness, which are characteristics of folk songs. Huang Gongwang wrote about the water of the West Lake with a sentiment different from his fellow poets. The two couplets are in response to each other and prominently reveal a consciousness of life.

《富春山居图》（无用师卷，局部）元　黄公望　台北故宫博物院藏

Dwelling in the Fuchun Mountains (The Master Wuyong Scroll, Partial),
Huang Gongwang, Yuan Dynasty, Taipei Palace Museum

世傳富春山居圖為麤于久
畫卷之冠邇年得其所謂無
用師卷以為真而又得是卷
凡黃子久畫約兩見於沈
趙等藏於諸家次第一幕
如其流落人間者一圖為
快兩宮冬永為盡永昔久
名辨真偽賞五幅鑑其可
沈文王辨矣五幕觀為尊
者是也因以三幕觀如怙
舊藏即富春山居圖真讀其
蒙藏偶遇富春二字四久之
為兩圖方孰辨其異與為謬
之雅也至量致而卷不久下
高而此卷筆力苓勁其高
雖與三兩幅潤如上自
如慢約丁真此等不相以同
并與以千金此出塞不石
集賢從此得九一件讀諸陸
遠而記其類末好斗山卯和
乎市駿秀後不周得珍如
藏之富者濱成為葉公豆
諸乾隆御識
乾隆御識

张可久

（1280—约 1352），字伯远，一说字仲远，号小山。庆元路（今属浙江宁波）人。一生仕途失意，纵情诗酒，放浪山水。工散曲小令，与乔吉齐名。有《张小山小令》《小山乐府》。

普天乐·西湖即事 [1]

蕊珠宫 [2]，蓬莱洞。

青松影里 [3]，红藕香中 [4]。

千机云锦重，一片银河冻。

缥缈佳人双飞凤 [5]，紫箫寒月满长空。

阑干晚风，菱歌上下 [6]，渔火西东。

【注释】

1. 普天乐：曲牌名。北曲中吕宫，其定格格式为十一句四十六字（衬字除外）。
2. 蕊珠宫：道教传说中的仙宫。
3. 青松："钱塘十景"中的"九里云松"。
4. 红藕："西湖十景"中的"曲院风荷"。
5. 双飞凤：与下句"紫箫"化用同一典故，即《列仙传》中记载的萧史、弄玉乘龙跨凤升天的故事，借此写西湖夜景引发的浪漫想象。
6. 菱歌：采菱人所唱之歌。

Zhang Kejiu

(1280 — c.1352) was a native of Qingyuan Route (now Ningbo, Zhejiang Province). With disappointing life experience as a government official, he indulged in poetry and alcohol and enjoyed natural views. Zhang was expert in Sanqu and Xiaoling (short lyric). There exist his collection of ci and qu poetry entitled *Zhang Xiaoshan's* (his art name) *Xiaoling* and *Zhang Xiaoshan's Yuefu* (Sanqu of northern tunes).

Putianle: With the West Lake as the Theme

Like the divine palace in heaven,

There are nine miles of green pines

And breeze-ruffled lotuses at Quyuan Garden.

The clouds in the sky are as brilliant as brocade;

The waves in the lake, like the Milky Way, shine.

The talent and the beauty fly away by phoenix and dragon;

Under the moonlight the gentle sound of flute echoes in the night sky.

The evening breeze blows through the railing;

The songs of picking water caltrops rise and fall one after another;

From west to east, the lights on fishing boats flicker.

　　这首曲子为张可久作于夏夜西湖之畔，头两句即由虚向实，先以蕊珠宫、蓬莱洞这两个道教仙地来比喻西湖的秀美繁华，继而写"九里云松"和"曲院风荷"这两个如梦如幻的西湖胜境。中间缀以神话传说，景色被充分虚化了。云彩如锦被重叠，湖面似冰冻的银河，上下辉映，恍若身处广袤仙境。萧史、弄玉飞升的遐想，将水天之际的恋慕情思，随月色与箫声洒满了长空。末句由虚返实，视野收回到岸边，风中菱歌与渔火此起彼伏，构成一幅真切可感的立体画面，情致无穷。

Comments and Tips

Putianle (Joy All Over the World): a pattern of the northern qu poetry, belongs to a kind of Xiaoling (a shorter length of qu). This qu poem was composed on the shore of the West Lake in a summer evening. Transferring from illusion to reality, the first two lines present the dream-like scenery of the West Lake. Then myths and legends are employed to completely blur the scenery. The last line returns back to the real world, constructing a tangible and perceptible three-dimensional picture with tremendous aesthetic appeal.

萨都剌

（约1307—约1359），字天锡，号直斋，出生于雁门（今山西代县）。泰定四年（1327）进士，曾任南台侍御史、淮西北道经历等。晚年寓居杭州。其诗歌风格清丽俊逸。有《雁门集》《萨天赐诗集》等。

次韵王侍郎游湖

绮席新凉舞袖偏[1]，赏心输与使君专。
螺杯注酒摇红浪[2]，彩扇题诗染绿烟。
一镜湖光开晓日， 万家花气涨晴天。
涌金门外春如海[3]，画舫笙歌步步仙。

【注释】

1. 绮席：盛美的筵席。
2. 螺杯：螺壳所作的酒杯，后用作酒杯的美称。
3. 涌金门：古代杭州西城门，门临西湖。

【阅读提示】

　　这首律诗是萨都剌在杭州春日酬答友人所作。前两联写湖船筵席间姬人歌舞、杯盏酬对、宾主奉和的情景。后两联写席外风光，"晓日""晴天""春如海""步步仙"等意象，将湖上花光之绮丽、画舫笙歌之闲适写得宛在眼前，又贴切地道出了作者与友人间的共同感受。结合诗歌题目来看，这是一首颇有难度的次韵即席之作，而全诗无雕琢之迹，与当时宴饮的情感基调切合，风格华美典雅，情致婉转含蓄，体现了作者高超的艺术手法。

Sa Dula

(c.1307—c.1359) was a native of Yanmen (now Dai County, Shanxi Province). He was a Jinshi in the fourth year of Taiding Period (1327) and resided in Hangzhou in his later years. The style of his poetry is natural and elegant. There exist *The Collection works of Yanmen* and *The Collected Poems of Sa Dula*.

Replying to Officer Wang's Poem on Trip to the Lake (According to the Rhyme of His Poem)

By singing and dancing the gorgeous banquet is accompanied;

For distinguished friends this happy atmosphere is embraced.

The glass is filled with wine and shaking;

The colourful fans with poems inscribed is more charming.

The sun rises and the lake reflects the light like a mirror;

Under the clear sky, the city is full of flowers competing with each other.

Outside the Surging Gold Gate, spring is like a sea without bounds;

The lake is simply like a paradise with a lot of boats and songs.

Comments and Tips

Sa Dula wrote this poem on a spring day in Hangzhou in response to a friend. The first two couplets describe the banquet on the pleasure boat with the singing and dancing of performers, the exchange of toasts and witty dialogues, and the guests and hosts contributing poems. The last two couplets present the scenery outside the banquet, bringing to life the gorgeous flowers and sunlight reflected on the lake water, as well as the leisurely entertainment on the boat. This is an extemporaneous composition with required meter and rhyme, which is not an easy task, revealing impressive artistic skills of the poet.

王 冕

（1287—1359），字元章，号煮石山农、梅花屋主，诸暨（今属浙江）人。本农家子，为人牧牛，窃入书塾听诸生读书，听毕辄默记。安阳韩性闻而录为弟子。至大都，泰不花荐以翰林院官职，不就。工于画梅，隐于九旦山。朱元璋取婺州，授冕以咨议参军，旋卒。有《竹斋集》。

素梅（组诗其二）

树头历历见明珠， 底用题诗问老逋[1]？
且买金陵秋露白[2]，小舟载月过西湖。

【注释】

1. 底用：何用。老逋：北宋诗人林逋。
2. 秋露白：一种酒的名称。

【阅读提示】

这首诗是王冕《素梅》组诗中的第二首。开篇即对梅花予以细节描写，点缀于枝头的一朵朵白梅，如明珠一样耀眼，起笔虽小而卓有情致。西湖之畔曾有林逋隐居于孤山，为世人所称道，而诗人之襟怀也如林逋一样孤高恬淡、皎洁纯粹。末二句抒写买酒乘舟，使全诗浸染于西湖的月色之中，兴象玲珑，情韵悠长。

Wang Mian

(1287—1359) was a native of Zhuji (now in Zhejiang Province). In Dadu, Wang refused to take the government position recommended. He was a master of painting plum blossoms. When Wang returned to Zhejiang, he retreated to the Jiuli Mountains. After Zhu Yuanzhang, the would-be first Emperor of Ming Dynasty, took Wuzhou, he appointed Wang to the position of his military adviser. Wang died soon in the same year. There exists *The Collection of Zhuzhai* (bamboo studio: name of his study).

White Plum Blossom (the Second in a Group)

The buds on the plum branches are clearly visible like pearls,
To ask Lin Bu, do I still need a poem to write?
Let's go to Jinling to buy Qiulubai, the finest wine,
And drive a boat to the West Lake under the moonlight.

Comments and Tips

This poem begins with a detailed description of plum blossoms, which is seemingly trivial but tasteful. People commend the reclusive poet Lin Bu for his living in seclusion at the foot of the Isolated Hill by the West Lake, and the poet here also shares the lonely and pure soul of Lin Bu's. The last line present the picture of buying wine by boat, so that the whole poem is immersed in the moonlight of the West Lake.

《南枝春早图》元　王冕
台北故宫博物院藏

Sunny Branches in Spring Morning,
Wang Mian, Yuan Dynasty,
Taipei Palace Museum

《西湖春晓图》

明　谢时臣

济南博物馆藏

Spring Dawn at the West Lake,
Xie Shichen, Ming Dynasty,
Jinan Museum

杨维桢

（1296—1370），字廉夫，号铁崖、东维子，诸暨人。泰定四年（1327）进士，官至建德路总管府推官，曾居西湖之畔七八载。他的古体、乐府诗风格奇诡，有《东维子文集》《铁崖先生古乐府》等。

嬉春体（五首其二）

西子湖头春色浓， 望湖楼下水连空¹。
柳条千树僧眼碧²，桃花一株人面红³。
天气浑如曲江节⁴，野客正是杜陵翁⁵。
得钱沽酒勿复较， 如此好怀谁与同！

【注释】

1. 望湖楼：位于西湖边，原昭庆寺前。
2. 僧眼碧：比喻柳条千树翠绿。
3. "桃花"句：唐崔护《题都城南庄》云："去年今日此门中，人面桃花相映红。人面不知何处去，桃花依旧笑春风。"作者此句似寓有今昔之慨。
4. 曲江：又名"曲江池"，原为汉武帝所造。唐玄宗开元年间大加整修，池水澄明，花卉环列。其南有紫云楼、芙蓉苑；西有杏园、慈恩寺。是当时著名的游览胜地。杜甫曾作《曲江》二首，其二颔联云："酒债寻常行处有，人生七十古来稀。"
5. 杜陵翁：指唐代诗人杜甫，这里为作者自喻。

Yang Weizhen

(1296—1370) was a native of Zhuji (now in Zhejiang Province). He was a Jinshi in the fourth year of Taiding Period (1327) and served as an official at Jiande Region. Yang used to live by the West Lake for seven or eight years. The style of his poetry is regarded as strikingly unusual, or even weird. There exist *Essays of Dongweizi* (his art name), *Old Yuefu by Master Tieya* (his another art name), and so on.

Spring Outing (the Second of Five)

The shore of the West Lake is in full spring;

The water is connected with the sky below Wanghu Building.

The willows are turquoise like the eyes of a monk;

The peach blossoms are rosy like a beauty's cheek.

The weather happens to be like late spring,

And I am a wild villager looking like Du Shaoling.

There is no need to count the money you get to buy barley-bree;

Is it good or bad to behave like this, and who was like me?

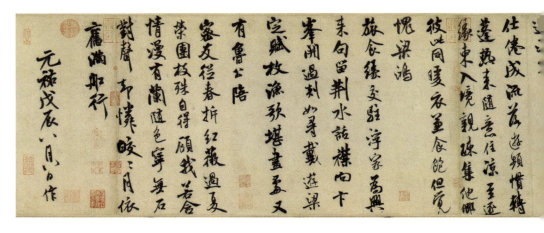

《苕溪诗帖》北宋　米芾　故宫博物院藏

Tiaoxi Poems, Mi Fu, Northern Song Dynasty, The Palace Museum

【 阅读提示 】

　　杨维桢写过不少歌咏西湖的诗作。这首诗写西湖春色，以"春色浓""水连空"白描写景，铺陈了一幅宏阔而富于禅意的画面。"僧眼碧"比喻柳条千树翠绿，映衬得一株桃花如人面娇红，写出了自然风光的瑰丽色彩，又有殊域风情。作者以"杜陵翁"自比，眼前的晴昼景象正似旧日之长安曲江，每到春日游人聚集娱嬉，繁华无限，正宜买酒自醉，而不必计较酒钱之多少。诗歌风格通俗直率，奇丽跳荡，可见世俗生活与乐府民歌的影响。

将之苕溪戏作呈诸友　襄阳漾仕黻

松竹留因夏，溪山去为秋。久赓白雪咏，更度采菱讴。缕会玉鲈堆。金橘润洲水宫无限景，载与谢公游。

半岁依修竹，三时看好花。懒倾惠泉酒，点尽壑源茶。主席多同好，群峰伴不哗。朝来还蠹简，便起故巢嗟。

余居半岁，诸公载酒不辍，而余以疾每约置膳，清话而已，复借书刘、李周三姓，好懒难辞，故徇以句。

通贪非理生，杜病觉亲切。小圃能留客，青冥不厌还。

Comments and Tips

This poem describes the spring views of the West Lake, presenting a grand and Zen-like picture. The poet compared himself to Du Fu, and the sunny scene in his view is just like the old days of Qujiang River in Chang'an city, which is just suitable for him to buy wine and get drunk without caring how much it costs. The style of the poem is plain and frank, yet strangely appealing, which shows the influence of secular life and folk songs.

Breeze-ruffled Lotuses at Quyuan Garden

《曲院风荷》

One Hundred Poems
on the West Lake in Hangzhou
Through the Ages

Ming Dynasty
(1368–1644)

高 启

（1336—1374），字季迪，号青丘子，长洲（今江苏苏州）人。与杨基、张羽、徐贲合称"吴中四杰"。明洪武初，召修《元史》，为翰林院国史编修。1374 年被朱元璋加罪腰斩。其诗风格多样，诗风豪放清逸。有《高太史大全集》。

谒伍相祠[1]

地老天荒伯业空[2]，曾于青史见遗功。

鞭尸楚墓生前孝[3]，抉目吴门死后忠[4]。

魂压怒涛翻白浪， 剑埋冤血起腥风。

我来无限伤心事， 尽在越山烟雨中[5]。

【注释】

1. 伍相祠：春秋时期吴国大夫伍子胥祠，位于西湖吴山上。
2. 伯业：霸业。
3. 鞭尸楚墓：《史记·伍子胥列传》："及吴兵入郢，伍子胥求昭王。既不得，乃掘楚平王墓，出其尸，鞭之三百，然后已。"后遂以"鞭尸"谓对有深仇大恨的人泄愤的典实。
4. 抉目吴门：伍子胥屡谏吴王灭越，但吴王听信谗言，反而令其自杀。伍子胥临死前告家人抉其眼悬于吴门，以观越军灭吴。抉：挖。
5. 越山：春秋时期杭州属于越国，因此称"越山"。

Gao Qi

(1336—1374) was a native of Changzhou (now Suzhou, Jiangsu Province). In the early years of Ming Dynasty's Hongwu Period, Gao was called on as an editor in the Imperial Academy to compose *The History of Yuan Dynasty*. In 1374 he was found guilty by the Emperor Zhu Yuanzhang and was executed by being cut into two from the waist. His poetry style is variant, though best known for its boldness and ease. There exists *Complete Works of Gao Taishi* (the government servant in charge of official history compositions).

Visiting Wu Zixu's Temple

In those years has long been buried in dust the ambition of hegemony;

Only from written records can people get a glimpse of history.

To avenge his father's murder Wu Zixu whipped the corpse of the King of
    Chu,

But his eyes were hung at the city gate when he was killed by the King of
    Wu.

His wronged soul turned into the raging tide on Qiantang River,

Which was also like a pair of dragon swords leaping into water.

I came here to pay my respect to his deceased spirit,

And melted into the misty rain of the vast mountains my sadness infinite.

《三绝图》明　文徵明　苏州博物馆藏

The Three Excellences, Wen Zhengming, Ming Dynasty, Suzhou Museum

【阅读提示】

　　这首诗为元末高启感张士诚政权覆灭而作。作者登临拜谒伍子胥祠，吟咏地老天荒的历史悲剧，借古鉴今之意尽显其中。伍子胥之父、兄皆被楚王杀害，后逃亡吴国，辅佐吴王阖闾、夫差成就霸业，对死后的楚平王鞭尸复仇，以尽孝节。事吴国忠贞不贰，而吴王夫差不听伍子胥直谏，听信谗言逼迫其自尽，终而导致灭国，暗合了元末张士诚的不听劝谏终于败亡的情境。此诗一变元代诗风，上接亘古时空，书写变化无常的时局。情感慷慨悲凉，风格浑厚雄壮。

Comments and Tips

This poem was written in response to the collapse of Zhang Shicheng's regime. The poet visited the shrine of Wu Zixu and lamented his tragedy, which implies that he was willing to find a solution to the present malady. The style of this poem is different from the dominating practice of Yuan Poetry. Despite its plaintive tone, this poem still creates a majestic realm.

于　谦

（1398—1457），字廷益，号节庵，钱塘人。明永乐十九年（1421）进士，官至兵部尚书、少保。正统十四年（1449）秋，蒙古瓦剌部进犯，英宗亲征被俘。于谦拥立景帝，并亲自督战击败瓦剌军，平息边患。英宗复位后，于谦遭诬陷被杀，后葬于杭州。万历间昭雪，谥"忠肃"。其诗风质朴刚健。有《于忠肃集》。

夏日忆西湖风景

涌金门外柳如烟，　西子湖头水拍天。

玉腕罗裙双荡桨[1]，鸳鸯飞近采莲船。

【注释】

1. 玉腕：洁白温润的手腕。亦借指手。

【阅读提示】

　　这首诗是于谦夏日回忆家乡西湖风光而成，因是追忆，对湖水与采莲船桨的描写也萦绕着静美的氤氲之气。诗中先写涌金门外柳叶葱茏轻盈如烟，湖水连绵不断涌向天际；次写采莲船上的女子身着罗裙，以玉手荡桨，两边的船桨对应着飞来的鸳鸯，成为画面的焦点。全诗有点有面有细节，动静结合，颇具唐人绝句的情调。

Yu Qian

(1398—1457) was a native of Qiantang. He was a Jinshi in the 19th year of Ming Dynasty's Yongle Period (1421) and was promoted to serve as the Minister of War. The autumn of the 14th year of Zhengtong Period (1449) witnessed attacks by the Oirat Mongols. The Emperor Yingzong captained an army to fight but was captured. Yu Qian supported the Emperor Jingdi to succeed and defeated the Mongols as the commander and thus brought peace to the country's border. When the Emperor Yingzong returned and restored himself to the throne, Yu Qian was falsely accused of treason and executed. He was buried in Hangzhou, and was later posthumously rehabilitated in Wanli Period and given the posthumous name Zhongsu (meaning loyal and stern). The style of his poem is plain and sturdy. There exists *The Collection of Yu Zhongsu*.

Memories of the West Lake in Summer

Outside the Surging Gold Gate, as hazy as smoke is a green willow forest;
The West Lake is boundless and the water is connected with sky.
The rowing woman swings the oars with her white wrist;
Towards the lotus-picking boat a pair of mandarin ducks fly.

Comments and Tips

This poem describes the lake and the lotus-picking boat with a prevailing dense atmosphere of quiet beauty. The whole poem offers different aspects and details of the lake views, with a combination of movement and stillness, which reminds readers of the taste of Tang Dynasty's Jueju (short poems of four lines) poetry.

岳忠武王祠

匹马南来渡浙河¹，汴城宫阙远嵯峨²。

中兴诸将谁降虏， 负国奸臣主议和³。

黄叶古祠寒雨积， 青山荒冢白云多。

如何一别朱仙镇⁴，不见将军奏凯歌！

【注释】

1. 匹马：一匹马，常指孤身一人。
2. 汴城：汴州，今河南开封市，北宋国都。嵯峨：山高峻貌。
3. 负国奸臣：指秦桧。
4. 朱仙镇：在今河南开封市西南，岳飞北伐最远处。

【阅读提示】

  这首诗吟咏南宋抗金名将岳飞。北宋灭亡，宋高宗南渡，在杭州建立南宋政权，苟且偏安，远离了汴都宫殿。岳飞力主恢复，浴血奋战，而卖国奸臣秦桧却议和投降。那些主张收复失地、试图中兴宋朝的将领们，有谁像岳飞一样英勇杀敌、战功赫赫呢？而岳飞却落得个被杀害屈死的千古奇冤。岳飞祠前寒雨飘零、黄叶堆积，青山荒冢、漫天白云，一派凄清荒凉，这不禁令人深思一代名将岳飞自"朱仙镇大捷"后，再也不能传来胜利消息的原因。诗人尖锐批判了投降派的负国议和，高度赞扬了岳飞，对其被害屈死深表悲愤，并借古讽今，委婉地表达了对"土木之变"后明朝政局的看法。

Yue Fei's Temple

Single-handedly crossing south to Zhejiang River;

The lofty palace in Bianzhou City was far away.

The generals supporting Song Court couldn't surrender to the invader;

However, the traitorous minister was advocating appeasement with the enemy.

Yellow leaves in the temple were scattered in the cold rain;

With the tomb white clouds and green hills accompany.

Since the general was recalled from Zhuxian Town by the emperor's
orders,

There were no more the news of the northern expedition victory.

Comments and Tips

With the fall of Northern Song Dynasty, the Emperor Gaozong crossed the Yangtze to the south and established the Southern Song regime in Hangzhou, away from palaces of the original capital city of Bianliang (now Kaifeng, Henan Province) and was content with the petty corner of the empire. Yue Fei keenly claimed the restoration of the land and the fearless fighting, while the traitor courtier Qin Hui negotiated for humiliating peace and surrender. It makes people ponder over the reason why Yue Fei, a distinguished general of his time, could not bring any news of triumph since the Great Victory of Zhuxian Town (located at the southwest of the Kaifeng city). The poet acutely criticized the surrendering faction's treasonable negotiation for peace, while highly praised Yue Fei. With the expression of deep sorrow and anger at Yue's death, the poet alluded to the present by relating the past, euphemistically revealing his views on the political situation of Ming Dynasty.

杨孟瑛

生卒年不详，字温甫，丰都（今属重庆）人。明成化二十三年（1487）进士，曾任杭州知州。杨孟瑛守杭州期间，疏浚西湖有功，修有"杨公堤"（堤以杨公姓冠名）"四贤祠"等，杭州人民塑像来纪念他。

谒和靖墓

无书封禅有诗传[1]，高节于今故凛然。

云宿断桥遮隐地， 花留老树殉逋仙。

孤山围水疑蓬阆， 病鹤巢松忘岁年。

冠剑新宫参俎豆[2]，秋风画栋出苍烟。

【注释】

1. 封禅：指宋真宗为挽回天威而设计的封禅事件。林逋《自作寿堂因书一绝以志之》："茂陵他日求遗稿，犹喜曾无封禅书。"
2. 冠剑：戴冠佩剑的官员。新宫：新建的宫室或宋庙。俎豆：俎和豆，是古代祭祀、宴飨时盛食物用的两种礼器，这里指祭祀。

【阅读提示】

　　这首诗为杨孟瑛拜谒孤山隐士林逋墓而作。宋真宗自澶渊之盟后为挽回颜面，祭泰山与梁父山，大兴土木，一些文人隐士竞进夸饰之词，而林逋却在此际归隐杭州孤山，写下《自作寿堂因书一绝以志之》一诗，中有"犹喜曾无封禅书"一句明志，其高情亮节令世人凛然生敬。林逋隐居的孤山，有断桥白云掩映而分外僻静，湖水环绕，如仙境一般，其"梅妻鹤子"的恬淡情怀长久流传。末两句写官员们在新宫祭祀，秋风吹过彩绘的栋梁生起苍茫云雾。全诗运用了对比反衬的手法，将林逋与当时的文人两相对照，烘托了林逋高标傲世的志趣。

Yang Mengying

was a native of Fengdu (now Chongqing), whose birth and death dates are not known. He became a Jinshi in the 23rd year of Chenghua Period (1487) in the Ming Dynasty. As once appointed the governor of Hangzhou, he managed to have the West Lake dredged, and built a long causeway called Yanggong Causeway (named after his surname), "Ancestral Temple of Four Wise Men" and so on. The local people erected a sculpture to memorize him after his death.

Mourning for Tomb of Lin Hejing

Instead of writing for the sacrifices to mountains, he wrote poems to the
　　world,
Such a high moral character is enough to make future generations hold him
　　in regard.
The clouds by the Broken Bridge obscure the place of privacy;
The flowers on the old plum tree still accompany the graveyard.
Isolated Hill surrounded by water is like Penglai Fairyland;
The sick cranes nesting in pine trees have long forgotten the years.
Officials chant poems to worship, wearing hats and swords;
The wind blew away the fog, and with flying roofs the pavilion appears.

Comments and Tips

This poem was made when the author climbed up the Isolated Hill to pay homage to the recluse Lin Bu at his tomb. In the Northern Song Dynasty, Emperor Zhenzong started a large scale of construction to worship Mount Tai and Mount Liangfu, so as to cleanse the insult to "The Chanyuan Treaty" (a treaty between Northern Song and Liao Dynasties). Many scholars competed for the compliments on it, while Lin Bu chose to return to Hangzhou, settled down on the Isolated Hill in seclusion, and then wrote a poem to express his pursuit of nobility and unyieldingness. Based on Lin Bu's story, the author portrays a picture of Lin Bu and the literati of the day by using the techniques of comparison and contrast.

《灌木丛筱图》
明 唐寅 苏州博物馆藏

Shrubs and Bamboos,
Tang Yin, Ming Dynasty,
Suzhou Museum

《钱塘景物图》
明　唐寅　故宫博物院藏

Qiantang Scenery,
Tang Yin, Ming Dynasty,
The Palace Museum

唐 寅

（1470—1524），字伯虎，号六如居士、桃花庵主等，吴县（今江苏苏州）人。性不羁，有才华，二十九岁时举乡试第一，会试时因牵涉科场舞弊案而被革黜。善书法，能诗文，擅画山水，兼工人物，与沈周、文徵明、仇英合称"明四家"。

题西湖钓艇图

三十年来一钓竿， 几曾叉手揖高官[1]。
茅柴白酒芦花被[2]，明月西湖何处滩？

【注释】

1. 叉手：拱手。
2. 茅柴白酒：村酿薄酒。芦花被：用芦花絮制成的被子。

【阅读提示】

唐寅富有才华，个性豪放不羁，因科场舞弊案而被革黜后纵情诗酒，此后再也没有踏入官场。首句"三十年"写出垂钓时间之长，次句则写出了他不受官场束缚、傲岸不羁的心态。末两句中"茅柴酒""芦花被""明月西湖"显示作者甘于贫寒清苦，明月小舟，飘荡于西湖，借疏散自适的垂钓来安顿身心。这首诗抒写了作者逍遥于山水生活，表达了安贫乐道之情趣。

Tang Yin

(1470—1524) was a native of Wu County (now Suzhou in Jiangsu Province). As a talented man, he was vigorous and unruly in nature. When he was 29 years old, he came first in the provincial examinations. Then he went to the capital to sit for the national examination, but was involved in bribing an examiner to give exam questions in advance. He was soon disqualified in disgrace. As a versatile in calligraphy, poetry, and landscape and figure painting, he is one of the Four Masters of Ming Dynasty which include Shen Zhou, Wen Zhengming and Qiu Ying.

Poem for the Painting of a Fishing Boat on the West Lake

For more than thirty years, I have lived only by fishing
And never begged a powerful official by knee bending.
With inferior wine and a reed catkins quilt as my companions,
On this moonlit night to which shore of the West Lake am I going?

Comments and Tips

In the poem, the first line tells the author's 30-year long seclusion of fishing; the second line, however, expresses his unrestrained attitude towards life. The last two lines show his willingness to live a poor and solitary life. The way he enjoys fishing gives him a sense of being happy to lead a simple, virtuous life.

文徵明

（1470—1559），初名璧，字徵明，以字行，改字徵仲，号衡山居士，长洲（今江苏苏州）人。曾任翰林院待诏，三年辞归。他擅书画，二诗词，是明代书画家、文学家，与沈周、唐寅、仇英并称"明四家"。今人辑有《文徵明集》。

满江红·题宋思陵与岳武穆手敕墨本 [1]

拂拭残碑，敕飞字、依稀堪读。

慨当初、倚飞何重 [2]，后来何酷！

果是功成身合死 [3]，可怜事去言难赎。

最无辜、堪恨更堪怜，风波狱 [4]。

岂不念，中原蹙 [5]？

岂不念，徽钦辱 [6]？

但徽钦既返，此身何属？

千载休谈南渡错，当时自怕中原复。

笑区区、一桧亦何能 [7]，逢其欲 [8]！

【注释】

1. 满江红：词牌名。双调，常用为九十三字，有仄韵和平韵两体。仄韵一般用入声。宋思陵：指宋高宗赵构，因其墓叫永思陵。岳武穆：指岳飞，其谥"武穆"。手敕：帝王亲笔写的诏令。墨本：拓本。

2. 倚：依靠。

3. 功成身合死：指大功告成却难逃一死，所谓："飞鸟尽，良弓藏；狡兔死，走狗烹。"喻帝王杀害功臣。合：应该。

4. 风波狱：指岳飞被害于南宋大理寺狱的风波亭。

5. 中原蹙：指宋朝广大中原地区沦陷。

6. 徽钦辱：指宋徽宗、钦宗二帝于"靖康之难"被金俘虏，饱受凌辱。

7. 桧：即力主议和投降的奸相秦桧。

8. 逢其欲：指迎合了宋高宗的心意。

Wen Zhengming

(1470—1559) was a native of Changzhou (now Suzhou in Jiangsu Province). He served as Daizhao (secretary) in the Imperial Academy, and then resigned from the post three years later. He was a painter, calligrapher and litterateur in the Ming Dynasty, particularly expert in poem writing. *The Collection of Wen Zhengming* was compiled in the 20th century.

Manjianghong: Written for the Edict of Emperor Song Gaozong to Yue Fei

Wiping away the moss marks on the stone tablet,

The handwriting of the edict of Zhao Gou to Yue Fei can be still read.

Back then, he was so dependent on Yue Fei to defend the country,

But later on he was so cruel to kill Yue by charge unwarranted!

It is true that one should be killed if he has made a great achievement;

Unfortunately; the matter has come to an end and cannot be repaired.

Yue Fei was innocently beheaded at Fengbo Pavilion,

Which is the greatest injustice in the world.

Didn't he care about the plight of the fall of the northern territory;

Nor pity his father and brother who were captured and suffering times hard?

He only worried, once the two emperors returned,

Could he still sit on the throne of the overlord?

Let's not argue today whether it is right or wrong of southward exile;

It is the emperor himself who was afraid of recovering the lost land.

What is the ability of Qin Hui, a trivial man?

He was only catering to the emperor's demand.

　　这首词作于嘉靖九年（1530），距岳飞被害已三百八十八年。作者文徵明拂拭当年的残碑，感慨精忠报国的岳飞所遭受的冤屈。抗金名将岳飞军纪严明，赏罚公正，率领岳家军所向披靡、屡立战功。但宋高宗和奸相秦桧等一意求和，以十二道"金字牌"下令岳飞退兵。岳飞遭诬陷被捕入狱，并因"莫须有"（即也许有，后指凭空捏造）的谋反罪被害风波亭。词中尖锐指出：正是宋高宗赵构为了一己私利，担心其父徽宗和兄钦宗回来，自己将失去皇位，从而勾结秦桧，导致了岳飞的千古奇冤。该词揭露深刻，鞭辟入里，表现了作者的高远识见和充溢才情。

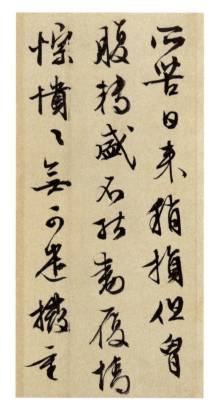

《尺牍册》明　文徵明　苏州博物馆藏

Calligraphy Album of Letters, Wen Zhengming, Ming
Dynasty, Suzhou Museum

Comments and Tips

Manjianghong (The River All Red), a pattern of ci poetry. This ci poem was made in the 9th year of Jiajing Period (1530). The author lamented over the loyal hero, Yue Fei's tragedy by cleansing the stone tablet and reading the edict engraved on it. This ci poem sharply points out the fact that owing to the Emperor Gaozong's selfishness, who feared that his father, Emperor Huizong and brother, Emperor Qinzong would be released by the Jurchen and then went back to threaten his claim to the throne, he, therefore, colluded with Qin Hui (Yue Fei's political enemy) and a brutal trial was held against Yue Fei. This ci poem discloses a profound meaning, with penetrating criticism, which presents the author's insight and talents.

明

王守仁

（1472—1528），初名云，字伯安，别号阳明子，余姚（今属浙江）人。弘治十二年（1499）进士，授刑部主事。世宗时封新建伯。嘉靖六年（1527）总督两广兼巡抚。其学以"致良知"为主，谓"格物致知"，当自求诸心，不当求诸事物。弟子极众，世称"姚江学派"。筑室阳明洞中，学者称"阳明先生"。有《王文成公全书》。

西　湖

灵鹫高林暑气清[1]，　竺天石壁雨痕晴[2]。

客来湖上逢云起，　僧住峰头话月明。

世路久知难直道，　此身那得尚虚名。

移家早定孤山计，　种果支茅却易成。

【注释】

1. 灵鹫：灵隐寺前飞来峰，传说由印度飞来。
2. 竺天：即天竺。飞来峰南麓以西有"下天竺""中天竺""上天竺"三寺。

【阅读提示】

　　这首诗吟咏西湖，系王阳明在明正德年间所作。灵鹫山即灵隐寺前的飞来峰，这里树木荫翳、冷泉清冽，能消暑气。山岩陡立，布满洞宇与佛像，在晴光中还可以看到雨滴的印痕。作者与友人游览西湖而来，与宿于飞来峰下的僧人相聚言谈甚欢，直到月上中天。多年的宦海与戎马生涯印证的是直道之难，让人早已淡泊虚名。诗人久已想举家归隐孤山，效仿林逋的生活，比起沉浮于仕途的蝇营狗苟，种果树、架茅屋该是容易做到的事啊！

Wang Shouren

(1472—1528) was a native of Yuyao (now in Zhejiang Province). He became a Jinshi in the 12th year of Hongzhi Period (1499) and then served as a secretary of the Ministry of Justice. Later he was the supreme commander and grand coordinator in Guangdong and Guangxi during the 6th year of Jiajing Period (1527). He believed that conscience can be possessed by studying: a person has to study the phenomena of nature in order to acquire knowledge, as well as to rely on himself instead of on others. He had numerous disciples, who were together entitled Yaojiang School. He built a chamber in the Yangming Cave, so scholars call him Master Yangming. There exists *The Complete Works of Duke Wang Wencheng* (his posthumous title).

The West Lake

The high and dense woods on Lingjiu Hill block the summer heat;
The rock walls around Tianzhu are left with the rain print.
I came to visit the West Lake when white clouds were dense;
I stayed here and talked with the monks until the bright moon rose.
Having already known that there is no straight path in nature;
How can I pursue fame and fortune regardless of danger?
It's better to retire to the Isolated Hill as soon as possible;
It's easy to build a hut and grow some fruit and vegetable.

Comments and Tips

This poem was made in Zhengde Period, Ming Dynasty. Lingjiu Hill is now the scenic spot the Flying Peak in front of Lingyin Temple. The author travelled along the West Lake, together with his friends. He realized it hard to be honest and straightforward in his official and military careers, and years of experiences taught him to be indifferent to fame and power. The author had a long-cherished dream to retire from the world to return to the Isolated Hill with his family, as the recluse Lin Bu did.

田汝成

（1501—约1557），字叔禾，别号豫阳，钱塘人。嘉靖五年（1526）进士，官至广西布政司右参议。有《炎徼纪闻》《西湖游览志》《西湖游览志余》等。

西湖游览

苏堤如带束湖心，　罗绮新妆照碧浔[1]。
翠幕浅搴怜草色[2]，华筵小簇占花阴[3]。
凌波人度纤纤玉，　促柱筝翻叠叠金。
月出笙歌敛城市，　珠楼缥缈彩云深。

【注释】

1. 碧浔：绿水边。
2. 翠幕：翠色的帷幕。
3. 华筵：丰盛的筵席。

【阅读提示】

　　这首诗为田汝成歌咏西湖苏堤一带的美景而作。首联即想象奇特，把苏堤比作一条环绕的腰带束住湖心，西湖好像一位身着罗绮的美人新妆方成，临碧水而自照，婉媚之致尽显。湖上的游人，在树木和花荫下的草坪上摆放丰盛的宴席，翠色的帷幕浅浅撩起，仿佛还在怜惜地上的草色。游船上的女子，如凌波而行，玉手纤细，弹拨弦筝翻出重叠金声。中间两联通过细节描写，生动描绘了湖边与湖上人们出游的场景，辞采华美，有声有色。尾联交代暮色中游人散去，歌声渐稀，而明月升起，彩云深笼在华美的楼阁之间，自有含蓄不尽之意。

Tian Rucheng

(1501−c.1557) was a native of Qiantang. He was a Jinshi in the 5th year of Jiajing Period (1526), and once served as an official of Guangxi Province. His works include *Yanjiaojiwen* (a work on the history of Southern nationalities with the main content of reflecting the nationalities in Guangxi), *Xihuyoulanzhi* (West Lake Sightseeing Chronicles), *Xihuyoulanzhiyu* (Supplements to the West Lake Sightseeing Chronicles).

Tour of the West Lake

The Su Causeway is like a green belt across the center of the lake;

The lake is a beautiful woman in new makeup on the blue water.

Lifting green willow curtains, the grass land looks more lovely;

A luxurious banquet is served under the branches of flower.

People in boats are paddling across the jade-like lake;

The rapid sound of string music is more like scattered gold and silver.

The moon rises, and the singing on the lake converges into the city;

Where pavilions and buildings twinkle as if they were in clouds of colour.

Comments and Tips

The poem is a chant about the splendid scenery around Su Causeway across the West Lake. The first couplet is full of unique imagination, where Su Causeway looks like a winded belt across the center of the lake, and the West Lake is a beautiful woman in new makeup, looking into the water to admire herself, with a graceful charm. The following two couplets depict the traveling scenes on and by the lake in detailed description. The words selected are rhetoric and flowery, forming a colourful and vivid picture. The last couplet tells the fact that when it's getting dark, the crowd disperse; the singing fade away, while the moon rises, and the sunset clouds hide themselves between the pavilions, implicitly imaginable.

徐　渭

（1521—1593），字文长，号天池山人、青藤道人，山阴（今浙江绍兴）人。诗文、戏曲、书画皆工。但科举不利，豪放不羁，蔑视传统。曾客胡宗宪幕，后宗宪受弹劾，徐渭被牵连下狱，获释后绝意功名，恣意山水，穷困而终。有《南词叙录》、杂剧《四声猿》及《徐文长集》等。

赠秦仲虚

冰玉山人本绝埃[1]，西湖自筑初阳台[2]。

何年养鹤曾飞去，　是水当门尽绕来。

道士忽逢松树下，　渔舟放在藕花隈[3]。

知余欲与为邻舍，　指点孤山一角梅。

【注释】

1. 冰玉：比喻人品高洁。
2. 初阳台：在杭州葛岭之巅，传为葛洪炼丹所设。
3. 隈：山、水等弯曲的地方。

Xu Wei

(1521—1593) was a native of Shanyin (now Shaoxing in Zhejiang Province). He showed his talents in poetry, traditional opera, calligraphy and painting. As he failed in the imperial examinations, he became unrestrained in behaviors and disregarded conventions. He worked in the general's office for Hu Zongxian (the supreme commander, who presided over the government's response to the pirate raids during Jiajing Period), but later on, he was implicated and sent to jail when Hu Zongxian got impeached. After his release, he decided not to pursue fame and power, but travelled around mountains and lakes. He lived a poor life till his death. There exists *The Collection of Xu Wenchang* (his style name).

Inscribing for Taoist Qin Zhongxu

The noble nature of the Taoist in the mountain abandons the mundane;

Beside the West Lake a platform was built at the top of Geling Hill.

Thousands of years, the white cranes have already flown away;

But there is boundless water in front of the door still.

Suddenly I met the Taoist priest under the pine tree,

And there was a boat by the lotus flowers bay.

Hearing that I wanted to be a neighbor with him, he pointed to the Isolated Hill

And told me: it is the place where Lin Bu planted plum blossoms, people say.

《墨梅图》明　徐渭　南京博物馆藏

Plum Blossoms of Ink Colour, Xu Wei, Ming Dynasty, Nanjing Museum

【阅读提示】

　　这首诗是徐渭吟咏西湖孤山、葛岭之作，抒发了诗人的隐逸情怀。葛洪曾在初阳台炼丹修道，作者称赞他高洁不染尘埃的品格，描绘初阳台附近超凡脱俗的仙家景象。全诗剪裁精炼，笔势飞动。鹤为仙禽，养之益寿延年，"曾飞去"与"尽绕来"使画面呈现流动不息之感。作者在松下与道士相逢谈话，藕花湾处有渔舟停放着，诗句营造出了一个清幽的修道氛围浓厚的环境。作者表达与道人秦仲虚为邻的志向，并得到了他的指点：在孤山僻静的一角，隐士林逋所居之处，"梅妻鹤子"的高风，可以效仿为之。全诗充满了恬淡质朴的栖隐意趣。

Comments and Tips

This poem is a chant about the Isolated Hill and Geling Hill beside the West Lake, which expresses the author's reclusive attitude. The author complimented Ge Hong (a Taoist priest), who studied Taoism and alchemy on the top of Geling Hill, on his noble and pure quality. The author, himself, wanted to be the neighbor of the Taoist Qin Zhongxu, who told him that the hermit Lin Bu once dwelled on the Isolated Hill. It was worthy of imitating this graceful conduct to view plum blossoms as his wife and cranes as his children. The poem, which is tranquil and simple, is full of secluded fun.

汤显祖

（1550—1616），字义仍，号海若、清远道人，临川（今江西抚州）人，戏曲作家、文学家。万历十一年（1583）进士，历任南京太常寺博士、浙江遂昌县知县等职。他反对程朱理学，批判拟古主义文学，追求个性解放。其戏剧代表作为《牡丹亭》《紫钗记》《南柯记》《邯郸记》，合称"玉茗堂四梦"（又名"临川四梦"）。另有《玉茗堂诗文集》。

天竺中秋

江楼无烛露凄清，风动琅玕笑语明[1]。
一夜桂花何处落？月中空有轴帘声[2]。

【注释】

1. 琅玕：指竹子。
2. 轴帘声：卷起帘子的声音。

【阅读提示】

　　此诗写中秋天竺的月下之景。作者闲坐江边小楼，夜晚却没有烛火，岂不令人感到凄清寂寥？然而正在此际，诗人却于风动竹子的刹那，听到了人们的欢声笑语。继而又描写了作者宁静空明的心境，他仿佛在体察着夜空中每一丝细微的声响：一夜扑簌的桂花都洒落在何处了呢？月光下只能听见不断卷帘的声音，令人清寂而怅惘。诗人善于捕捉声音，以动写静，描写细腻精到。

Tang Xianzu

(1550—1616) was a native of Linchuan County (now Fuzhou in Jiangxi Province). He is a playwright and litterateur in the Ming Dynasty. He was a Jinshi in the 11th year of Wanli Period (1583), and then served as Boshi (Erudite) in the Nanjing Court of Imperial Sacrifices and later the commander of Suichang County, Zhejiang Province. As a man in pursuit of individual emancipation, he disregarded Cheng-Zhu School of Neo-Confucianism and criticized the archaistic literature. His major plays are collectively called The Four Dreams at Yumingtang (the name of the place where the author lived) or called The Four Dreams of Linchuan, which includes *Mudanting* (The Peony Pavilion), *Zichaiji* (The Purple Hairpin), *Nankeji* (Record of the Southern Bough) and *Handanji* (Record of Handan). He also wrote *The Poem Collection at Yumingtang*.

Mid-Autumn Night in Tianzhu Hill

Without candlelight in the building, only desolation of the night dew can
    be felt;
Autumn breeze blows the bamboo forest, and a sound of laughter comes
    from it.
Where do the osmanthus petals fall tonight?
Only the sound of rolling up curtains can be heard in the moonlight.

Comments and Tips

This poem depicts a moonlight scene of Tianzu Hill on the Mid-Autumn night. The author sat at a building in the dark, feeling so lonesome and desolated. But when a gust suddenly blew the bamboo curtain, he heard a flurry of laughter outside. The following lines portray the author's clear and tranquil state of mind. It feels as if he were sensing the slightest sounds in the night, which indicates an air of chilliness and wistfulness. The poet has an eye for sounds and details, who also creates a state of quietness in the description of motion scenes.

胡应麟

（1551—1602），字元瑞，号少室山人，兰溪（今属浙江）人。万历间举人，久不第。筑室山中，购书四万余卷，记诵淹博，多所撰著。有《少室山房类稿》《少室山房笔丛》《诗薮》等。

西湖竹枝歌（四首其三）

倚棹汀洲草色齐 ¹，回船涛浪满苏堤。
万家杨柳青门外 ²，一片芙蓉绿水西。

【注释】

1. 倚棹：靠着船桨，即划船。汀洲：水中的小洲。
2. 青门：《汉书》："霸城门，民间所谓青门也。"此处指杭州城临西湖一带的城门。

【阅读提示】

　　此诗为胡应麟所作《西湖竹枝歌》四首的第三首，诗人以生动优美的语言描绘了夏季人们在西湖洲渚间泛舟的景象。起句写在四周都是茂盛青草的湖中划动船桨，意境悠远浑朴。继而写船头调转回旋出的波浪铺满了苏堤岸，诗人的视角也随之望向了岸边：只见荷叶田田，碧波荡漾，家家户户门外，杨柳垂下翠绿的枝条。后两句，"青"字和"绿"字，描绘出满眼盎然的生机。全诗浑厚流畅而富于情韵，遣词运笔真挚自然、毫无雕琢痕迹。

Hu Yinglin

(1551—1602) was a native of Lanxi County in Jinhua (now in Zhejiang Province). He was a Juren (a rank achieved by a person who passed the provincial exam in the imperial examination) during Wanli Period, but failed several times in the higher-leveled exams. Then he constructed a chamber in the Shaoshi Mountains and bought over forty thousand of books to read and study. With a wide knowledge of learning, he was prolific in writing. His works include *The Poem Collection of Shaoshishanfang* (his chamber in the Shaoshi Mountains) *Notes from Shaoshishanfang*, and *On Poetry*,.

Song of Bamboo Branch at the West Lake (the Third of Four)

Rowing a boat near the isle, which is covered with green grass;
Turning the bow rolls up the waves to the causeway surging.
The east bank outside the city is green with willows;
While the lotuses in the west of the lake look more flourishing.

Comments and Tips

In a lively and elegant language, the poet depicts the scene of boating on the West Lake in the summer season. The first two lines are about a boating trip in the lake. In the last two lines, the two characters "qing" (blue) and "lü" (green) present a magnificent view of vitality. The poem has a vigorous and fluent flow, full of charm. The words selected and applied are sincere and simple, without a trace of deliberate modification.

袁宏道

（1568—1610），字中郎，号石公，公安（今属湖北）人。万历二十年（1592）进士，官至吏部郎中。与兄袁宗道、弟袁中道并有才名，时称"三袁"。抨击拟古文风，主张诗文以抒写性灵为主，时称"公安体"。有《袁中郎集》。

初至西湖（二首其一）

山上清波水上尘， 钱时花月宋时春[1]。
看官不识杭州语[2]，只道相逢有北人。

【注释】

1. 钱时：五代十国时期，钱镠建立吴越国时。
2. 看官：话本和小说中对听众和读者的称呼，此处泛指外来的游客。

【阅读提示】

　　这首诗是明万历年间袁宏道首次游览西湖时所作，以精省的意象、综括的视角，点出了作者对西湖的最初感受。诗人第一次到杭州，因而此前关于西湖的种种历史记忆，都化作无穷的诗情游兴，只是一睹山色湖光，就已令诗人目酣神醉。一、二句中，"清波""尘"与"花月""春"形成精巧对仗，几个意象浓缩了数百年的时空，包含了无穷的韵味。三、四句以"看官"戏称外地游客听不懂此际仍留有汴京口音的杭州话，还以为是遇到了北方的游人，将诗人沉醉于游赏的意趣、兴致，写得生动自然而又情态毕现。

Yuan Hongdao

(1568—1610) was a native of Gong'an County (now in Hubei Province). He was a Jinshi in the 20th year of Wanli Period (1592) and served as the Director of the Ministry of Personnel. Yuan Hongdao and his brothers Yuan Zongdao and Yuan Zhongdao are known as Yuan's Three Brothers. He criticized the archaistic writing style and advocated a genuine and true feeling in poem writing. His verses are known for "Gong'an Style". His works include *The Collection of Yuan Zhonglang* (his given name).

First Visit to the West Lake (the First of Two)

The hills undulate like tumbling water waves;

The moon in the reign of King Qian, and spring of Song Dynasty.

Tourists are not used to hearing Hangzhou dialect,

And they think they have met northerners here excitedly.

Comments and Tips

The author conceived this poem when he visited the West Lake during Wanli Period. It was the first time that the poet had been to Hangzhou. Only one glimpse of the landscape had drawn the poet's attention and let him drunk in the beauty of the scenery. In the first and second lines, several images can represent hundreds of years of history, leaving a lingering charm. The third and fourth lines show a vivid and natural picture of his traveling taste and mood.

Warblers Singing in Willow Waves

《柳浪闻莺》

清

One Hundred Poems
on the West Lake in Hangzhou
Through the Ages

Qing Dynasty
(1616–1911)

钱谦益

（1582—1664），字受之，号牧斋，晚号蒙叟，江苏常熟人。明万历三十八年（1610）进士，南明弘光帝时，起为礼部尚书。后降清，授礼部侍郎，任职五月而归。后两次因大案牵连入狱，终均得幸免。晚境颇颓唐。诗文极有造诣，有《初学集》《有学集》《国初群雄事略》等，编有《列朝诗集》。

西湖杂感（组诗其二）

潋滟西湖水一方，　吴根越角两茫茫[1]。

孤山鹤去花如雪，　葛岭鹃啼月似霜[2]。

油壁轻车来北里[3]，梨园小部奏西厢[4]。

而今纵会空王法[5]，知是前尘也断肠。

【注释】

1. 吴根越角：原指吴越故地之边陲，后多泛指江浙一带。
2. 葛岭：在杭州西湖之北宝石山西面，相传东晋时著名道士葛洪曾于此结庐修道炼丹，故而得名。
3. 油壁轻车：古人乘坐的一种车。此指苏小小事。北里：唐代长安平康里。因在城北，故称"北里"。
4. 小部：唐代宫廷中的少年歌舞队。袁郊《甘泽谣·许云封》："值梨园法部置小部音声，凡三十余人，皆十五以下。"
5. 空王：佛的尊称。

Qian Qianyi

(1582–1664) was a native of Changshu, Jiangsu Province. He was qualified as a Jinshi in the 38th year of Wanli Period (1610). In Southern Ming Emperor Hongguang's reign, he was appointed as the Minister of Rites. Before long, he surrendered to the Qing Dynasty and was appointed as an assistant minister of the Ministry of Rites, but served for merely five months. He then was twice imprisoned for being implicated in major cases, but was spared somehow. Qian was in a rather decadent position in his later years and was considerably accomplished in verse and prose. There include *Chuxueji* (a collection of his poems written in the Ming Dynasty), *Youxueji* (a collection of his poems written in the Qing Dynasty), and *A Brief Account of Great Men in Early Ming Dynasty*. Qian also compiled *The Poetry Collections of Previous Dynasties*.

Miscellaneous Feelings of the West Lake (the Second in a Group)

The water of the West Lake is rippling with clear waves;

The mountains and rivers in Wu and Yue are boundless really.

The cranes in the Isolated Hill had gone, leaving the plums bloom like snow;

The cuckoo's cry on Geling Hill, shaking off the moonlight frosty.

Painted carriages could travel through erotic alleys,

As if there come sound of music from the palace distantly.

Now, even if I understand the dharma of the emptiness of everything;

Realizing that this is an illusionary realm makes me heartbroken deeply.

【阅读提示】

这是钱谦益《西湖杂感》二十首中的第二首。首联以苏轼"潋滟"词意入笔，而归以"茫茫"，苍凉之感顿生；颔联融入历史典故，鹤去、鹃啼，说尽物是人非；颈联以昔日繁华映衬当前的衰败，而与尾联"而今"相接。作者不由得悲伤肠断，一切都已是往日陈迹，空无而没有意义。全诗用典丰富自如，境界阔远，感慨深沉。颔联拗救应用，更是表达出悲不自胜、痛定思痛的情感波澜。

《孤山放鹤图》

明　项圣谟　台北故宫博物院藏

Releasing Cranes in the Isolated Hill, Xiang Shengmo, Ming Dynasty, Taipei Palace Museum

Comments and Tips

The first couplet of this poem is written with the allusion from Su Shi's words. The second couplet incorporates historical allusions, elaborating the vicissitudes of life. The following couplet offers a contrast of the present decay and the past prosperity, introducing the last couplet which starts with "Now". The poet could not help but feel sad and broken, while everything is a relic of the past, empty and meaningless. Abundant allusions are naturally employed in the poem, which presents a remarkable scope and deep feelings.

清

张　岱

（1597—1689），字宗子、石公，号陶庵，山阴（今浙江绍兴）人。生于官宦家庭，但一生未仕。明亡后，隐居剡溪山中。是晚明小品文大家，有《石匮书》《四书遇》《陶庵梦忆》《西湖梦寻》等。

钱王祠

扼定东南十四州，　五王并不事兜鍪[1]。

英雄球马朝天子[2]，带砺山河拥冕旒[3]。

大树千株被锦绂[4]，钱塘万弩射潮头[5]。

五胡纷扰中华地，　歌舞西湖近百秋。

【注释】

1. 五王：吴越国历三代五王。兜鍪（móu），古代作战时戴的头盔。
2. 球马：犹裘马，谓轻裘肥马，形容生活豪华。
3. 带砺（lì）：亦作"带厉"，比喻长久。《史记·高祖功臣侯者年表》："封爵之誓曰：'使黄河如带，泰山若厉。国以永宁，爰及苗裔。'"后因而以"带厉"为受皇家恩宠，与国同休之典。冕旒（liú）：天子的礼帽和礼帽前后悬垂的玉串。借指皇帝、帝位。
4. 被锦绂（fú）：覆盖彩色的丝带。《西湖梦寻》载："梁开平元年，封镠为吴越王。……是年，省茔垄，延故老，旌钺鼓吹，振耀山谷。自昔游钓之所，尽蒙以锦绣。"
5. 射潮头：指吴越王钱镠射潮之事。

Zhang Dai

(1597—1689) was a native of Shanyin (now Shaoxing, Zhejiang Province). He was born to a family of officials, but never served in the government. After the fall of Ming Dynasty, he lived in seclusion in Shanxi Mountain. He was a master of short essays in the late Ming Dynasty. His works include *Stone-Case Book*, *Encountering the Four Books*, *Recollected Dreams of Tao'an* (his art name) and *Tracing the West Lake in Dreams*.

The Temple of Qian Liu, King of Wuyue State

Stabilizing the territory of the fourteen southeastern states,

All the five kings did not honor martial power.

A generation of heroes prayed for the prosperity of the country and the
    people,

Remembering the grace of the emperor, and vowing to submit to the
    emperor.

Thousands of trees were wrapped around the golden silk ribbon;

Tens of thousands of arrows were launched towards the spring tide frontier.

Northern China was suffering from foreign aggression year after year;

Only the singing and dancing on the West Lake had continued for a long
    era.

这是一首吟咏古迹的诗，前两联叙写钱镠平定两浙，辖一军十三州，保境安民而善事中原之事。钱王射潮，多有记载。宋孙光宪《北梦琐言》："杭州连岁潮头直打罗刹石，吴越钱尚父俾张弓弩，候潮至，逆而射之，由是渐退。"在战乱频仍、民不聊生的时代，唯两浙安宁，"民至于老死不识兵革，四时嬉游，歌舞之声相闻，至于今不废。其有德于斯民甚厚"。张岱言诗要有"冰雪"之气，重古朴、凝重、冷峭的艺术风格，此诗可以说是这一风貌的代表。

Comments and Tips

This is a poem that traces the historical site. The first two couplets describe how Qian Liu brought peace to Zhejiang Province. He protected the land and the people and served the imperial court well. King Qian shooting the tide remains a popular subject matter. Sun Guangxian (Song Dynasty) wrote in his notes: "Hangzhou was threatened by strikes of the tide for years. King Qian Liu of Wuyue commanded archers to wait for the tide and shoot. From then on the tide gradually retreated. " When people could hardly survive in an era of war and chaos, only those who were in Qian Liu's reign could enjoy peace. Zhang Dai claimed that poetry should possess the air of "ice and snow". This poem is a case of his simple, grave, steep and unsentimental style.

清

黄宗羲

（1610—1695），字太冲，号梨洲、南雷，余姚人。明末清初杰出的思想家、文学家。早年参加"复社"，明亡后屡拒清廷征召，发愤著述。有《明夷待访录》《宋元学案》《明儒学案》《南雷文定》等。

寻张司马墓

草荒树密路三叉，　下马来寻日色斜。
顽石鸣呼都作字[1]，冬青憔悴未开花。
夜台不敢留真姓[2]，萍梗还来醉晚鸦[3]。
牡蛎滩头当日客[4]，茫然隔世数年华。

【注释】

1. 都作字：到处都有题词。
2. 夜台：坟墓。张煌言殉难后，不敢公开下葬，托为"王先生墓"。
3. 萍梗：浮萍断梗，喻人行止无定。
4. 牡蛎滩：旧说椒江北岸有金鳌山，为宋高宗驻跸处。山下有一浅滩，名曰"牡蛎滩"。此非确指，只是表达作者自己当年海上的抗清活动。

【阅读提示】

　　此诗写对张司马的哀悼之情。张司马，即张煌言。古代司马掌管军政，故称为"张司马"。全诗写张煌言墓埋没蒿莱的衰败苍凉之景。张苍水逝后不敢公开埋葬，墓前仅草立一碑石，石上题"王先生墓"。黄宗羲撰写《张苍水墓志铭》前来寻访，已是荒僻难寻，不由感慨万千，一洒追思之泪。末联回想自己的抗清生涯，又恍有隔世之感。全诗情感沉郁，哀转低回，撼人心魄。

Huang Zongxi

(1610－1695) was a native of Yuyao. He was a member of the "Restoration Society" in his early years. After the fall of Ming Dynasty, he repeatedly refused the call of Qing court and was resolute in his writing career. His major works are *Mingyi Daifang Lu* (Waiting for the Dawn: A Plan for the Prince), *Song-Yuan Xue'an* (Survey of Song and Yuan Confucianists), *Mingru Xue'an* (Survey of Ming Confucianists), *Nanlei Wending* (Fixed Prose Writings of Nanlei; Nanlei being Huang's art name) and others.

Searching for Zhang Huangyan's Tomb

At the crossroads of barren grass and dense forest,
I got off horse to look for Zhang's grave under soil layer.
There are only stones everywhere to mark his tomb;
And evergreen trees looked haggard without flower.
The martyr's tomb dared not inscribe his real name,
So I can only pour wine on the ground attracting crows to fly near.
Back then, we fought the invaders together at the seaside,
Now I am the only one alive, feeling at a loss in different Nature.

Comments and Tips

This poem is an elegy for Zhang Huangyan, also known as Zhang Cangshui (his art name), who was the Minister of Military Affairs of Southern Ming Dynasty. The whole poem describes the bleak and desolate scene of Zhang's tomb buried in weeds. Huang Zongxi came to look for the tomb with his "Epitaph of Zhang Cangshui", only found it difficult to spot the location in the wild, upon which he could not help but feel emotional and shed tears of remembrance. In the last couplet Huang recalled his own anti-Qing experience, which happened as if in a previous life. The whole poem reveals grave feelings in a sorrowful and touching way.

张煌言

（1620—1664），字玄著，号苍水，浙江鄞县人。明末举人，清顺治二年（1645）起兵抗清。后桂王称永历帝，张煌言为大学士兼兵部尚书，与郑成功联军抗清。康熙三年（1664）因叛徒出卖被捕，同年九月在杭州英勇就义。有《张苍水集》。

甲辰八月辞故里[1]

国亡家破欲何之？　西子湖头有我师。

日月双悬于氏墓，　乾坤半壁岳家祠。

惭将赤手分三席[2]，敢为丹心借一枝[3]。

他日素车东浙路[4]，怒涛岂必属鸱夷[5]！

【注释】

1. 甲辰：清康熙三年（1664），是年，张煌言被押解去杭州，临行时作此诗。
2. 赤手：即徒手，在此表示自己对复兴明朝毫无寸功的愧叹。
3. 一枝：用《庄子·逍遥游》"鹪鹩巢于深林，不过一枝"之意，表示所占微小，这里喻作一席葬身之地。
4. 素车：古代丧事所用之车，在此以死明志，以示绝不向清朝妥协让步，誓死捍卫明朝。
5. 鸱夷：皮革制的口袋。这里借代伍子胥。

Zhang Huangyan

(1620—1664) was a native of Yin County, Zhejiang Province. He was a Juren by the end of Ming Dynasty. In the second year of Shunzhi Period (1645), Zhang raised an armed force against the Qing Dynasty. Later, when Ming's Prince Gui was enthroned as Emperor Yongli, Zhang served as a Grand Secretariat and Minister of War, and allied forces with Zheng Chenggong against the Qing Dynasty. He was betrayed by traitors and was captured in the third year of Kangxi Period (1664). September of the same year witnessed his heroic death in Hangzhou. There exists *The Collection of Zhang Cangshui* (his art name).

Farewell to My Hometown

My country is broken, and where is my way to go?

On the shores of the West Lake two of my teachers slept eternally.

Here is the tomb of Yu Qian, who preserved the Great Ming Dynasty;

Here is the shrine of Yue Fei, who protected half of the Song's territory.

I am now empty-handed and hopeless to serve the country,

But I dream of being buried with them, feeling so guilty.

People will come to mourn for me one day in future.

The spring tide of Qiantang River will once again sweep with fury.

《玉带桥诗意图》清　徐扬　故宫博物院藏

Poetic Contemplation of the Jade Belt Bridge, Xu Yang, Qing Dynasty, The Palace Museum

【阅读提示】

　　这首七律系 1664 年张煌言抗清被俘，押解杭州途中所作。诗的开篇即以设问句式坦陈自己宁死不屈、矢志以身报国的心迹。颔联承上，说明自己的榜样是于谦和岳飞。"日月双悬"与"乾坤半壁"，不但对仗工整，而且高度赞扬了两位英雄的光辉业绩。颈联表明自己不惜身死的决心，以及未能实现抗清复明大业的遗憾。尾联则巧用伍子胥化为潮神的传说，言己身虽死，但抗清之志不灭，如同钱江大潮一般，汹涌澎湃，奔腾不息。本诗抒情明志，慷慨激昂，悲壮苍凉，洋溢着强烈的民族气节和凛然正气，可谓字字血、声声泪，读之令人感奋。

One Hundred Poems on the West Lake in Hangzhou through the Ages

Comments and Tips

This poem was written in 1664 when Zhang Huangyan was captured for resisting the Qing Dynasty and was sent to Hangzhou under escort. The first couplet states that he would rather die than give in and was determined to serve his country with his life. The second couplet continues to claim that his role models were Yu Qian and Yue Fei. The following couplet expresses his determination to sacrifice and his regret of not being able to achieve the final success of the great cause of overthrowing the Qing regime and restoring the Ming Dynasty. The last couplet skillfully employs the legend of Wu Zixu's incarnation as the tide god, claiming that his will to resist the Qing regime will never die despite his physical cessation of life. The poem is lyrical and expressive, impassioned yet mournful and desolate, full of intense patriotism and awe-inspiring noble spirit.

275

陈维崧

（1625—1682），字其年，号迦陵，宜兴（今属江苏）人。康熙十八年（1679）举博学宏词科，授翰林院检讨，参与编修《明史》。为清初阳羡词派创始人，词学苏轼、辛弃疾，风格豪放，又善诗和骈文。有《湖海楼诗文词全集》。

春从天上来·钱塘徐野君王丹麓来游阳羡余以浪迹梁溪阙焉未晤词以写怀 [1]

烟月杭州。

记徐卓当年，诗酒风流。

水市露井 [2]，桂桨莲舟。

老铁吹裂龙湫 [3]。

奈十年一梦，断桥上、落叶飕飕。

恨年来，只无情皓月，犹挂湖头。

Chen Weisong

(1625—1682) was a native of Yixing (now in Jiangsu Province). In the 18th year of Kangxi Period (1679), he passed a special test for expert scholars upon the order of the emperor. Serving as an official in the Royal Academy, he participated in the composition of *History of Ming Dynasty*. Chen was the founder of the Yangxian (the dated name of his hometown Yixing) ci poetry school in the early Qing Dynasty, whose bold style was learned from Su Shi and Xin Qiji. He was an excellent poet and was expert in "Pianwen" (a highly stylized prose form featuring rhythm and rhyme as well as regular lines arranged in couplets so that it is pleasant to read and chant). There exists *The Complete Collection of Verse and Prose from Huhailou* (the building by the lake and sea).

Chuncongtianshanglai: My Friends Visiting but Not Meeting

Blossoming in spring, Hangzhou is a beautiful place.

I still remember how romantic Xu was

When he wrote poems and drank with grace,

Walking through the alleys and streets

And boating on lake surface.

The cold wind cracked the waterfall at the cliff edge.

Falling leaves whizzed across the Broken Bridge.

It has been ten years, as if in a fantasy.

Since then, only the bright moon

Still mercilessly hangs above the West Lake,

leaving nothing but regret only.

王郎清歌绝妙，邀白发词人，同下长洲。

瑟瑟丹枫，濛濛白雁，秣陵总不宜秋⁴。

叹龙峰归后，人去远、烟缆难留。

漫登楼。

数枝残菊，还替人愁。

【注释】

1. 春从天上来：词牌名，调见《中州乐府》。徐野君：即徐士俊，字三有，号野君，仁和（今浙江杭州）人，生活于明末清初，工杂剧，有《洛水丝》《春波影》等六十余种，还有《尺牍新语》存世。王丹麓：即王晫，字丹麓，号木庵，钱塘人，生活于明末清初，淡泊科举，工诗文，有《今世说》《遂生集》《霞举堂集》《墙东草堂词》及杂著多种。
2. 水市：水边的市集。露井：口沿没有覆盖的井。
3. 龙湫：温州市雁荡山著名瀑布。
4. 秣陵：南京的古称。

【阅读提示】

　　这首词是陈维崧因未能赴好友徐士俊与王晫之约而作。整首词布局非常巧妙，上阕和下阕呈平行状态。上阕回忆与好友徐士俊的交游景况，记得当年在西子湖畔，与好友诗酒流连，但时光荏苒，物是人非，现在只能怀想当年与好友的交游岁月，表现出了此次未能赴约的伤感之情。下阕回忆与王晫的交游景况，当年一起同游苏州，但现在却只能独自登楼，无限怅惘，都付于对友人的深深怀念。从词中，我们不仅可以看出一位重情重义且多愁善感的词人形象，更能感受到从昔至今那份真挚友谊的可贵。

I also remember that Wang's singing was clear and brilliant,

Inviting me, a grey-haired poet,

To view Taihu Lake, beautiful and magnificent.

The red maple leaves rustling,

The wild geese flying,

The autumn scenery is always heartbreaking.

Sadly, since that departure,

I have drifted to nowhere and have failed to meet you further.

Going upstairs anyhow,

I picked a few chrysanthemums,

And returned to soothe my sorrow.

Comments and Tips

Chuncongtianshanglai (Spring Coming from Heaven): a pattern of ci poetry. This ci poem was composed upon Chen's missing the appointment with two of his friends. The entire ci is very skillfully laid out. In the first half, the poet recalled how he used to enjoy trips with his close friend Xu Shijun. As time had passed and things were still there, but people were not the same. Failing to meet his friend this time made him sorrowful. The second half recalls his friendship with Wang Zhuo. They used to travel together in Suzhou, but now the poet could only ascend the building alone, and was tremendously frustrated missing his friend. This ci poem reveals the image of an affectionate and sentimental poet, exposing the preciousness of the sincere friendship from the past to the present.

清

洪　昇

（1645—1704），字昉思，号稗畦，钱塘人。生于世宦之家，历经二十年科举不第，白衣终身。清代著名戏曲家、诗人，代表剧作《长生殿》，他与《桃花扇》作者孔尚任并称"南洪北孔"。有《洪昇集》。

岳武穆王墓

老树残碑风露寒，　忠魂千载照湖干。

汾阳大略垂成易[1]，诸葛雄心欲遂难[2]。

共恨相公终误国[3]，谁知天子乐偏安[4]。

两宫未返身先死[5]，泪洒中原血肯干。

【注释】

1. 汾阳：即郭子仪，唐代中期名将，后得封汾阳郡王，后世称"郭汾阳"。
2. 诸葛：即诸葛亮，三国蜀汉丞相，曾辅佐刘备建立蜀汉，在刘备去世后，鞠躬尽瘁辅佐刘禅，六出祁山欲收复中原，无奈最终失败。
3. 相公：这里指宋高宗时的奸相秦桧，主张对金求和，并迫害主战派大臣，尤其是协助宋高宗以"莫须有"之罪害死了名将岳飞，最终使收复中原化为泡影。
4. 天子乐偏安：指宋高宗放弃北伐收复中原，最终偏安于杭州，建立了南宋朝廷。
5. 两宫：指在靖康之变中被俘虏的宋徽宗和宋钦宗二帝。

Hong Sheng

(1645—1704) was a native of Qiantang. He was born into a family of officials, and after twenty years of failing to pass the imperial examinations, he remained a civilian all his life. He was a famous dramatist and poet, whose representative work is *The Palace of Eternal Life*. He and Kong Shangren, the composer of *The Peach Blossom Fan*, were known as "Southern Hong and Northern Kong".There exists *The Collection of Hong Sheng*.

Sacrificing Yue Fei's Tomb

Old trees and ruined monument immersed in cold wind and dew;

The soul of the hero has been shining on the lake for a thousand years.

Guo Ziyi's strategy is easy to succeed;

But it is difficult to realize Zhuge Liang's ideas.

All the people hated the traitor for destroying the country,

But the faint ruler was happy to be in peace with the invaders.

Unable to welcome the two emperors but died himself,

Tears mixed with blood watering the Central Plain areas.

　　这首诗是洪昇拜谒岳飞墓祠而作。首联表现了诗人对岳飞千载忠魂的敬仰，以一片萧瑟的冬景为背景，更衬托出岳飞墓祠的庄严与诗人拜谒时心情的肃穆。颔联用两位著名历史人物典故的鲜明对比，郭子仪成功平定安史之乱，而诸葛亮却无法实现克复中原的夙愿，以渲染岳飞壮志未酬的悲剧色彩。颈联批判了宋高宗与宰相秦桧为求偏安一隅，将矢志收复中原的岳飞迫害致死的罪孽。最后从悲凉中来，又回到悲凉中去，君臣偏安一隅，只剩被俘的徽、钦二帝羁押在北国，而岳飞只能含冤九泉，最终以悲剧收场。整首诗沉郁悲怆，通过对岳飞的悲剧人生的沉痛吊唁，深刻表现了诗人的爱国思想和民族情怀。

Comments and Tips

This poem was written by Hong Sheng when he visited the tomb shrine of Yue Fei. The first couplet expresses the poet's admiration for the loyal soul of Yue Fei which has been revered for thousands of years. The second couplet employs allusions to two famous historical figures, Guo Ziyi and Zhuge Liang. Through the sharp contrast between the two, the tragedy of Yue Fei's unfulfilled ambition seems even more impressive. The following couplet criticizes Emperor Gaozong of Southern Song Dynasty and his chancellor Qin Hui. From sorrow the poem starts, and with sorrow the poem ends: the emperor and ministers were content to retain sovereignty over their petty corner, leaving the two captured previous emperors Huizong and Qinzong in custody in the northern Jin Kingdom. The whole poem has a somber mood with a tone of pathos. It vividly expresses the poet's profound love for his country and people through sorrowful condolences to the tragic life of Yue Fei.

《两江名胜图》册（十之五《西湖岳坟图》）明　沈周　上海博物馆藏

Yue Fei Temple by the West Lake in the album of *Southeast Scenic Spots*, Shen Zhou,
Ming Dynasty, Shanghai Museum

《苏堤联骑图》明 谢时臣 天津博物馆藏

Riding on Su Causeway, Xie Shichen, Ming Dynasty, Tianjin Museum

查慎行

（1650—1727），初名嗣琏，字夏重，号查田，后改名慎行，改字悔余，号他山，海宁（今属浙江）人。康熙三十二年（1693）举人，四十二年以献诗赐进士出身，授翰林院编修。雍正间，受弟嗣庭狱株连，旋得释，归后即卒。诗学苏轼、陆游。有《他山诗钞》《敬业堂集》。

临江仙·西湖秋泛 [1]

记得棕亭春待宴，满湖灯烛熏天。

一番光景换尊前。

残荷犹泻雨，疏柳已无蝉。

望望西泠桥外去 [2]，吟过第六桥边 [3]。

商声辊上十三弦 [4]。

晚风吹不断，凉透鹭鸶肩。

【注释】

1. 临江仙：词牌名。本为唐教坊曲名，多用以咏水仙，故名。
2. 西泠桥：在杭州西湖上，孤山西北尽头处，是庄孤山入北山的必经之路。
3. 第六桥：杭州西湖苏堤北端的"跨虹桥"。
4. 商声：五音中的商音，比喻秋声。辊（gǔn）：机器上能滚动的圆柱形机件。这里作动词，即旋转之意。十三弦：唐宋时教坊用的筝均为十三根弦，因代指筝。

Zha Shenxing

(1650－1727) was a native of Haining (now in Zhejiang Province). He was a Juren in the 32nd year of Kangxi Period (1693). Ten years later, he dedicated a poem to the emperor and was offered the title of Jinshi and served as a royal secretary. During Yongzheng Period, he was involved in the case of his brother siting and was put into prison. Zha was soon released, but passed away not long after he returned back home. His poetry followed the style of Su Shi and Lu You. There exist *Poetry Collection of Tashan* (Zha's art name) and *The Collection of Jingyetang* (Dedication Hall).

Linjiangxian: Wandering Around the West Lake in Autumn

I remember that we had a banquet in Hangzhou in the spring of that year;

The lights of the boats on the West Lake reflected the night sky curtain.

The sight was far better than a table full of banquets.

It is now late autumn, with water dripping from the crumbling lotus leaves

And no more cicadas on the sparse willow branches.

I walked towards Xiling Bridge,

Chanting poems along the way to Kuahong Bridge.

Someone was playing the music of zither in the distance.

The evening wind was blowing,

And the egrets by the lake with their wings tightened.

【阅读提示】

这首词主要写西湖秋色与作者心绪之间的互动，作者借西湖秋色的渲染，来表达自己无限落寞悲愁的心情。上阕首句回忆了当年在西湖上诗酒流连的盛况，但第二句一转笔就将思绪从记忆中拉回了现实，现在已经是满湖残荷、蝉鸣不再的萧瑟秋季了。下阕作者站在西泠桥上远望，隐隐听见耳畔传来秋声，时间将晚，寒气逼来，更显凄凉。这首词虽然表面上写的是西湖晚秋之景，但结合作者的人生遭遇，又何尝不是作者的命运自况呢？查慎行出身于江南名族，早年进士及第，春风得意，正像作者在首句回忆的那样，但命运无情，受弟弟文字狱牵连，入狱罢官，从此人生转入低谷。作者在此临秋湖自照，情景交融，悲愁无限。

Comments and Tips

Linjiangxian (The Descent of River God): a pattern of ci poetry. This ci poem is mainly about the intercourse between the autumn colours of the West Lake and the desolate and sorrowful sentiments of the poet. The first half starts from the recall of his lingering about the West Lake with poetry and wine, and then shifts soon back from memory to the reality of the bleak autumn with the lake full of withered lotus leaves and no more cicada songs. The second half describes the poet standing on Xiling Bridge looking far into the distance, the faint sound of autumn overheard; it was getting late and the cold air came in force, which reinforces the sense of bleakness. This ci poem is ostensibly about the late autumn scenes of the West Lake, but is actually a revelation of the poet's own bumpy life. The autumn lake scenes offer a perfect reflection of his own endless sorrow.

爱新觉罗·玄烨

（1654—1722），即清圣祖，康熙是其年号。1161—1722 年在位期间收复台湾、驱逐沙俄，是统一的多民族国家的捍卫者，奠定了清朝前期兴盛的根基。组织编写了《康熙字典》《古今图书集成》等。《康熙诗词集注》录其诗词凡一千一百四十七首。

行宫雨中望吴山

槛外青山纵目收[1]，繁花初落叶新稠[2]。
更教点染烟云色， 添得窗前翠欲流。

【注释】

1. 槛外：栏杆之外。
2. 稠：多而密的样子。

【阅读提示】

这首诗创作于康熙三十八年（1699），亦即康熙帝第二次南巡来杭州时，他站在行宫处远望吴山，见江南春末景致，心情畅快，乃有此作。康熙帝此次南巡杭州，天下太平，江南已然在明末清初的战乱中复苏，重新呈现出一派繁华景象，同时，康熙帝正值壮年，身临胜景，一草一木在他眼中都是那么的娟娟可爱。全诗虽是写景，但在字里行间透露出这位君主的从容与雅趣，以及帝王身份与士大夫情致在其身上的融合。

Aisin-Gioro Xuanye

(1654—1722) is the personal name of Qing Dynasty's Shengzu (his temple name) Emperor. Kangxi is his era name. During his reign as the defender of a unified multi-ethnic nation, he unified Taiwan and expelled forces of Tsarist Russia, and laid the foundation for the prosperity of the early years of Qing Dynasty. The Emperor gave orders to compose invaluable reference books, among which are *Kangxi Dictionary*, *Gujintushujicheng* (also known as *Imperial Encyclopaedia*) and so on. *The Collection and Annotation on Poetry of Emperor Kangxi* lists about 1147 pieces of his works.

Looking at Wu Hill in the Rain at the West Lake Palace

Outside the balustrade, you can see the green hills in the distance;
The flowers are beginning to fall, and the new leaves are getting denser.
If there are some clouds and fogs dyeing,
The vegetation in front of the window will flow in green colour.

Comments and Tips

This poem was composed in the 38th year of Kangxi Period (1699) when Emperor Kangxi was on his second southern inspection tour to Hangzhou. Viewing Wu Hill from his palace at the southern foot of the Isolated Hill, he was pleased by the late spring scenery of the south of Yangtze and contributed this verse. This tour was made when China finally enjoyed peace and the south of Yangtze had revived from war and civil disturbance of the late Ming and early Qing Dynasties and reclaimed its prosperity. The poem is about the scenery, but the monarch's ease and grace is revealed between lines. His identity as an emperor and the sentiment of a scholar gentleman find a perfect blend here.

厉 鹗

（1692—1752），字太鸿，号樊榭，钱塘人。康熙五十九年（1720）举人。清代文学家、学者。有《樊榭山房集》《宋诗纪事》《南宋杂事诗》等。

冷泉亭

众壑孤亭合，泉声出翠微[1]。

静闻兼远梵，独立悟清晖。

木落残僧定，山寒归鸟稀。

迟迟松外月，为我照田衣[2]。

【注释】

1. 翠微：泛指青山。
2. 田衣：袈裟的别名，亦称"田相衣"。袈裟多方格形图案，类水田畦畔纵横，故名。

【阅读提示】

这首诗围绕着清幽的山水景致展开。首联就为读者描绘了一幅清幽雅致的山水小品画，青山幽涧与孤亭完美地融合，读者置身其中，还可以听见潺潺泉水声。颔联通过首联景致的烘托，将禅意渗透其中；听着远处传来的诵经声，使人进入一种妙悟自得的境界。颈联更进一步渲染了这种由清净而入禅定的状态，在不知不觉中，时间将晚，飞鸟归林，而诗人尚流连山间。在尾联中我们可以看到，诗人虽非出家人，但满心禅意，身披袈裟，似乎已经陶醉在这玄妙的山水禅境之中，忘却尘世，超然物外。全诗不仅呈现了一派令人沉醉的山水幽境，而且可以看出作者对佛教的倾心与理解，虽然诗人眼中的冷泉亭景致有一丝淡淡的清冷落寞，但依然令人神往。

Li E

(1692—1752) was a native of Qiantang. He was a Juren in the 59th year of Kangxi Period (1720) and a renowned writer and scholar. His works include *Works Composed in Fanxie's Mountain Cottage* (Fanxie was Li's art name), *Recorded Occasions in Poetry of Song Dynasty* and *Miscellaneous Poems in Southern Song Dynasty*.

The Cold Spring Pavilion

Many hills and gullies coincide with the solitary pavilion;

The sound of spring water flows out of the rocks green.

The running water is like the chanting sound in the distance,

Which makes people comprehend the clear brilliance.

The leaves are withering; the elderly monk has entered meditation.

Even the returning birds appear to be sparse in the cold mountain.

Covering the pine woods is the moonlight

Which shines on my lonely monk's robe bright.

Comments and Tips

The Cold Spring Pavilion is located in Lingyin Temple of Hangzhou, and the poem revolves around the secluded landscape there. The first couplet offers a vignette of the quiet and elegant landscape, in which the green hills and remote streams perfectly blend with the lone pavilion. In the second couplet the remote sound of chanting inside the temple serves as a guide to a moment of epiphany and a sense of enlightened ease and freedom. The following couplet further reinforces the state of Zen meditation resulting from the quiet and peace of mind. The last couplet reveals that although the poet was not a Buddhist monk, he was indulged in Zen meditation. The poem not only presents an enchanting secluded landscape, but also reveals the poet's devotion to and comprehension of Buddhism. The scenery is attractive despite the fact that it is somewhat desolate.

爱新觉罗·弘历

（1711—1799），即清高宗，"乾隆"是其年号。在位期间（1735—1796）使清朝的社会经济达到了"康乾盛世"以来的最高峰，进一步完成了多民族国家的统一。还倡导并编成中国历史上规模最大的丛书《四库全书》。据说一生作诗四万多首。《乾隆诗词集》收录其诗词一百九十四首。

坐龙井上烹茶偶成

龙井新茶龙井泉¹，一家风味称烹煎。

寸芽出自烂石上， 时节焙成谷雨前²。

何必凤团夸御茗³，聊因雀舌润心莲⁴。

呼之欲出辩才在⁵，笑我依然文字禅⁶。

【注释】

1. 龙井：位于杭州西湖西面之风篁岭，原名龙泓，泉水清冽甘甜，周围是"西湖龙井"名茶主产地之一。龙井茶因色、香、味、形俱佳而被列为茶中上品。
2. 谷雨：二十四节气之一，是春季的最后一个节气。此时采制的龙井茶被称为"雨前茶"，味道可口，是龙井茶中的名品。
3. 凤团：宋代贡茶名，用上等茶末制成团状，印有凤纹，此处泛指好茶。
4. 雀舌：绿茶中的精品，以其形似张口鸣叫的雀嘴而得名。
5. 辩才：释元净（1011—1091），字无象，於潜（今浙江临安区於潜镇）人，俗姓徐。十岁出家，十八岁学于天竺慈云师，二十五岁赐紫衣及辩才号，后退居龙井寿圣院。
6. 文字禅：用诗文阐发的禅理。

Aisin-Gioro Hongli

(1711—1799) is the personal name of Qing Dynasty's Gaozong (his temple name) Emperor. Qianlong is his era name. During his reign (1735—1796), the social economy reached its peak (booming and golden age of Qing Dynasty from Kangxi to Qianlong emperors) and the unification of the multi-ethnic country was further completed. He advocated the compilation of the largest series of books *Complete Collection in Four Treasuries* in Chinese history. It is said that he composed over 40,000 poems in his lifetime. *The Collection of Poems by Qianlong* lists 194 of his poems.

Cooking Tea by the Dragon Well

New tea of the Dragon Well Village is brewed with local spring water,
Which really has its own unique flavor.
The new leaves less than an inch grow on the rock hump,
And the finished tea product is baked before Guyu solar term.
Why do I need to boast that Fengtuan is royal tea?
This bird tongue shaped leaf bud is the best for me.
I ask Monk Biancai to come out soon;
He is laughing at me that I still use poems to express Zen.

　　此诗是乾隆皇帝南巡到杭州时所作。乾隆帝虽然是一代帝王，但在清代诸帝中，其文人情趣是最浓重的。其中，对于龙井茶的喜爱，更是无以复加，龙井茶也因其钟爱而成为皇家贡品，享誉全国，杭州至今流传着他御封十八棵龙井茶树的故事。诗人在首联、颔联和颈联中对龙井茶不惜笔墨进行称赞，在尾联中，诗人将茶与禅意相连，从形而下的饮品提升到了形而上的禅思，充分体现了"禅茶一味"的雅趣与内涵。

Comments and Tips

This poem was composed when Emperor Qianlong was going on his southern inspection tour to Hangzhou. As a monarch, he showed more literati interest than any other Qing emperors. For instance, his love for Longjing tea was beyond compare. As a result, Longjing tea became exclusive to royalty and has enjoyed a nationwide fame ever since. The story of how the 18 tea trees of Longjing won their imperial acclaim is still circulating in Hangzhou. The poet spared no effort to praise the Longjing tea in the first three couplets. The last couplet introduces the connection between tea and Zen: The physical drink is promoted to the metaphysical Zen meditation, which fully reveals the elegance and connotation of "the identical taste of Zen and tea".

袁　枚

（1716—1798），字子才，号简斋，晚号随园老人，钱塘人。乾隆四年（1739）进士。曾任溧水、江宁等县知县，有政绩。四十岁即告归，在江宁小仓山下筑园名"随园"，吟咏其中。论诗主"性灵说"，古文骈体亦自成一格。有《小仓山房集》《随园诗话》《子不语》等。

谒岳王墓

江山也要伟人扶，　神化丹青即画图。
赖有岳于双少保[1]，人间才觉重西湖。

【注释】

1. 岳于：即南宋的岳飞和明代的于谦。少保：高级官衔的一种，为太保的副职。但一般不拥有实权，而是一种荣誉虚衔，作为恩赐给予功臣或重臣。

【阅读提示】

　　此诗是作者拜谒岳飞墓祠时有感而作，全诗语句流畅，浑然一体，气势雄浑。通过简洁明了的诗句，一种对英雄的崇敬之感跃然纸上。特别是最后两句，以一种较为隐晦的对比，将英雄人物对西湖精神塑造的重要性凸显了出来。西子湖本来在人们看来是个温柔乡，犹如美女一般柔媚，但正是因为在西子湖畔长眠着像岳飞和于谦这样浩气长存的英烈忠良，使得西湖，乃至整个杭州为之变换气质，于柔媚中增添了一份义胆忠肝与铮铮铁骨，令人怀想，催人振奋。

Yuan Mei

(1716—1798) was a native of Qiantang. He was a Jinshi in the fourth year of Qianlong Period (1739). Yuan made considerable achievements serving as the head magistrate in counties such as Lishui and Jiangning. However, he retreated in his forties to build Suiyuan Garden at the foot of Xiaocangshan Hill in Jiangning, where he wrote and chanted. He stressed the importance of one's true self revealed in poetry and his works of prose had a unique style of his own. There exist *Collection of Xiaocangshanfang* (his study), *Suiyuanshihua* (poetry talks in Suiyuan Garden) and *Zibuyu* (ghost stories censored by Confucius).

Paying Homage to Yue Fei's Tomb

Mountains and rivers shall also be graced by great men;
When the colours of red and green are spiritualized, a picture is produced then.
It is because of the two heroes buried here
That the West Lake is more admired by the people under heaven.

Comments and Tips

This poem was written upon the poet's visit to the shrine of Yue Fei. The natural flow of his language results in consistence and forcefulness. The brief and explicit lines vividly reveal his reverence for the heroes. The last couplet, in particular, presents the significance of the heroic characters to the shaping of the spirit of the West Lake with a rather subtle contrast: the West Lake was generally seen as a place of sweet romance which is as tender and charming as a lovely woman. But the existence of the martyr souls like Yue Fei and Yu Qian on the lake shores has altered its temperament so that the West Lake, and even Hangzhou, has righteousness, loyalty and fortitude added to the original softness, which is thought-provoking and inspiring.

黄景仁

（1749—1783），字仲则，号鹿菲子，武进（今江苏常州）人，清中叶诗人。清高宗乾隆东巡，召试，中二等。曾谋为县丞，未补官而卒。他富有才情，诗学唐人，尤重李白，但能兼容众家之长。有《两当轩集》。

吴山写望

云蒸海气欲浮城，　雨过江天旷望清。

踏浪人归歌缓缓，　回帆风定鼓声声。

湖头前后英灵在，　浙水东西王气平。

回首西湖真一掬[1]，几番花月送人行。

【注释】

1. 一掬：两手捧物的动作，亦表示数量少。

Huang Jingren

(1749—1783) was a native of Wujin (now Changzhou, Jiangsu Province) and a poet of Mid-Qing Dynasty. He was summoned to take an exam during Emperor Qianlong's eastern inspection tour, and won the second grade. He once sought to become a county executive, but died before he could fill the post. He was considerably talented and learned from the Tang poets, especially Li Bai, but was able to integrate the merits of various literary schools. There exists *Collection of Liangdangxuan* (the name of his study).

Climbing Wu Hill and Looking Far away

The river is foggy, and the city seems to be floating in the clouds.

After the heavy rain, the river and the sky look vast and clear.

The wave-treaders in the river slowly return with singing;

The ship arriving at the wharf stows its sails in the drums' sound you can

hear.

There are heroes buried on the shore of the West Lake;

Both sides of Qiantang River are ushering in auspicious atmosphere.

Looking back, the West Lake is like a handful of clear water;

And how many rounds of flowers and moons sending people away are

there?

　　全诗是作者站在吴山之巅，俯瞰钱塘江与西湖而作。诗歌充满着一种苍茫辽阔之感，诗人在首联和颔联中，生动描绘了雨后钱塘江面水天一色、壮阔苍茫的景象，伴随着踏浪人归来的缓缓歌声与归帆到岸的阵阵鼓声，似乎通过这江水，将诗人的思绪流向了历史的纵深。在颈联中，诗人历数曾经在钱塘江和西子湖畔建功立业的英杰们，他们连同他们的功业，现在何处？同时将视线从钱塘江转移到了西子湖，通过将辽阔苍茫的钱塘江与西子湖作对比，更显西子湖"一掬"之小，从而联想到了万古时空与一己人生的对比，真是"几番花月送人行"。在尾联中，诗人对人生的短暂和渺小发出慨叹，呼应前文，深化诗旨，从景物描写上升到历史怀想，最终升华到人生感悟，情景交融，步步深化，发人深省。

《西湖画舫》明　程嘉燧　台北故宫博物院藏

The Decorated Boat on the West Lake, Cheng Jiasui, Ming Dynasty,

Taipei Palace Museum

Comments and Tips

This poem was composed when the poet was standing on the top of Wu Hill overlooking Qiantang River and the West Lake. The first two couplets vividly depict the magnificent scene of the sky and water of the vast Qiantang River blending with each other after the rain, accompanied by the singing of wave-treaders going back home and the rolling drums of returning boats. In the third couplet, the poet's concern shifted from Qiantang River to the West Lake. The poet named the heroic souls of those who accomplished their careers on the shore of the West Lake: now where are those great men and their glorious deeds? In the last couplet, the poet lamented the insignificance of life, which echoes the previous text and enhances the theme of the poem. The description of scenery is sublimated to historical reminiscence and finally to perception of life.

阮　元

（1764—1849），字伯元，号芸台，江苏仪征人。乾隆五十四年（1789）进士，曾任浙江学政、浙江巡抚，官至体仁阁大学士，加太傅。谥"文达"。清嘉庆五年（1800）时任浙江巡抚的阮元主持疏浚西湖，以浚湖淤泥堆积成岛，故后人称之为"阮公墩"，今成"新西湖十景"之"阮墩环碧"。有《研经室集》。

秋日西湖泛舟

三面青山倚夕阳，桂花天气半温凉。
不须泊岸寻花去，湖上秋风镇日香[1]。

【注释】

1. 镇日：整天。

【阅读提示】

　　这首绝句写于嘉庆七年（1802），是阮元描写带着幕僚游西湖的诗篇。前两句描绘了杭州西湖的山水、天气；后两句采用因果关系倒置的修辞手法，言说既然在湖中船上就飘着桂花香，又何必泊舟登岸去寻找桂花呢。全诗用语轻巧，波澜不惊，意境平淡素雅，展现出从容自若、宁静惬意的风貌。

Ruan Yuan

(1764 – 1849) was a native of Yizheng, Jiangsu Province. He was a Jinshi in the 54th year (1789) of Qianlong Period. Ruan used to serve as the Superintendent of Education and then Governor of Zhejiang Province. He retired as the Grand Royal Secretary and was given a posthumous title of Wenda (learned and informative). When Ruan served as the Zhejiang Governor in the 5th year of Jiaqing Period (1800), he had the West Lake dredged, and the lake mud was piled up into an islet, which was known as Ruan Gong Dun (Master Ruan Gong Islet). One of the New Top Ten Scenes of the West Lake is "Ruan Gong Islet Submerged in Greenery". There exists *Collection of Yanjingshi* (the name of his study).

Boating on the West Lake in Autumn

The green hills surrounding the West Lake look particularly beautiful in
    the sunset;

It is the season of osmanthus and the weather is not warm nor cool, a
    feeling of delight.

There is no need to stop the boat and go ashore to look for osmanthus
    trees;

The fragrance is wafting in the autumn breeze on the lake day and night.

Comments and Tips

This poem was written in the 7th year of Jiaqing Period (1802) upon Ruan's visit to the West Lake with his counselors. The first couplet describes the scenery and weather of the West Lake of Hangzhou. The last two lines employ the inverted order of speech to show the cause-and-effect relationship: If you can smell the fragrance of osmanthus from the boat, why bother to disembark? The whole poem offers simple yet artful diction as well as an unperturbed, plain and elegant tone, showing a relaxed, peaceful and agreeable style.

林则徐

（1785—1850），字元抚，一字少穆，侯官（今福建福州）人。嘉庆十六年（1811）进士，曾任湖广总督，作为钦差大臣赴广东查禁销毁鸦片。第一次鸦片战争后被腐败的清政府革职，遣戍伊犁。他是晚清关心国计民生的政治家、思想家和诗人。有《林文忠公政书》《云左山房诗文钞》等。

六和塔 [1]

浮屠矗立俯江流 [2]，暮色苍茫四望收。
落日背人沉野树， 晚潮催月上沙洲。
千家灯闪城南市， 数点帆归海外舟。
莫讶山僧苦留客， 有情江水也回头。

【注释】

1. 题目为编者所加。该诗原题《春暮偕许玉年（乃穀）、张仲甫（应昌）诸君游理安寺、烟霞洞、虎跑泉、六和塔诸胜，每处各系一诗》，共七律四首，此为其四。
2. 浮屠：佛教语，梵语"Buddha"的音译，指佛塔。此指六和塔。江流：指钱塘江。

Lin Zexu

(1785—1850) was a native of Houguan (now Fuzhou, Fujian Province). He was a Jinshi in the 16th year of Jiaqing Period (1811). He served as the Governor-General of Hunan and Hubei and went to Guangdong as the Imperial Commissioner to eliminate the opium trade and destroy opium. After the First Opium War, he was dismissed by the corrupt Qing government and exiled to Ili (located in the northwestern border of the present-day Xinjiang Uygur Autonomous Region). He was a statesman, thinker and poet who was concerned with the national economy and people's livelihood in the late Qing Dynasty. There exist *Political Writings by Lin Wenzhong Gong* (his posthumous title) and *Collected Verse and Prose of Yunzuoshanfang* (the name of his study).

Six Harmonies Pagoda

The pagoda standing on the river bank overlooks Qiantang River;
The scenery in all directions is in sight and the twilight is pale and
　　whopping.
The sunset seems to be hiding behind the wild woods;
The evening tide is coming, urging the moon to rise on the sandbar,
　　shining.
Where thousands of lights are lit, there is a temple in the south of the city.
The sails are dotted on the river, which are the fishing boats from the sea
　　returning.
Don't be surprised that the monks want to keep me for a stay,
And the river will flow backwards as long as it has love, the true feeling.

【 阅读提示 】

　　此诗作于 1841 年暮春，作者在巡视钱塘江防务时曾游览六和塔。首联写六和塔高耸矗立，俯视钱塘江，诗人在暮色苍茫中登上六和塔，举目四望，无限风光尽收眼底的情形。起势不凡，境界开阔。中间两联写即目所见，远山夕阳在不知不觉间落入荒野古树林里，钱塘江潮水一浪紧似一浪冲上江边的沙洲，仿佛催促月亮快快升起。城南的集市里，无数灯火闪耀；钱塘江上，从遥远的海上晚归的帆船，星星点点，构成一幅动人画卷。尾联由景及人，极富情味；末句"有情江水也回头"，是指六和塔下的钱塘江蜿蜒曲折呈"之"字状，似有不忍远离的情态，描摹惟妙惟肖。全诗写得大气磅礴，情景交融，给人无限遐想。

《禹航胜迹图》册（十八之十六《六和塔》）清　佚名　杭州西湖博物馆藏

The Six Harmonies Pagoda in the album of *Spots Traversed by the Great Yu*, Anonymous, Qing Dynasty,
West Lake Museum of Hangzhou

Comments and Tips

This poem was written in the late spring of 1841 when the poet visited the Six Harmonies Pagoda during his inspection of the defense of Qiantang River. The first couplet describes how the pagoda stands tall and upright, overlooking the river. Such extraordinary opening lines reveal a broadened horizon. The following two couplets are about the appealing picture in the poet's view. The last couplet shifts its concern from the scenery to the people, and is rich in emotion. A vivid description is found in the ending line, which refers to Qiantang River zigzagging beneath the Six Harmonies Pagoda, as if reluctant to leave. The whole poem presents a majestic atmosphere and is quite absorbing with a blend of scenes and emotions.

龚自珍

（1792—1841），字璱人，号定盦（ān），浙江仁和人。道光九年（1829）进士，授内阁中书，官礼部主事。博学负才气，是近代改良主义运动的先驱。诗文均自成一家，以奇才名天下。有《定盦全集》。

湘月·甲戌春泛舟西湖赋此

湖云如梦，记前年此地，垂杨系马。

一抹春山螺子黛，对我轻颦姚冶[1]。

苏小魂香[2]，钱王气短[3]，俊笔连朝写。

乡邦如此，几人名姓传者。

平生沈俊如侬[4]，前贤倘作，有臂和谁把。

问取山灵浑不语，且自徘徊其下。

幽草黏天，绿荫送客，冉冉将初夏。

流光容易，暂时著意潇洒[5]。

【注释】

1. 姚冶：妖艳。
2. 苏小：即苏小小。
3. 钱王：即钱镠，吴越国开国国君。
4. 沈俊：即沉俊，埋没的俊才。
5. 著意：留意，注意。

Gong Zizhen

(1792—1841) was a native of Renhe, Zhejiang Province. He was a Jinshi in the 9th year of Daoguang Period (1829). Gong served as a secretary of the Cabinet and later a chief official of the Ministry of Rites. Learned and talented, he was a pioneer of China's early modern reform movement. He was accomplished in both verse and prose and was known for his unusual gift. He is the author of *Complete Works of Ding'an* (his art name).

Xiangyue: Boating on the West Lake in Spring

I remember tying horse under the weeping poplar here the year before last,

And over the West Lake was dreamlike the cloud.

The green and black spring hill gestured to me

Like the eyebrows on a beauty's forehead slightly furrowed.

Su Xiao's soul exuded fragrance,

While the kingdom of Qian's family had not lasted long;

And history has always been written this way.

My hometown is like this.

How many people have left their names since ancient day?

You are so deep and handsome in my eyes.

If you are a senior,

How can I put my arms around you with my love feeling?

When I go to ask the mountain god,

But he doesn't answer,

And I am just lingering.

Early summer is approaching.

The deep grassland is connected to the sky;

In the shade of the dense green trees I reluctantly bid farewell.

Years are rushing by,

And I am temporarily pretending to be well.

《西湖泛月图》清　宋葆淳　天津博物馆藏

Boating on the West Lake in the Moonlight, Song Baochun, Qing Dynasty, Tianjin Museum

【阅读提示】

　　这首词作于嘉庆十九年（1814）。此前两年，龚自珍曾同妻子段美贞至杭州，泛舟西湖，写下另一首《湘月·天风吹我》词。此词采用相同词牌，显系续作。但作者心境已迥然不同，癸酉（1813）七月，段美贞离世。甲戌（1814）三月，龚氏携其妻灵柩归杭，物是人非，自然情绪低沉。词的上阕有无限凄凉之感，一句"湖山如梦"，为全词奠定了伤感的基调。虽然湖山如故，妖冶明艳，但自己科场失意，妻子逝去，已经无心欣赏了。在乡邦名人中，苏小小仅因艳质丽骨令后人咏叹；钱镠又是志气狭短，故而龚氏发出了"几人名姓传者"之喟叹。下阕亦是抒写孤独和伤悯之情。作者虽有才情如许，但科场无名，沉俊下僚。孤独本是龚自珍固有的人生体会，这首词更因妻子逝去，而强化了痛楚。如今，谁还能和自己把臂言欢，入林赏景呢？"冉冉物华休"，作者只能发出"暂时著意潇洒"这一对身世的感叹。全词情感细腻，意象和情感水乳交融，在伤感、孤独中有着对人生的憧憬。

Comments and Tips

Xiangyue (The Moon on Xiangjiang River): a pattern of ci poetry. This ci poem was written in the 19th year of Jiaqing Period (1814), obviously a sequel to one also entitled "Xiangyue" (the first line being "Driven by the Celestial Wind"), which was composed two years ago when Gong visited Hangzhou and boated on the West Lake with his wife Duan Meizhen. However, the poet reveals a very different state of mind here. The first half of this ci poem reveals a sense of infinite desolation. The second half is also about loneliness and sadness. Loneliness is an inherent experience of Gong Zizhen's life, and this ci poem reveals his pain intensified by the death of his wife. Now who could share merry talks and lovely woods with him? The poet could only sigh for his sorrowful life The whole ci poem reveals delicate sentiments with a blend of images and emotions, yet a longing for life is to be found in sadness and loneliness.

俞　樾

（1821—1907），字荫甫，号曲园，浙江德清人。道光三十年（1850）进士，曾任河南学政，未几罢归。主讲苏州紫阳、上海求志等书院和杭州诂经精舍。清末学者、文学家、经学家、古文字学家，章太炎、吴昌硕等皆出其门下。所著多达五百余卷，编为《春在堂全书》。

水龙吟

卅年抛却渔杆，浮生惯欠烟波债。

虚名误我，莼鲈秋味¹，鸡豚春社²。

旌节辎轩³，旂常钟鼎⁴，到今都罢。

向沙堤十里，芒鞋布袜⁵，渔樵辈、同闲话。

Yu Yue

(1821—1907) was a native of Deqing, Zhejiang Province. He was a Jinshi in the 30th year of Daoguang Period (1850). Yu used to serve as the Superintendent of Education in Henan Province, but was dismissed socn. As a distinguished scholar and expert in literature, Confucian classics and paleography, he taught in academies of Suzhou, Shanghai and Hangzhou and wrote prolifically. Zhang Taiyan and Wu Changshuo were among his best known d.sciples. His works are as many as over 500 volumes, composed as *Complete Works of Chunzaitang* (the name of his study).

Shuilongyin

For thirty years without fishing rod,

I have owed countless debts to a life of mist and water.

For table delicacies from land and sea

And various banquets and parties,

I had been misled by vanity ever.

All those ceremonial grand occasions

Have gone forever.

Wearing straw sandals and carrying a fishing rod,

I walked on the sand bank

In the company of the angler.

潇洒。

西湖精舍。

谢东坡、头衔容借。

玉堂梦断，天教管领，湖山图画。

风月平章⁶，烟云供养，鸥鹭迎迓⁷。

问封侯万里，金章斗大⁸，是何人也。

【注释】

1. 莼鲈：《晋书·张翰传》："翰因见秋风起，乃思吴中菰菜、莼羹、鲈鱼脍，曰：'人生贵得适志，何能羁宦数千里以要名爵乎！'遂命驾而归。"后称思乡之情为"莼鲈之思"。
2. 鸡豚：鸡和猪。春社：古时于春耕前祭祀土神，以祈丰收，谓之"春社"。
3. 旌节：古代使者所持的节，以为凭信。辎轩：古代使臣乘坐的一种轻车。
4. 旗常：旗与常。旗画交龙，常画日月，是王侯的旗帜。钟鼎：钟和鼎。喻富贵荣华。
5. 芒鞋：用芒茎外皮编织成的鞋，亦泛指草鞋。
6. 风月平章：指品评美好的景色。
7. 迎迓：迎接。
8. 金章：金质的官印。一说即铜印，因以指代官宦仕途。

【阅读提示】

　　这首词是为了回应作者被封为"西湖长"而作。作者当然觉得自己不配拥有这个头衔，但他对自己是西湖诂经精舍山长感到欣慰和高兴。在词的前半首，"莼鲈秋味"和"芒鞋布袜"表达了他对自由和简单生活的渴望。词的后半首以无拘无束的生活理念开始。它暗借苏东坡作为"西湖长"的典故，虽然仕途受挫，还是以做大自然的伴侣为乐。这首词让我们想起了苏东坡关于"草鞋"的诗句。诗人一定是在欣赏这种生活方式，字里行间不加修饰，却充满了生活中的乐趣。

It's a dashing feeling.

By the West Lake there is an exquisite cottage for worshipping.

I really have to thank Su Dongpo

For the title of West Lake Chief borrowing.

The ideal of serving the court has been shattered,

And Heaven asked me to take charge of this natural landscape painting.

Tasting the wind and the moon

And fed by clouds and mists,

There are gulls and herons greeting.

Even if he is a marquis with a big golden seal,

To me, that means nothing!

Comments and Tips

Shuilongyin (Water Dragon Chant): a pattern of ci poetry. This ci poem was composed in response to a seal given to the author as "West Lake Chief". Although Yu certainly felt that he did not deserve this title, he took comfort and amusement for being the head of Gujingjingshe (Academy of Confucius Classics) of the West Lake. In the first half of the poem, "table delicacies from land and sea" and "straw sandals" express his longing for a life of freedom and simplicity. The second half of the ci begins with the ideal of unrestrained life. It alludes to the story of Su Dongpo as "West Lake Chief". Though he was frustrated in his official career, he took comfort in being a companion of nature. The ci reminds us of Su's poem regarding "straw sandals". The poet must admire this lifestyle; because in this poem the words are unadorned and yet filled with many delights in life.

《南屏晚钟》

Evening Bell Ringing from Nanping Hill

近 代

One Hundred Poems
on the West Lake in Hangzhou
Through the Ages

Modern Times
(1840–1919)

康有为

（1858—1927），字广厦，号长素，南海（今属广东佛山）人，人称"南海先生"。近代重要的政治家、思想家、教育家，资产阶级改良主义的代表人物。光绪二十一年（1895）进士。上书光绪帝，建议变法。光绪二十四年（1898），得光绪帝召见，促成"百日维新"。戊戌变法失败后逃亡日本。作为保皇党领袖，他反对孙中山的民主革命。有《新学伪经考》《康南海先生诗集》等。

闻意索三门湾以兵轮三艘迫浙江有感 [1]

凄凉白马市中箫 [2]，梦入西湖数六桥 [3]。
绝好江山谁看取 [4]？涛声怒断浙江潮 [5]。

【注释】

1. 意：指意大利。三门湾：为我国重要的港湾，位于浙江宁海东面的象山半岛南端。兵轮三艘迫浙江：指光绪二十五年（1899），意六利以武力威胁强租三门湾之事。
2. 白马：指伍子胥。《录异记》载：春秋时，大夫伍子胥助吴伐越，屡建功勋。后多次劝谏吴王夫差拒绝越国求和并停止攻伐齐国，吴王不听，反信谗言，命其自杀。越国灭吴后，曾在苏州东南的三江口设坛杀白马祭祀伍子胥。后又在此立白马庙。市中箫：《史记·范雎蔡泽列传》载，伍子胥原为楚国人，为报楚王杀父之仇，逃亡吴国。初至吴时，伍子胥鼓腹吹箫，乞食吴市。
3. 六桥：即杭州西湖苏堤上的映波、锁澜、望山、压堤、东浦、跨虹六桥。
4. 谁看取：谁守护的意思。取，语助词。
5. 怒断：怒极、怒煞。浙江潮：即钱塘江潮。

Kang Youwei

(1858—1927) was a native of Nanhai, (now in Foshan, Guangdong Province), and hence was known as Master Nanhai. He was a prominent early modern politician, thinker, educator, and a representative of bourgeois reformism. Kang was a Jinshi in the 21st year of Guangxu Period (1895). He submitted a written statement to Emperor Guangxu and suggested constitutional reform. In 1898, he was summoned by the emperor and precipitated the "Hundred Days' Reform", which failed soon and he managed to flee to Japan. As a leader of the royalists, Kang consistently opposed Sun Yat-sen's democratic revolution. There exist *A Study of the False Traditional Chinese Classics and Collected Poems of Master Kang Nanhai*.

Heard that Italy Used Warships to Claim Sanmen Bay

When Wu Zixu fled Wu Kingdom, he played flute in street for food;
Now I walk across the six bridges on Su Causeway dreamily.
Who cares about the survival or perish of our great motherland?
And there is only ever rising tides of Qiantang River, furiously.

　　这首诗写于 1899 年。清光绪二十四年（1898），戊戌维新变法失败后，康有为在英国人的保护下逃至香港，转往日本。次年（1899）夏历正月，意大利命驻京公使玛尔士诺向清政府提出租借三门湾的无理要求，并把军舰开进浙江。康有为在日本得知这一消息，忧愤异常，写诗抒发了自己对时局的关切之情。此诗首句借用伍子胥的典故来喻己抒怀；二句通过记梦，表达诗人对祖国的眷恋；三、四两句，用自问自答的句式，向清朝统治者发出了讽劝。诗中暗喻国事沦丧，心忧祖国，苦于无力施展抱负，咏此以寄其一腔忠愤，表达对祖国的思念和对时局的关切。全诗用典贴切自然、苍凉悲壮，落句以景结情，诗人结合叙事来抒发情感，写得至深、至透、至痛，愤愤然大有立足千钧之势，令人感愤不已。

Comments and Tips

This poem was written in 1899. After the failure of the Reform in 1898, Kang Youwei fled to Hong Kong under the protection of the British and then went to Japan. In February 1899, upon the order of the Italian government, its ambassador Renato De Martino in Beijing raised excessive demands on the Qing government for the lease of Sanmen Bay and brought warships into Zhejiang. When Kang Youwei learned about the news in Japan, he was worried and indignant and wrote this poem to express his concern about the current situation. The first line of the poem employs an allusion to Wu Zixu to express the poet's own feelings. The second line reveals the poet's sentimental attachment to his homeland by the view of walking "on Su Causeway dreamily". The following lines send an allegorical advice to the ruler of Qing Dynasty with a rhetorical question. The poem alludes to the decline of the empire. All he could do was contribute this verse to express his loyalty and indignation as well as his concern about the current situation and how he missed his country.

朱祖谋

（1857—1931），原名孝臧，字古微，号彊村，归安（今浙江湖州）人。光绪九年（1883）进士，官至礼部右侍郎，因病假归作上海寓公。工倚声，为"清季四大词人"之一，著作丰富，有《彊村词》。

采桑子（五首其二）

三潭月上西湖好，载酒来过。
髡柳无多[1]。
奈此彭郎白发何[2]。

凭阑才觉秋香重，万笠风荷。
万点秋螺。
浩翠如潮赴镜窠。

【注释】

1. 髡（kūn）柳：剪削枝条后的柳树，柳枝短而不下垂，画家常用来画作秋末或春初的柳树形象。
2. 彭郎：原指江西彭泽县南岸有澎浪矶，此处指湘军将领彭玉麟。

Zhu Zumou

(1857—1931) was a native of Guian (now Huzhou, Zhejiang Province). He was a Jinshi in the 9th year of Guangxu Period (1883). Zhu asked for sick leave from his last post of Vice Minister of the Ministry of Rites and retreated to Shanghai. As one of the four grandest ci poets of late Qing Dynasty, he was skilled in writing ci poems to a specific pattern. Zhu was a prolific writer. There exists *Ci Poems of Jiangcun* (his art name).

Caisangzi (the Second of Five)

The most beautiful view of the West Lake

Is the bright moon rising over the three pools.

I come here with wine by a boat,

Looking at sparse the willow branches,

Like the gray hair on the head of General Peng.

It is only when you climb the island

That you feel the strong fragrance of osmanthus.

Lotus leaves swing like hats in the wind;

The hills by the lake look like a group of snails;

Or like boundless greenery tide flows into the lake's center.

此词应作于 1906 年，时年朱祖谋年五十，居于苏州、上海，这一年曾至杭州西湖游览。其模仿欧阳修颍州西湖《采桑子》十首，创作了一组《采桑子》西湖词，序言："湖上逭暑，日课小词。仿六一。"此词为第二首。词意亦仿欧阳修。上阕以"西湖好"总领，描写丝丝细柳，疏朗如画。述及彭郎之事（彭郎，此似指晚清名臣、湘军将领彭玉麟。彭玉麟晚年隐居在三潭印月东北的退省庵）。下阕写词人凭栏远望，秋香阵阵，万顷风荷，如万点碧螺，在波平如镜的西湖中荡漾，作者已完全沉醉于大自然的美景之中。诚如《尊瓠室诗话》记诗人之言云："予暮春尝宿退省庵中，时当夕阳欲下，徙倚门前，峰峦环互，苍翠扑人如雨，洵异景也。"全词用语轻灵，情感氤氲，含味醇厚，与欧阳修原词相较有过之而无不及。

《苏堤消夏图》清 朱偁 旅顺博物馆藏

Taking a Summer Holiday on Su Causeway,
Zhu Cheng, Qing Dynasty, Lüshun Museum

Comments and Tips

Caisangzi (Song of Picking Mulberries): a pattern of ci poetry. This ci poem is allegedly written in 1906. Residing in Suzhou and Shanghai, Zhu visited the West Lake of Hangzhou in that year and composed a set of ci poems about the West Lake entitled "Caisangzi", imitating Ouyang Xiu's ten pieces of Caisangzi about the West Lake in Yingzhou. This ci poem is the second piece of Zhu's set. The first half of this ci poem is introduced by the "beautiful view of the West Lake". The term "Peng Lang" in this ci poem seems to refer to Peng Yulin, a famous official of late Qing Dynasty and a general of the Xiang army. In his later years, Peng retreated to Hangzhou and lived a reclusive life by northeastern of "The Moon Printed in Three Pools". The latter half depicts how the poet leaned upon the balustrade and looked far away. The poet could not but be completely absorbed in the beauty of nature.

况周颐

（1859—1926），字夔笙，号蕙风，临桂（今广西桂林）人。光绪五年（1879）举人，授内阁中书，充会典馆纂修。后为两江总督张之洞、端方幕客。精词学，为"清季四大词人"之一。有《蕙风词》《蕙风词话》等。

隔浦莲近·杭州人来言湖上荷花盛开为占此调依梦窗体

蘅皋不度佩响[1]。

飞梦成来往。

画里楼台换，迷金碧、千波晃。

鸥鹭知怅惘。

天机锦[2]，未了云霞想。

影娥上[3]。

含情怕问，玉容别久无恙。

夕阳芳草，误了红衣双桨。

香色年年送去浪。

休忘。

踏摇归路妍唱[4]。

【注释】

1. 蘅皋：长有香草的沼泽。
2. 天机锦：《月令广义·七月令》引南朝梁殷芸《小说》："天河之东有织女，天帝之子也。年年机杼劳役，织成云锦天衣。"
3. 影娥：汉代未央宫中池名。《三辅黄图·未央宫》："影娥池，武帝凿以玩月。其旁起望鹄台，以眺月影入池中，亦曰眺蟾台。"
4. 踏摇：唐崔令钦《教坊记》："以其且步且歌，谓之踏摇。"妍唱：谓美妙的歌词、曲调。

Kuang Zhouyi

(1859—1926) was a native of Lingui (now Guilin, Guangxi Province). He was a Juren in the 5th year of Guangxu Period (1879). He served as a Cabinet Secretory and Editor of Political Records. When he resigned, Kuang was invited as a staff member by Zhang Zhidong and then Duanfang, who served in turn as the Governor of Liangjiang (Jiangsu, Jiangxi and Anhui Provinces). As an expert in the study of ci poems, Kuang was one of the four greatest masters of ci poetry of late Qing Dynasty. There exist *Ci Poems by Huifeng* (his art name) and *Notes on Ci Poems by Huifeng*.

Gepulianjin: The Lotus Flowers on the West Lake in Full Bloom

The fragrant herbs in a pool can't play jingling sound of jade pendant,

So I can only pursue it in my dream brilliant.

The platform in a picture varies,

But lotuses in the lake

Are still in blue waves rippling elegant.

Gulls and herons are also in a state of confusion.

The brocade woven by fairies

Evokes endless wonderful reveries.

Viewing the moon high above in the sky;

I am full of feelings but dare not ask,

Is your appearance still delicate after a long goodbye?

Here is the grassland in sunset;

No chance for me to enjoy lotus flowers in lake boating.

The beauty and fragrance of lotuses are so year after year.

Don't forget

To return all the way, stepping and singing.

【阅读提示】

　　此词创作于民国四年（1915）。《况周颐词编年》载：是年夏，闻杭州人言西湖荷花盛开，依吴文英词韵作《隔浦莲近》（蘅皋不度佩响）。此词调依梦窗（吴文英）体，风格亦有所相似。只是吴文英词言榴花，此词言荷花。况周颐此词意象密集，引人遐想。上阕言荷花盛开，浓烈如画，如天机织锦，绚烂如七宝楼台。下阕则有相思之情，由景而及人，美妙的音声浮荡在一片碧波之中，给人以无限的想象空间。后人评其二十岁前，词作主"性灵""好为侧艳语""固无所谓感事"（赵尊岳《蕙风词史》），此词虽为后期所作，但仍有作者前期创作的风致，既有对吴文英词作的色彩与意象的模仿，又有超脱洗练之处，拂叶披花，清致可掬。

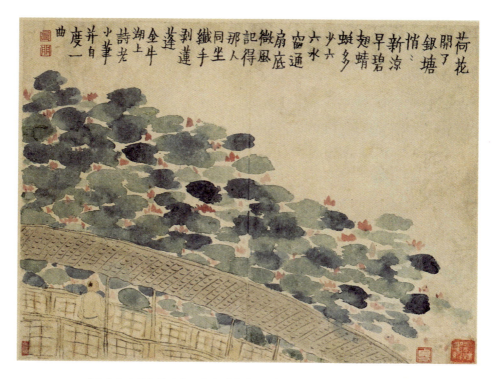

《人物山水图》册（十二之十《荷花开了》）清　金农　上海博物馆藏

Lotus Blossoms in the album of *Landscapes and Figures*, Jin Nong, Qing Dynasty, Shanghai Museum

Comments and Tips

Gepulianjin (Song of Lotus in the Water of Other Side): a pattern of ci poetry. This ci poem was composed in the fourth year of the Republic of China (1915). According to *The Chronicle of Kuang Zhouyi's Ci Poetry*, in the summer of that year, he heard from natives of Hangzhou that the lotuses in the West Lake were in full bloom, and then composed this "Gepulianjin" according to the tune pattern of Wu Wenying's ci poem. This ci poem offers dense images and stimulates reveries. The first half describes lotus blossoms in full bloom, whose rich colour is as intense as a painting, a piece of heavenly brocade, and is as splendid as a tall building decorated with all precious jewels. The second half extends from natural views to emotions and reveals how the poet missed his love. Although this is a late composition, it still reveals the style of Kuang's earlier works. It is an imitation of the colours and imagery of Wu Wenying's ci poem, but also shows a unique transcendent and refined feature.

章太炎

（1869—1936），浙江余杭人。初名学乘，字枚叔（以纪念汉代辞赋家枚乘），后易名为炳麟，号太炎。世人常称之为"太炎先生"。后自认"民国遗民"。清末民初民主革命家、思想家、学者、朴学大师，研究范围涉及小学、历史、哲学、政治、朴学等。死后葬于杭州西湖南岸，现建有章太炎纪念馆，与张苍水先生祠相邻。章太炎著述甚丰，有《章太炎全集》。

归杭州

故园时一至，　妻子又携将。

为有西山爽，　而宜首夏凉[1]。

明湖澹云月[2]，垺郭下牛羊[3]。

旦晚胡箈动，　莼羹不易尝[4]。

【注释】

1. 首夏：初夏，多为农历四月。
2. 明湖：明圣湖，即西湖。
3. 垺郭：破败的城市。下牛羊：牛羊回家。《诗·王风·君子于役》："日之夕矣，牛羊下来。"
4. 莼羹：又名"莼菜羹"，杭州名菜，以莼菜叶为之，食之淡雅。

Zhang Taiyan

(1869—1936) was a native of Yuhang, Zhejiang Province, who was commonly known as Master Taiyan. He later identified himself as a "descendant of the Republic of China". Zhang was a democratic revolutionary, a thinker, a famous scholar and a master of philologist in the late Qing Dynasty and early Republic of China. He was buried on the south shore of the West Lake in Hangzhou, where Zhang Taiyan Memorial Hall has been built, adjacent to the Shrine of Zhang Cangshui. There exists *Complete Works of Zhang Taiyan*.

Back to Hangzhou

Sometimes I make occasional trips to my hometown,

And this time I take my wife with me to pay a call on.

In order to feel the refreshing air of west hills area,

It is just the right season in the early summer.

The lake is wonderful with a clear moon and light clouds;

Returning to the decaying city are the sheep and cows.

Heard from morning till night are sad military songs,

How can I have the mood to taste brasenia soup delicious?

据《申报》记述，1923 年 5 月 2 日，章太炎乘"早车赴杭，游览西湖"，"曾在第一中学讲学两日，及于省教育会开五四纪念会时演讲一次"，于 8 日"乘车返沪"。这首诗即当时所作。首联点明主题，章为杭州余杭人，此次杭州之行也即携妻归故乡。中间两联写景，游西山之爽，是因初夏时节，杭州还未到炎热时候。西湖之美妙又与破败的城市形成鲜明的对比。尾联忽然跳开，切入国事与战乱，就连美味的莼羹也没有心情去品尝。全诗层次井然，在最后达到高潮，表达了章太炎先生时刻不忘国家的胸怀。

《篆书七言联》近代　章太炎

Seven-Character Couplet in Seal Script,
Modern Times, Zhang Taiyan

Comments and Tips

According to *Shun Pao* (a. k. a. Shanghai News), Zhang Taiyan took "an early train to Hangzhou and visited the West Lake" on May 2, 1923. He "lectured at the No. One Middle School for two days, and gave a speech at the May Fourth Memorial Meeting of the Provincial Education Association", and "returned to Shanghai by train" on the 8th. This poem was written at that time. The first couplet states the theme: as a native of Yuhang, Hangzhou, he was actually returning to his hometown with his wife to Hangzhou. The following two couplets describe the scenery. However, the charming beauty of the West Lake is in sharp contrast to the decaying city. The last couplet makes a surprising shift to national affairs and war turmoils, so that even the delicious brasenia soup was not appealing to the poet. The poem is well structured and reaches a climax at the end, revealing Zhang Taiyan's quality as a statesman who would always bear the country in his mind.

秋 瑾

（1875—1907），字璿卿，号竞雄，别署鉴湖女侠，浙江绍兴人，清末杰出的女革命家。1904 年赴日留学，次年加入孙中山领导的同盟会。回国后创办《中国女报》，鼓吹革命。1907 年与徐锡麟共谋起义，事泄被捕，1907 年 7 月慷慨就义。有《秋瑾集》。

题乐天词丈《春郊试马图》[1]

白苏堤柳绿丝丝，　正是词坛纵马时。

三月烟花千里梦，　半林风月一囊诗[2]。

元龙湖海增豪气[3]，庾信江关寄远思[4]。

可向此君堂畔过，　瓣香亲拜水仙祠[5]。

【注释】

1. 乐天：别号，清末诗人，生平事迹不详。词丈：对前辈诗人的尊称。

2. 一囊诗：《新唐书·李贺传》载：（李贺）"骑弱马，从小奚奴，背古锦囊，遇所得，书投囊中"。

3. 元龙：指东汉末年将领陈登。《三国志·魏书·吕布臧洪传》："陈登者，字元龙，在广陵有威名。又掎角吕布有功，加伏波将军，年三十九卒。"

4. 庾信：南北朝时期文学家，文藻绮艳。侯景陷建康，信奔江陵，奉使聘西魏，被留不返。入周，累迁骠骑大将军、开府仪同三司，世称"庾开府"。这句连上句是说壮美的山河给自己增添豪情壮志与思乡之情。

5. 瓣香：师承，敬仰。水仙祠：《西湖志纂》："水仙王庙本伍胥祠。胥浮尸江上，吴人称为水仙。见《越绝书》。宋时水仙祠在苏堤第四桥，名水仙王庙，后人误为水仙女神。"

Qiu Jin

(1875—1907) was a native of Shaoxing, Zhejiang Province. She was a distinguished revolutionist by the end of Qing Dynasty. In 1904, she went to Japan for further education, and next year joined the Tongmenghui (United League) of China led by Sun Yat-sen. After returning to China, she founded *China Women's News* and advocated a revolution. In 1907, she plotted an uprising with Xu Xilin, but the plan was divulged. As a result, she was arrested and executed in July of the same year. There exists *Collection of Qiu Jin*.

Inscribing for the Painting "Riding a Horse in the Outskirts in Spring"

The willow branches are green from Bai Causeway to Su Causeway,
And this is also the time when a poet is riding a horse on the way.
In mid-spring, warblers sing in flowers sea, taking you into dreams;
A clear wind and bright moon urge you to be poetically gay.
I want to be like an ancient hero with lofty ambition,
And also to be like a poet with his deep feeling ray.
Today, I ride a horse by the painter's pond,
To go in person to Wu Zixu's temple to pray.

【 阅读提示 】

　　这首诗写于 1904 年秋瑾从北京返回浙江途中，诗前原有一小序，交代写诗缘
由：“甲辰南归，适见南海乐天词丈有《春郊试马图》之咏，一时和作如林，无美
不备。自忘谫陋谨和二律，兴之所至，未能步原韵也。”最初发表于上海《时报》
1907 年 9 月 26 日的“投收”栏。诗的前两联叙写江南美景，初春三月，绿柳吐绿，
草长莺飞，正是驰骋情思、纵情吟咏之时，诗人对家乡的一种热爱之情油然而生。
面对此情此景，想象家国山河。第三联引入陈登和庾信，既可以给人增添豪俊之气，
又能触发思乡之情。最后呼应题旨。全诗层次井然，辞气俊爽，表现出即将摆脱封
建旧家庭的豪迈气概。

Comments and Tips

This poem was written in 1904 when Qiu Jin was on her way back to Zhejiang from Beijing. The first two couplets of the poem describe the beautiful scenery of Jiangnan, and reveal her love for the hometown. The third couplet involves Chen Deng (a military general and politician by the end of Han Dynasty) and Yu Xin (a poet, politician, and writer of Liang and Northern Zhou Dynasties) to offer a grand and heroic tone and a feeling of homesickness at the same time. The last couplet serves as a response to the title of this poem and its implication. The whole poem is well structured and the style is smart and candid, showing Qiu Jin's heroic boldness when she was about to get rid of her old feudal family.

《春游晚归图》明　戴进　台北故宫博物院藏

Spring Outing and Returning Late, Dai Jin, Ming Dynasty, Taipei Palace Museum

余至自西湖遇太史聞之
以舟相待要余黃寺廬
貞父將中夜話貞父寓
居靈隱山寺呂山人鍊
藥處

《纪游图》明　董其昌　台北故宫博物院藏

Painting as Travelogue Album, Dong Qichang, Ming Dynasty, Taipei Palace Museum

陈独秀

（1879—1942），字仲甫，号实庵，怀宁（今安徽安庆）人。中国共产党创始人和早期领导人之一，思想家、语言学家。早年留学日本，1915 年创办《新青年》杂志，1917 年任北京大学教授、文科学长。1918 年和李大钊创办《每周评论》，宣传马克思主义，是五四新文化运动主要领导人之一。1921 年 7 月在上海举行的中国共产党第一次全国代表大会上，被选为中央局书记。大革命后期思想右倾，1927 年被撤销总书记职务，1929 年被开除党籍。1942 年 5 月病逝。主要著作收入《独秀文存》。

游虎跑 [1]（二首其一）

昔闻祖塔院 [2]，幽绝浙江东。

山绕寺钟外， 人行松涧中。

清泉漱石齿， 树色暖碧空。

莫就枯禅饮， 阶前水不穷。

【注释】

1. 虎跑：杭州著名的旅游景点，位于杭州西湖区大慈山麓。相传元和十四年（819），高僧寰中与弟子云游至杭，居大慈山下，适逢天旱无水。夜梦神人告知："南岳有童子泉，当遣二虎驱来。"天明，果见二虎刨地做穴，须臾，清泉涌出，故名"虎跑泉"。遂依此作寺，寺名"定慧禅寺"，又称"虎跑寺"。
2. 祖塔院：宋太宗时，改定慧禅寺为"祖塔法云院"。

Chen Duxiu

(1879—1942) was a native of Huaining (now Anqing, Anhui Province). As a major leader of the May Fourth Movement, he was also a co-founder and early leader of the Communist Party of China (CPC) as well as a thinker and linguist. In 1915, he founded the magazine *New Youth*. In 1917, he was appointed as a professor and dean of liberal arts at Peking University and then he founded *Weekly Review* with Li Dazhao to advocate Marxism in 1918. Chen was elected General Secretary of the Central Bureau at the First National Congress of the CPC held in Shanghai in July 1921, but was removed from the post in 1927. He was expelled from the Party in 1929. Chen died of illness in May 1942. His major works can be found in *Collected Works of Chen Duxiu*.

Touring the Tiger Spring Temple (the First of Two)

Having heard the story of tiger spring for a long time.

It's really a quiet and extraordinary place you will stay.

Walking in the hills, you can hear the bells in distance;

And water trickling around pine forest all the way.

The clear spring rushes, washing the rocks in stream brightly;

The dense shade is full of vitality, to whom the blue sky will repay.

Don't rush to drink as soon as you sit down.

In front of stone steps the spring will run from day to day.

《西湖十景》（局部）清　王原祁　辽宁省博物馆

Ten Scenes of the West Lake (Partial), Wang Yuanqi, Qing Dynasty, Liaoning Provincial Museum

【阅读提示】

　　《游虎跑》原有两首，此为其一。此诗前三联写景，生动地描绘了虎跑清幽的环境。颈联"漱""暖"两字用得极妙，使山涧流淌的清泉和碧空下茂盛的树木都显得富有生命和活力。而尾联则富有禅意，令人联想到大诗人苏轼《病中游祖塔院》中"道人不惜阶前水，借与匏樽自在尝"之诗意。

Comments and Tips

This is the first of two poems entitled "Touring the Tiger Spring Temple". The first three couplets vividly depict the peaceful and secluded environment of the Tiger Spring Temple. The clever choice of verbs in the third couplet makes the clear spring and the trees under the blue sky seem so vital and lively. The final couplet offers a Zen-like connotation.

李叔同

（1880—1942），初名文涛，改名岸，又名广侯、成蹊，字惜霜，号叔同，浙江平湖人。曾留学日本，归国后任教浙江第一师范学校、两江师范学堂。1918年在杭州虎跑寺出家为僧，法名演音，号弘一。今杭州虎跑寺有弘一法师舍利塔。其人多才艺，编歌演剧、作画治印无所不擅。诗好作长短不齐之句，奇趣洋溢。词豪婉兼具。有《弘一法师文钞》。今人辑有《李叔同诗全编》。

玉连环影·为丏尊题小梅花屋图 [1]

屋老。

一树梅花小。

住个诗人，添个新诗料。

爱清闲。

爱天然。

城外西湖，湖上有青山。

【注释】

1. 丏尊：夏丏尊（1886—1946），名铸，字勉旃，后改字丏尊，号闷庵。浙江绍兴市上虞人。近代文学家、语文学家、出版家和翻译家。

Li Shutong

(1880—1942) was a native of Pinghu, Zhejiang Province. He studied in Japan and taught at Zhejiang Official Level-Two Normal School and Liangjiang Normal School after his return to China. In 1918, he was accepted by the Tiger Spring Temple in Hangzhou as a Buddhist monk and was known as Hongyi (his Buddhist name) since then. There is a relic pagoda of Master Hongyi in the Tiger Spring Temple in Hangzhou. He was multi-talented as an excellent song writer, stage actor, painter and seal cutter. He enjoyed composing poems of uneven lines that are curiously interesting. His ci poems are both spirited and graceful. There exists *Writings of Master Hongyi* and *The Complete Works of Poetry by Li Shutong*.

Yulianhuanying: Inscription for "Little Plum Blossom House" Painting

An old room.

A small tree of plum blossom.

There lives a poet in it,

Which adds new interest in writing poem.

He loves leisure,

And likes to be close to nature.

There is a lake outside the city,

And around the lake the green hills stand as guarder.

据《弘一大师年谱》一九一四年条引夏丏尊对此《玉连环影》的说明："民初余傔居杭城，庭有梅树一株，因名之曰'小梅花屋'。陈师曾君（诗人陈三立之子，著名美术家、艺术教育家）为作图，一时朋友多有题咏。图经变乱已遗失，此小词犹能记育，亟为录存于此。丏尊记。"知为文人雅集题咏之作。全词寥寥数句，不避口语，写实逼真，饶有情趣。

Comments and Tips

Yulianhuanying (Shadow of Jade Ring Chain): a pattern of ci poetry. Xia Mianzun once explained this poem: "I rent a house in Hangzhou in the early years of the Republic of China. There was a plum tree in my yard, so I named it 'Little Plum Blossom House'. Chen Shizeng (a famous artist and art educator, son of the poet Chen Sanli) painted a picture featuring the house, to which my friends eagerly offered their inscriptions and poems. The picture was lost after the years of turmoil, while this little poem remains on my mind, and it is urgent to record it here. Noted by Mianzun. " So we understand that this poem is a fine response to a cultivated practice of the genteel literati. The poem consists of few lines; the vernacular language employed here offers a vivid picture of real life and much fun.

苏曼殊

（1884—1918），名玄瑛，字子毂，后为僧，号曼殊，香山（今广东中山）人。留学日本，漫游南洋各地。能诗文，善绘画，曾任报刊编辑及学校教师。与章太炎、柳亚子等人交游，参加南社。诗悱恻芬芳，并翻译拜伦、雨果等人作品。有《苏曼殊全集》。

住西湖白云禅院作此

白云深处拥雷峰[1]，几树寒梅带雪红。
斋罢垂垂浑入定[2]，庵前潭影落疏钟。

【注释】

1. 雷峰：指雷峰塔，在杭州西湖南面的夕照山上。五代时吴越王钱俶所建，1924年倾塌。"雷峰夕照"为西湖十景之一。现今的雷峰塔系 2002 年重建。
2. 入定：佛教徒的一种修行方法，谓安心一处而不昏沉，了了分明而无杂念。

【阅读提示】

此诗写于 1905 年，当时苏曼殊住在西湖雷峰塔下的白云禅院。首两句描写西湖白云禅院的景色：白云悠悠，雷峰塔耸峙其间；几树寒梅，在白雪的映衬下显得格外红艳。一远一近，一高一低，将禅院的清旷幽寂点染得如诗如画。尾两句写斋定生活。疏钟潭影，融为一体，给人以清澄虚远的妙境。句中巧用三潭印月和南屏晚钟，创造了一个十分清远的境界。一个"落"字，写得亦真亦幻，亦虚亦实，静中有动，动中有静，全诗营造出一种静寂悠远的禅境，反映出了诗人宁静、恬淡的心情。曼殊诗风"清艳明秀"，此诗基调轻松，色彩鲜明，极富形象化，宛如一幅画卷，清新之气扑面而来，具有较高的艺术性。

Su Manshu

(1884—1918) was a native of Xiangshan (now Zhongshan, Guangdong Province). He became a Buddhist monk and adopted Manshu as his Buddhist name. He studied in Japan and travelled around Southeast Asia. Su was a gifted poet, author and painter and used to work as a newspaper editor and a school teacher. He made friends with famous intellectuals such as Zhang Taiyan and Liu Yazi, and was a member of Nanshe (Poetry Club in Southern China). His poems are sweetly sentimental. He translated works of internationally important writers such as Lord Byron and Victor Hugo. There exists *Complete Works of Su Manshu*.

Living in Baiyun Temple by the West Lake

Leifeng Pagoda stands deep in white cloud;
Several plum blossoms are red in white snow.
After Buddhist ceremony I begin to meditate, entering the Zen state;
Outside the Buddhist hall sparse bells fall in the pool shadow.

Comments and Tips

This poem was written in 1905 when Su Manshu lived in Baiyun Temple at the foot of Leifeng Pagoda by the West Lake. The first two lines describe the scenery of Baiyun Temple. The last two lines are about his experience of Samadhi as a result of fasting, revealing an amazingly intangible world of transcendental clarity by the clever employment of the famous views of "The Moon Printed in Three Pools" and "The Evening Bell Ringing from Nanping Hill". The choice of the word "fall" makes the scene both real and illusionary, with movement and stillness found themselves in each other. The whole poem creates a peaceful and otherworldly Zen realm, revealing the poet's tranquil and modest state of mind.

图书在版编目（CIP）数据

历代杭州西湖诗词一百首：汉英对照 / 张梦新, 柏舟主编.
-- 杭州：浙江大学出版社，2023.7（2024.4重印）
ISBN 978-7-308-24009-3

Ⅰ.①历… Ⅱ.①张… ②柏… Ⅲ.①古典诗歌–诗集–中
国–古代–汉、英 Ⅳ.①I222

中国国家版本馆CIP数据核字(2023)第125832号

历代杭州西湖诗词一百首

张梦新　柏　舟　主编

策划编辑	宋旭华	
责任编辑	韦丽娟	
责任校对	董齐琪	
封面设计	李腾月	
出版发行	浙江大学出版社	
	（杭州市天目山路148号　　邮政编码　310007）	
	（网址：http://www. zjupress.com）	
排　　版	杭州林智广告有限公司	
印　　刷	浙江海虹彩色印务有限公司	
开　　本	710mm×1000mm　1/16	
印　　张	24	
字　　数	412千	
版 印 次	2023年7月第1版　2024年4月第2次印刷	
书　　号	ISBN 978-7-308-24009-3	
定　　价	128.00元	

版权所有　侵权必究　印装差错　负责调换

浙江大学出版社市场运营中心联系方式：0571-88925591；http://zjdxcbs. tmall.com